STEPPING OFF

ALSO BY
JORDAN SONNENBLICK

Drums, Girls & Dangerous Pie

Notes from the Midnight Driver

Zen and the Art of Faking It

Curveball: The Year I Lost My Grip

After Ever After

Falling Over Sideways

JORDAN SONNENBLICK

STEPPING OFF

SCHOLASTIC PRESS
NEW YORK

All rights reserved. Published by Scholastic Press, an imprint of Scholastic Inc.,
Publishers since 1920. SCHOLASTIC, SCHOLASTIC PRESS, and associated logos are
trademarks and/or registered trademarks of Scholastic Inc.

The publisher does not have any control over and does not assume any
responsibility for author or third-party websites or their content.

No part of this publication may be reproduced, stored in a retrieval system, or
transmitted in any form or by any means, electronic, mechanical, photocopying,
recording, or otherwise, without written permission of the publisher. For information regarding permission, write to Scholastic Inc., Attention: Permissions
Department, 557 Broadway, New York, NY 10012.

This book is a work of fiction. Names, characters, places, and incidents are
either the product of the author's imagination or are used fictitiously, and
any resemblance to actual persons, living or dead, business establishments,
events, or locales is entirely coincidental.

Library of Congress Cataloguing-in-Publication Data available

ISBN 978-1-339-02317-5

10 9 8 7 6 5 4 3 2 1   24 25 26 27 28

Printed in Italy   183
First edition, June 2024

Book design by Christopher Stengel

To Mark Chou and Matt Lambiase. I was a painfully awkward teen, and without the two of you beside me, I would have made an even bigger mess of high school, my teenage love life (such as it was), my driving escapades, and just about everything else.

Just don't think this means I forgive you for touching the back of my neck when we were watching Arachnophobia and making me throw my popcorn everywhere. That wound is still too raw.

There's a picture of me pinned to the corkboard over my desk at my dad's house. It's a couple of years old. I took it myself with a timer. In it, I have my beloved Fender Precision electric bass guitar strapped around my neck. I'm wearing a lake-blue hoodie with block letters on it, but you can only see the tops of a couple of words over the instrument.

Anybody who looked at the photo without knowing me would just see a pale, freckly, scrawny teenage boy with shaggy brown hair, a slightly-too-big nose, and hazel eyes. They would guess he probably plays the bass and likes hoodies.

They wouldn't be wrong about any of that. But there is just so much they wouldn't see. They wouldn't know how nervous and insecure that kid is. They wouldn't know he was taking the photo to send to a girl, or that he was trying desperately to impress her, like *See? I'm cool! I'm a bass player!* They wouldn't even know he had bought that bass used online, specifically because it was finished in a rare shade called "Charcoal Frost" that reminded him of the color of the girl's eyes.

The girl wouldn't know that part, either.

The back of the hoodie said: *The real world isn't real!* That was the official motto of Tall Pines Landing, the Pennsylvania vacation-home community where I'd spent all my summers and weekends since I was a little kid. I loved that hoodie for the same reason I loved the place itself. My "real world" was Staten Island, New York. It was crowds and traffic, pollution and endless noise. It was commuting to my incredibly high-pressure math-and-science magnet high school in Manhattan five days a week by bus, ferry, and subway. It was feeling alone and afraid in a vast, rolling sea of people. It was watching my parents growing further and further apart every year.

I spent the first sixteen and a half years of my life trying as hard as I could to escape to the mountains of Pennsylvania. Every chance I got, I went there physically, and when I couldn't actually be there in body, I would close my eyes, put on some music, play my bass, and be there in spirit.

I needed to believe that the real world wasn't real.

1. The Pause Button

Have you ever wished that life came with a pause button? I've wished it over and over again, and I know exactly when I would freeze everything: late in the afternoon on Saturday, May 18, 2019.

It was hot. Sunny. I was standing in bright orange swimming shorts and my favorite old black Converse All Stars on top of the concrete vehicle barrier that ran along the edge of the Ledgedale Bridge, looking down at the dark, shadowed waters of the lake forty feet below, trying to work up the nerve to jump.

When you jump off the Ledgedale Bridge, the sneakers are necessary so you don't break your feet.

I was between two girls, halfway in love with both of them at the same time. Chloe Conti was holding my right hand loosely, her thin fingers dry against mine. Ava Green was squeezing my left hand in a death grip, her round fingers slick with sunscreen. "Don't let go of me," Ava hissed. The sun was coming through the chain-link fence over her shoulder, and it was so bright that I couldn't really make out her features. She was just a flash of white teeth and a golden halo of long hair above a bubblegum-pink swimsuit and the smooth skin of a hip against my leg.

"Never," I said.

We were all leaning back against the fence. The links were burning into my back. I closed my eyes and tried to breathe slowly, in through my nose, out through my mouth—just like my asthma doctor always said to do when I was feeling panicky about my breathing. Or, you know, about jumping off something really high and drowning. As soon as I inhaled, the coconut scent of Chloe's lotion and the flowery smell that always came off Ava's hair almost overwhelmed me.

Chloe squeezed my hand with birdlike gentleness, and I turned to her. She was staring right at me, which did not make me less lightheaded. I could see the soft, haunting gray around her pupils. I looked down, because sometimes making eye contact with Chloe was too much for me to handle, even when we weren't balanced on an alarmingly narrow ledge.

That was the thing about being with Chloe and Ava that summer: I'd never been so happy, so nervous, so uncomfortable, so miserable, and so *thrilled* before—all at the same time. Being with them was hot sauce and honey on my tongue.

My calves were starting to get shaky, so I knew we couldn't just stand there much longer. Plus, the police might come. But I didn't quite have the guts or the leadership or

4

whatever it would require to get us to take that one big step forward. It was Chloe who finally said, "So, guys, are we doing this or what?"

Well, I sure wasn't going to look like a chicken in front of my two best friends. Who were also my two crushes. "Oh, we're doing it," I said. "If the birthday girl is ready?"

For some reason, it was a Tall Pines Landing tradition—a highly illegal tradition—to climb out onto the middle of the Ledgedale Bridge and jump into the water as a sixteenth-birthday rite of passage. I was already sixteen, and so was Chloe. Our birthdays were in the winter, but it was Ava's actual birthday weekend, so this was officially the birthday jump for all of us. We had come up with the idea of a triple jump years ago, probably when we were around eleven, lying on the ratty old mattresses on the floor of Ava's treehouse. We'd had five years to think about this moment, but it hadn't totally sunk into my head how scary it would be until now.

Ava's grip, which had already been bone-crushing, cranked up another notch. I was pretty sure I felt a knuckle in my pinkie crack. "I'm ready," she said. "Kinda."

"So, do we just, like, count down?" I asked.

"I guess so," Ava replied. "But from a high number, okay?"

"Are we talking five? Ten? Twenty?" I felt my voice crack on that last syllable, which I was pretty sure hadn't happened since I was thirteen.

"No," Chloe said, "we count down from three, like this: three . . . two . . . one . . . go!"

My knees bent, and I almost involuntarily started to spring forward. Chloe and Ava both yanked me back against the fence, hard.

"That was just a practice countdown, Superman," Chloe said.

"I knew that," I replied weakly.

Chloe let go of my hand for a second, put the back of her hand against my chest, and gently pushed me against the fence. "Just breathe for a second, okay?" she said. Then she shouted, "Hey, Jake, are there any boats coming?"

Oh, that's right, I realized. My older sister and her boyfriend were down on the rocks on one side below. Nobody ever jumped off this bridge without an audience, because if you didn't have spotters, you might just land on the deck of somebody's sailboat.

"You're good!" Jake yelled. "By the way, I'm totally filming this, so try to make it cinematic, okay?"

Perfect, I thought.

Chloe took my hand again. "All right, kids. Remember what everyone always says: Bend both knees. Jump off with both feet at once. Don't tense up. Keep your body straight up and down in the air. Legs together. Let go of each other when we hit the water so everybody's hands are free for swimming. Then swim straight up toward the light. Got it?"

I wanted to throw up. I wanted to cry. I wanted to forget this whole thing.

"You're still clear!" Jake shouted.

Ugh, I thought. *It's gonna be a long summer if we don't go through with this.*

"You good, Ava?" I asked. Ava relaxed her death grip for an instant, only to clamp down even harder.

"Never better," she gritted out through clenched teeth.

"Count it, Chloe," I said.

I forced myself to look straight ahead into the air as Chloe, the girl of half my dreams, said, "Three . . . two . . . one . . . GO!"

I felt Chloe's and Ava's hands drop down and swing back a bit, then forward. My knees almost buckled, but they held as I swung my arms with theirs and took the leap.

For that one perfect second, maybe a second and a half, we were flying.

2. After the Fall

If I could have paused the world right then, when we were still all holding hands in a line, maybe a quarter of the way down, before we entered the deep shadow of the bridge, that would have been great. Even if you'd offered the option to me then, before I knew what was coming, I would have been pretty tempted to take it. If Chloe on my right and Ava on my left—frozen in all the potential of that day, just as that summer was starting up—could have been my eternity, that would have been a sweet deal.

Looking back now, after all the things that have torn us up, all the things that have ripped my family apart, everything that's gone wrong in the world, and the unstoppable wave of deaths that was going to crash over Ava first and knock me down less than a year later, pushing that button would be the simplest decision in the world.

But you can't really protect anybody from the future. You can count down, hold hands, and brace yourselves the best you can, but that isn't the same thing as a guarantee. We learned that the hard way when my left foot got tangled up in Ava's. We both tried to pull our feet apart, but all that did was spread our legs a bit more and make all of us tip backward slightly just before we hit the water.

By the way, I've done the math since then, on a physics calculator I found online. A person falling forty feet reaches a speed of over thirty-four miles per hour at the time of impact. So you can see why all the older kids emphasized the parts about wearing sneakers, landing in a vertical position, and keeping one's legs together.

We managed to keep our sneakers on, so hey, that was a plus. We found out how much the other stuff mattered when we went ka-SPLAT against the surface of the lake at a respectable automotive speed. The first thing I felt was a tremendous slap against the backs of my thighs and my lower back. Then I shot forward and down in the water, diagonally, as dirty lake water shot up my nostrils. Somewhere along the way, I let go of everybody's hands. I was stunned for a moment, and then I realized I had to swim. I could see the light above me, so I kicked for the surface, which must have been about ten feet above me. I came up, sputtering, and spat out a mixture of silty water and blood.

Apparently, I had bitten my cheek. Also, I was becoming increasingly aware that the legs-akimbo landing had not been kind to my most sensitive boy parts, and a deep throbbing was setting in.

Even more pressingly, I couldn't see my friends. I looked around frantically. Chloe was nowhere to be seen, but Ava was floating just a few feet behind me. She smiled when she saw me, but I also thought I saw a grimace flash across her face. "Are you okay?" I asked.

"Yeah," she said. "Bit of a rough landing."

"We have to find Chloe!" I said. "Leah! Jake! Chloe isn't up!"

I could see my sister scrambling toward the canoes, although I was pretty sure Jake was still sitting on a rock, filming. I turned toward where I thought Chloe should be, in front and to the right of where I had popped up. Suddenly, I saw a bunch of bubbles break the surface. I swam over, took a breath, and ducked beneath the water—

—just in time for the top of Chloe's skull to ram into the bridge of my nose.

Several minutes later, the three of us were all lying on our backs on the steeply sloped, sun-warmed slate rocks of the shore. Leah had brought me a bag of ice from the general store up by the top of the bridge, and then she and Jake had gone back up to get themselves some ice cream.

I was pretty sure my nose had stopped bleeding. Ava and Chloe were comparing war wounds. Chloe said, "I would have come up faster, but wow! I had to, uh, fix my suit first. I had, like, the worst wedgie I have ever had in my life. Jesse, cover your ears."

By this point, I had a pulsating headache from where her head had smashed into me. It was like a whole throbbing party everywhere, from my nose to my groin. Good times!

"Chloe," I groaned, "you know you're supposed to say the 'cover your ears' part *before* the embarrassing part, right?"

"Good point," Ava said. "By the way, I absolutely whacked the bottom of my boobs when I landed. And my ass. Don't look when I walk—my cheeks are probably bright red! Cover your ears, Jesse. Oops. Chloe, we suck at this. Maybe we should change the subject before our rescue hero faints. He's really quite sensitive, you know."

When we were little kids, we had all been able to talk about anything in the world without getting embarrassed. To be fair, Chloe and Ava still could. But sometime around puberty, which had happened for both of them way before it had for me, things had gotten super weird for me. Maybe it was because there were two of them and only one of me, or maybe it was true what everyone always says about girls being more mature than boys, but all I knew was that they loved to talk about stuff that would make me blush. Sometimes I felt like they were flirting with me, sometimes I felt like they were competing for me, and sometimes I was so confused I just wanted them to stop—while also wanting them to tease me *more*.

"I'm not sensitive," I said, probably with more edge than I'd intended. "I'm in actual, physical pain. Chloe smashed into my face, in case you forgot, plus I landed with my legs open and smashed my . . . you know."

Ava laughed, but Chloe sat up a bit, reached out toward me, and said, "Aww, let me take a look."

I flinched away, and she said, "At your *nose*."

I was kind of afraid to pull the ice pack away, because I had visions of a plume of bloody mucus spewing out all over both of us, but Chloe was as gentle as usual and my face was pretty numb, so I barely felt anything.

She leaned in close to examine my nose, then turned my head from side to side with her hand and took a careful look at the area under each of my eyes. "Jesse, your right eye might be getting a bit black-and-blue, but I think you're going to pull through," she said.

"Yeah," Ava said, "but what about his *boys*? Will he ever be able to reproduce?"

"This isn't the time or the place for that investigation, Ava," Chloe said, her hand still on my cheekbone.

"Well, keep me posted, okay?" Ava said. Maybe I was imagining things, but she almost seemed mad.

Just then, Leah and Jake came around the edge of the rock formation. "You guys recovered yet?" Leah asked. "I told Dad we'd be back in time to light the grill for dinner. Ooh, Jess, I think you might have a black eye. Pretty savage, Klo!" Everybody we knew called Chloe "Klo" except me. I loved the sound of her whole name too much to ever shorten it.

Chloe's hand dropped away from my face and she moved back. Even with the numbness and the weird, thick feeling of the swelling, I could still feel the light, ghostly imprint of her fingers. I almost reached out and grabbed her hand without even thinking about it.

Like *that* wouldn't have been weird.

"Chloe, it's okay," I said. "The injury just makes the story better, right?"

"Yeah," Jake added. "And the clip already has *dozens* of likes!"

Swell. No pun intended.

We went to our canoes, grabbed life jackets off the seats, and dragged the boats down into the shallows. Leah and Jake got into one and started paddling back across the lake to where Leah's car was parked. I held the back of the other steady while Chloe and Ava climbed into the front and middle positions. Then I hopped into the rear seat and started back-paddling us out into the deep water.

We had done this together so many times that I didn't have to say anything. Chloe and Ava both started paddling in rhythm with me, and despite how banged up we were, we caught up with my sister's boat only a hundred feet or so past the bridge. Jake looked surprised. "Wow, Bird," he said, "you've got some strong girls in that boat. I know *you're* not the one rowing that hard."

Until that moment, I hadn't known it was possible to have a swollen nose and a developing black eye, and still manage to burst into a full-blown blush at the same time. But I could feel my face heat up like someone had just stuck it in a microwave. I hated it when people called me Bird, which had been my nickname back home in Staten Island since I was in sixth grade or so. It was short for Bird Chest, because of how scrawny I have always been. That was bad enough when we were in the city, but out in Pennsylvania in front of Chloe and Ava, it was much, much worse. I wasn't sure which I felt like doing more: bursting into tears or shoving my canoe paddle so far down Jake's throat that he crapped maple splinters for the rest of his life.

Ava leaned way, way back, turned partway around, patted my thigh, smiled at me, looked at Jake, and said, "We *are* strong, Jacob. But also, Jesse is just way stronger than *you* look."

Oh, snap. Suddenly, I felt better. My blush didn't go away, though.

When we got back to the little cul-de-sac in Tall Pines Landing where all three of our houses were and got out of the car, both girls gave me long, damp hugs, and the smells of coconut, flowers, and lake water combined to make me feel lightheaded again. Jake had already started walking up our steep gravel driveway, but Leah waited for me. As Chloe and Ava walked away, she said, "You know you're gonna have to choose one, right?"

"What are you talking about?" I smiled like I was kidding. But I wasn't relaxed enough to be kidding. In fact, my brain was going a million miles a minute, almost like I couldn't stop texting myself in a panic.

-Does Chloe like me?

-Does Ava like me?

-Why would either of them like me?

-My nickname is Bird Chest. What beautiful girl likes a guy named Bird Chest?

-But they flirt with me all. the. time.

-And Ava sticks up for me.

-And I saved Chloe's life under the bridge!

-No, I didn't. That was just sad. Also, must go inside and check out how my nose looks.

-Ava touched my thigh.

-Ava TOUCHED my THIGH.

"Are you coming, Jesse?" my sister asked. I snapped back to reality. "Or are you just going to stand here in the driveway until Dad pulls in and runs you over? No offense, but you look a little dazed all of a sudden. Maybe Dad should take you into town and get your nose checked out. You might have a concussion or something."

"I'm fine," I said, although I had no idea whether that was true or not.

3. The Problem with Normal

In the real world, Chloe and Ava were way, way out of my league.

In the real world, Chloe had never been without a boyfriend for more than a week. She was incredibly beloved, popular, beautiful in a fragile and cute way that made everybody in the world want to protect her, and also—very importantly—tragic. Until we were twelve, she seemed to lead a fairy-tale kind of life. Her parents were semi-rich and semi-famous, because her dad owned an art gallery on Long Island and had discovered some well-known street artist back in the early 2000s, so they hung out with royalty, billionaires, and movie stars. Then, all of a sudden, it fell apart. Her mom left her dad, and then died in a random car accident. Chloe was in the back seat, and spent a month in the hospital with several broken ribs and really bad internal injuries. For like a year, she had a slight limp, and her dad once told me she cried herself to sleep every night for months.

She never showed any of that out here at Tall Pines Landing, or talked about it. In fact, she was the one who always cheered everybody else up.

Which came in very handy when Ava was around. Ava wasn't exactly popular; her moodiness put some people off. Their loss, because she was also fierce and loyal and perceptive and funny and *hot*.

Unfortunately, Ava was also tragic. Her real world was the Connecticut suburbs. Her parents had a super-ugly breakup before I ever even met her. Her dad bought the Tall Pines house when Ava was maybe seven years old and her little sister, Annie, was three. The tragedy started a few years later, when her dad, Richard, met and married her stepmom, Tracy, because Ava is 100 percent convinced Tracy hates her. It intensified when Ava's mom moved to Florida without any warning four years ago. And it reached a raging new level last fall, when Ava's mom was diagnosed with breast cancer. Since then, whenever all three of us were at Tall Pines at the same time, I felt like it was some kind of therapy session and Chloe was the guru, because she was the one who'd been through all the bad stuff already.

I can't even tell you how many hours we had spent that year looking up at the bare rafters of Ava's treehouse, listening to Ava cry and rage as her mom slowly faded. The worst was in April, because Ava and Annie had just come back from flying down to see their mom in Florida for Easter.

A typical conversation went like this. Ava would say, "I hate her."

Chloe would say, "I know, sweetie, I know." Meanwhile, Ava would be lying between us on the mattresses, turned into my side, crying so hard that I could literally feel the tears and snot running down from the edge of my chest to my shoulder blade. I would stroke Ava's soft golden hair and try not to think about what it felt like to have her body snuggled up against me, while also racking my brain for something—anything—useful to say.

But there was nothing, because my parents weren't divorced. My mom wasn't dead or dying. My life was just regular, normal, and boring. I mean, it wasn't like I wanted to trade. I just felt small and unimportant sometimes.

So I'd play with Ava's hair some more, until she suddenly punched my ribs and yelled, "I mean, I really hate her!" Then she'd whack me again and again, once per word, as she barked out, "WHY! ISN'T! SHE! HERE? WHY! AREN'T! WE! ENOUGH?"

On the one hand, I loved this girl. But on the other hand, they call me Bird Chest for a reason. She was basically just slamming me in the cartilage, a mere spare rib away from my pounding heart. She was hurting me.

This was going to leave a bruise.

Chloe would eventually notice the look of distress on my face, reach over, grab Ava's wrists in that barely-there grip of hers, and say, "I get it. I'm *still* mad at my mom. And I still wish I could climb into bed with her when I'm scared."

Then Ava would flip over to face Chloe, and just start wailing a stream of things that were barely even words while Chloe kept nodding and saying, "I know." The thing is, she really *did* know. Meanwhile, I just sat there, steadily patting Ava's back.

. . . .

All three of us had summer jobs at the recreation center at Tall Pines, which is a community center all year, but also has a day camp for little kids in July and August. We started working on weekends in the spring. Chloe worked at the front desk, which was perfect because everyone loved talking to her. Ava was a lifeguard at the pool, which was perfect because she loved wearing a swimsuit all day and getting tan. And me? I was a tennis court attendant. I even taught lessons to the little kids, and to the random tennis ladies. I wasn't a great player or anything, because first of all, the asthma wasn't exactly a big performance booster, and second of all, as my first tennis teacher once told me, I had "less than zero killer instinct." But I was patient and gentle, so I was perfect for the kids and the old ladies. My favorite student was Ava's twelve-year-old sister, Annie. By 2019, I'd been giving her lessons whenever I could for years. She was sweet and bubbly most of the time, and nothing like Ava. My nickname for her was Sunshine.

About a week after Ava and Annie's Easter trip, I was hitting with Annie at the end of my shift, and she seemed unusually blue—almost mopey. She hit a bunch of balls into the net in a row, which was not like her, and then I could have sworn I heard her curse under her breath, which was even more out of character. When we stopped to pick up a basket of balls, I asked her to sit next to me. Then I said, "Feel like talking, Sunshine?"

Annie turned to me, and I could see that her brown eyes, which were the exact same milk-chocolate shade as Ava's, were brimming with tears. "I can't talk about it," she whispered. So I put my arm around her, and we sat there for what felt like an eternity, until Ava came out of the pool area and found us there. By then, we were just sitting calmly, or at least, it must have looked that way.

"Sorry I'm late," Ava said. "I had to jump in the pool because some rug rat tried to stand up on a kickboard and banged his head on the edge of the pool. So then I took a quick shower to get the chlorine out of my hair. I didn't dry it, though, because I knew you'd be waiting. See?" With that, she gathered up a handful of her blonde locks, leaned over very close to me, and wrung a stream of water out onto my shoulder.

Annie jumped up and shouted, "Why do you have to be such a *jerk* all the time?"

I leapt to my feet and stood between them with my palms outstretched, like some kind of extremely ineffective crossing guard. "It's okay, Sunshine, she was just playing around. I don't mind or anything."

"Well, of course *you* don't mind, Jess."

"What's that supposed to mean?" Ava asked.

"Oh, like you don't know," Annie sneered. I was shocked. I hadn't really known Annie *could* sneer. "Jesse and I were having a moment over here, until you showed up being your usual oblivious self and hogging all the attention, shoving yourself in his face and—"

"I did *not* shove myself in his face. And how were you 'having a moment'? Please. You're, like, five. Was he giving you some Goldfish crackers and a juice box?"

"See?" Annie shrieked. "This is what you do to everyone. This is why people hate you!"

This was getting so loud that two old ladies on the next court over had stopped playing to stare at us. One of them was a regular student of mine. I waved at her reassuringly and explained, "It's okay, Mrs. Wasserman. Just a little dispute over a line call!"

"A line call?" Ava said, the pitch of her voice rising alarmingly. "What line is that?"

"*This* ought to be good," Annie muttered.

I took a deep breath. I felt all shaky, and my chest was constricting like it did at the start of an asthma attack. There was literally nothing I hated more than conflict, especially between people I cared about. Annie was right that Ava liked to suck up all my attention, but on the other hand, I liked it, too.

Sort of.

Annie needed me, and I liked protecting her. I forced myself to make direct eye contact with both of them in turn.

"Listen," I said, "I love *you* and I love *you*. Okay? Now, can we please stop humiliating me at my workplace?"

Nothing happened for a couple of seconds. A mixture of water from Ava's hair and sweat from my own rapidly developing panic dripped down the back of my shirt. Then, out of nowhere, both Annie and Ava started cracking up.

Annie made a little puppet hand in the air in front of my mouth, scrunched up her face, and in a pretend-deep voice, said, "I love yoooouuuuu!"

Then Ava made her own puppet hand from the other side, and in an even deeper voice, said, "And I love yyyyyooooouuuuuu!"

"No, I looovvvveeeeeee youuuuuuu!"

"Noooo, liiiiiii looooovvvvveeee yyyyyooooouuuuuu!"

I grabbed my racket bag and started walking away from them off the court in the direction of the parking lot, but they followed me with their "I love you" and "I looovvvveeee yyooouuuu" act, which didn't stop until they were both gasping for air and leaning against me for support.

Ava and Annie were terrible when they were fighting, but they weren't that much less terrible when they were getting along. My car was next to a rack that held Annie's bike. I had my Pennsylvania driver's license, which you can get when you're sixteen and a half, but I was only legally allowed to drive one passenger who wasn't a relative. That meant Annie was going to have to pedal the half mile to our little street.

I started throwing my stuff in the trunk, and Annie said, "Oh no, he's pouting."

Ava looked me up and down and said, "You're right. He is pouting. What do we do?"

"Staring contest?"

"Tickling?"

"Group hug?"

"Group hug!"

I tried to pull away, but not very hard. Annie whispered into my ear, "I'm sorry I got mad. I really *do* love you." When she pulled away, her eyes were glistening again.

As soon as the car door closed, Ava said, "You know, I hate when she's sad. She actually does better when she's mad at me."

Something clicked in my head. "Wait a minute. Are you saying you picked a fight with her on purpose?"

"Not exactly. But I didn't back down, either. I mean, sometimes she just needs to explode. Which I totally get. I even respect her for it."

I didn't know what to say, so I concentrated on starting the car, releasing the emergency brake, and shifting into gear. As I pushed my right foot down on the gas pedal, Ava said, "What was your little *moment* about, anyway?"

I stopped at the edge of the lot and signaled to turn

left onto the street. "She didn't say, but she wasn't her usual self. She kept slamming balls into the net, and when I asked what was wrong, she almost cried. So I sat there with my arm around her, not saying anything. I'm probably an idiot, but I have no idea what to say about any of this."

"Oh, J," Ava said, "you have no idea how good you are with her. You might not be able to relate to what she's going through, but you are exactly what she needs. You're such a good listener, and you just . . ."

Ava's voice got kind of husky, almost like she was going to cry. I wanted to look, but I also wanted to not crash and die, so I kept my eyes on the totally empty road.

"I just what?"

"You just . . . when, um, when a person is with you, even when things are all screwed up, she feels calm. Making girls feel calm is your superpower."

At that point, I wasn't sure whether Ava was still talking about Annie, or whether she had switched to talking about herself. But what I did know was that she reached over the parking brake lever and squeezed my leg.

I almost swerved off the road into a tree. I wasn't sure what Ava's superpower was, but it most definitely was not making boys feel calm. The problem was, I didn't want to make her feel calm, either. I wanted to make her scalp tingle. I wanted to make her break out in a sweat every time we hugged. No, I wanted to make her break out in a sweat every time we even came *close* to hugging.

Even worse, I wanted to have that same effect on Chloe. Maybe even more so.

Instead, apparently, I was like a big old human sleeping pill.

4. I Don't Get My Skills from Dad

After the big bridge jump, my sister and Jake hooked up the propane tank and fired up the grill on our back deck while I showered. My parents were supposed to go traveling in Spain and France for a couple of weeks that summer with some old friends, so they had stayed in Staten Island to have lunch with the other people and make plans. Then they were supposed to be coming up to the Landing in time for dinner. One thing about my dad was that he hated being late, especially for meals, which was why getting the grill started was such a big deal. I toweled off my hair, came downstairs, and was pretty surprised to find that my parents still hadn't arrived.

"Where are they?" I asked.

"I don't know, but I'm hungry," Jake said. Jake was always hungry. Well, hungry and hyper and a bit goofy. He was always joking around in a way that often irritated me, but I had to admit, he made my sister happy.

"They haven't called or texted," Leah said. "Can you check your phone?"

"I got nothin'," I said, "but don't panic. We can call them—"

"Oaw oo coog ook inga gwibeway!" Jake had grabbed a banana off the counter and had about two-thirds of it shoved in his mouth. He spoke around the edges of the mushy mess.

"What?" my sister asked.

He swallowed. It was like watching a cartoon boa constrictor eat. I could see the huge lump slide down his throat. Then he repeated, "Or you could look in the driveway."

Now that he mentioned it, I could hear the crunch of tires on gravel. We all rushed to the screen door in time to see our father getting out of the driver's side of the car, alone.

Leah looked at me. I looked at her. She shrugged. This was weird. There had been times when one parent came up for the weekend without the other, but never without us knowing about it in advance.

"Jake," Leah said, "why don't you go throw the meat on the grill?"

We had a whole ritual greeting for when our father walked into the Tall Pines house. One of us asked, "What's the news from the real world?" Then he said, "It's still ticking."

But this time, when I started to say, "What's—" he

27

cut me off with, "Sorry I'm late. Did you start the grill?" He didn't even mention our missing parent.

As soon as Leah nodded yes to the grill question, he brushed past us and out onto the patio. "Thanks, Jake, but I've got this now," he said. Then I heard the grill tools clanking around against the grates. It sounded a lot louder and more violent than usual. Jake walked in and Leah hissed, "What the hell's going on?"

"I don't know," Jake said, "but I'm thinking tonight isn't the night to ask your father to pay for those Ariana Grande tickets you wanted."

We all hustled around, grabbed stuff to set the table, and then sat in silence playing on our phones until my father came in with the big ceramic platter he always used to carry food in from the grill. It had Leah's and my handprints on it from when we were little kids, in bright primary colors. I'm pretty sure it was a Father's Day gift from our mom.

As soon as I saw the platter, I had a thought. I messaged Leah: *Should someone be texting Mom?* She shook her head, then put her phone on the table, screen down. My orders were clear: We were going to ignore the whole situation.

"So, Dr. Dienstag," Jake said, before we could even start serving ourselves, "how was lunch? You went to the Panini Grill, right? I love that place."

Freaking Jake.

My dad was holding a pair of grill tongs. He had been about to serve himself a big chunk of Italian sausage, but he slowly put the meat and the tongs down. Then he rubbed his eyes with the backs of his hands, which was something he usually only did when he was super tired, like if he had been called out of bed in the middle of the night for a psychiatric emergency at the hospital where he worked.

He sighed. "We never made it to lunch." Then he just sat there with his mouth a little bit open, like someone had yanked the air out of his lungs before he could say the rest of his words.

Leah leaned toward him. "Dad, is everything okay? Is Mom okay?"

When Dad answered, his tone was scornful. "Oh, *Mom* is fine," he said. "*Mom* is great. Apparently. I mean, she says she's great. Mom just doesn't want to go to Europe with *Dad*."

Leah looked at me. I looked back at her. She turned and looked at Jake. But even Jake wasn't insensitive enough to blunder off the cliff of this awkward silence.

I felt like I was going to have a heart attack if nobody said anything, so I stared straight down at my plate, cleared my throat, and choked out, "Do you want to, um . . . I don't know . . . talk about it?"

I'd noticed that things had seemed strange between my parents lately, but this was way worse than I could have imagined.

My father sighed again. He was a champion sigher. Leah and I generally found the sighing irritating, but in this case, it was definitely preferable to the dripping bitterness he'd been displaying the moment before. "Can we serve ourselves some food first?" he asked. "I'm sorry, Jess, but I haven't eaten anything since breakfast, and I'm having a little trouble thinking straight."

You should have seen us whipping that food around the table. You've never seen a more intensive display of platter piling. I was pretty sure I even saw Jake take a vegetable.

I decided to imagine some music in order to relax myself, concentrating on the bass parts. What I loved about the bass was that it was the anchor for all the other instruments. They could all be going crazy around it, play-ing melodies, harmonies, solos, countermelodies, horn punches, whatever. They could drop in and out. Singers could start and stop. But throughout everything, the bass was right there, defining the rhythm and the key, tying the drums to the melodic instruments.

Holding it all together.

To avoid thinking about the fact that my mom had apparently just canceled a big vacation with my dad, I concentrated on feeling the bass line from the classic White Stripes song "Seven Nation Army." It was pretty much impossible to concentrate on this song without also bopping my head to the beat, which must have been noticeable. Plus, I suppose I stopped eating. When the song was over (and I have to say, I really killed the ending), I opened my eyes to find everyone staring at me.

Normally, my parents and my sister were fairly accustomed to these little interludes of mine. I'd even say my dad had been known to find them amusing at times. But from what I could tell, this wasn't times.

I forced myself to smile weakly at everyone, grab my fork, and take a big bite of grilled peppers just as my dad said, "So, um, Europe is off, and your mother is . . . somewhere."

"Somewhere?" Leah echoed. "What do you mean, *somewhere*? Is she in Staten Island? New York City? New York State? Should we be worried?"

Dad's voice was strained and quiet as he said, "Well, I'm worried."

My dad was a psychiatrist. He never said he was worried. He was sometimes *perturbed* or *concerned* or *monitoring the situation*, but *worried* was way too strong a word for him to be throwing around.

"What do you mean, you're worried?" I asked. "Are you actually worried about Mom's safety?"

He looked at me blankly. I wanted to add, *Or are you worried about your marriage?* But I didn't want to hear the answer.

After a silence so long that Jake managed to eat an entire chicken leg, my dad said, "I'm sure your mother is physically safe. She's just extremely angry. And I don't understand why."

Nobody responded to this. Jake grabbed a wing. My dad continued.

"It was time for us to head out to the restaurant, and she wasn't coming downstairs. So I said, 'Are you coming?' And she said, 'No.' I said, 'What do you mean, no?' She said, 'I mean, I'm not coming with you.' I said, 'To the restaurant? But the Rudermans are going to be waiting for us.' She came stomping down the steps and said, 'I mean, I'm not coming to Europe with you.'"

I'm pretty sure my mouth was literally hanging open in shock. I know Leah's was.

My dad swallowed, then dove right back into his tale of terror. "I said, 'But we already paid for the tickets.' Then she started screaming and yelling about how this was my fault. None of it made any sense. She was the one who *wanted* this trip. I asked her to calm down and be reasonable, but everything I said just made her angrier. Finally, she grabbed her purse, stormed out, and slammed the door. That's all I know."

My father looked crushed. He looked—I don't know—defeated.

I didn't know where my mother was. I didn't know what had happened, or what all of this meant for the future of my family. One thing was for sure, though. Keeping women calm was *not* a skill I had inherited from Dad.

5. Chloe Makes It Weird

The whole first half of that summer, it was like the weather gods were trying to push me toward Chloe. I mean, it wasn't like I was devoutly praying for rain or anything, but I was low-key rooting for it. And I was definitely getting what I wanted.

See, the recreation center had an indoor pool and an outdoor pool, but it only had outdoor tennis courts. That meant when it rained, Ava still had a pool to work at, but I couldn't be a court attendant, so I ended up hanging out behind the desk with Chloe. The rec center director, a cranky old guy named Larry, sometimes walked by and yelled, "What the hell am I paying you for, Dienstag? To keep the pretty girls company?"

In reply, I would blush cleverly. But when he walked away, I would say something devastatingly witty under my breath, like, "Has it ever occurred to you that maybe you're paying the pretty girls to keep *me* company?"

Then I would blush again at my own comment.

Anyway, Chloe and I got to talk all day. And I know this sounds stupid or pathetic or whatever, but there was a padded wooden crossbar under the desk that nobody could see from the front, so Chloe would take off her sandals and put her feet up on the bar. Then I'd put mine up there, too, and for hours on end, our feet would either briefly touch, or almost touch, or actually *be* touching, and no matter what we were talking about out loud, I felt like a pretty massive percentage of the conversation was happening below the knees. I spent weeks wondering whether Chloe meant to be flirting, or whether she was feeling totally innocent about the whole thing.

Also, we made friendship bracelets. Like, yards and yards of friendship bracelets.

The first full week we worked that summer was the July Fourth week. July 3 was a Wednesday. It was drizzly and overcast, and the rec center was totally deserted. Chloe was trying to tie a friendship bracelet onto my wrist next to two others she'd already made for me. I also had two from Ava on my other wrist.

Not that it was some kind of contest or anything.

Chloe was having trouble with the knot, even though she was the queen of friendship bracelets. She asked me to stand up and face her. Then she kind of pulled my arm to her and hugged it while she tried again to tie the bracelet.

"Hmm, that's weird," she said, her fingers caressing my wrist and then pressing a bit harder against it.

"What's weird?" I replied. "Nothing's weird. I don't think anything's weird." *Except that you smell like coconuts and sunshine and the abject surrender of total happiness and little baby angels getting their wings and I think your hair just brushed against my face but I can't look because I closed my eyes and I have no idea when I did that or why, but anyway as I was saying nothing's weird.*

"Your pulse is weird. Your heart is pounding. Are you okay? Maybe we should sit down."

Oh, yikes. Of course my pulse was weird! My heart was probably always pounding when I was touching Chloe. But I couldn't say that. I opened my eyes as she kind of pressed me down into my chair. Now our knees were touching. That wasn't going to be therapeutic. Ecstatic, yes. Therapeutic, no.

I thought fast. "Well, actually, I've been hiding something from you. From you and Ava. From everyone, really."

This was true. I had been keeping the new strangeness of my family life a secret, partly because I didn't understand what was going on. I had tried a couple of times to ask my mom what the deal was with the canceled vacation, and all she would say was that she was "too stressed" to go. And then she would pivot to some totally random topic.

I was tangled up in a crisis I couldn't begin to comprehend. I didn't know what to say around either of my parents. I didn't know what to do about any of it. And I wasn't sure why, but I was embarrassed by the thought of even discussing it with anyone.

Chloe took both my hands in hers. "What is it, sweetie? You know you can tell me anything, right?"

I half wanted to say, *I love you. You are my dream girl. I love how gentle you are. I love how you listen. I love how you always notice when somebody's unhappy. I love how you always know what's cool before the rest of the world figures it out. I love how you are the one who got us to jump off the bridge.*

But, you know, awkward.

So instead I said, "My parents haven't been up here at the same time in weeks."

"What do you mean?"

"I mean, they had some kind of big fight about a trip they were supposed to take to Europe this summer, and ever since then, they barely talk when we're in New York. And they don't say anything about this, but somehow when it's time to get in the car and drive to Pennsylvania, suddenly there's only one parent coming."

One thing about Chloe is that she generally tries to see the sunny side of things. "Are you sure it isn't just a coincidence? Like, maybe that one time they had the fight, and then these other times, they really do just have different plans?"

"I don't think so, Chloe. This was a pretty explosive fight. I mean, my parents don't have confrontations like that. And now they're just kind of civil. Like roommates."

"Oh."

"Yeah. And I've tried to remember other times in the past when only one parent came up. I think we always knew way in advance, like it would be because my dad was on call at the hospital, or my mom was visiting her college roommate for the weekend. Now there's just this weird last-minute mumbling, like, 'Oh, your father has a thing, but don't worry, it's fine.' And if I ask, 'What kind of thing?' my mom is just like, 'Get in the car, it's almost rush hour.'"

Chloe lifted my hands up so they were in front of her face and pressed them to her cheek. "Oh, Jess, I'm sorry. You must be so worried," she said.

"I'm . . . concerned," I said. *Ugh*, I thought. *Now I sound like my dad.* "Honestly," I mumbled, "I just don't know how to make things *right*."

Chloe dropped my hands so fast I thought I had offended her. She was almost glaring at me as she said, "Jess, it's not your *job* to make things right. Believe me, you can't."

"Did I say something wrong?" I asked.

She stepped closer, wrapped her arms around me, and put her hands in my hair. "No, you just made me sad for you. Jess, you're a people fixer. You always want to calm everyone down. But you know I went through this with my family, so please trust me. You can't calm your parents down. You have to worry about you."

When she said that last *you*, her breath against my ear made me tremble. At that moment, I was the most miserably excited I had ever been in my entire life. Who knows what might have happened next if the desk phone hadn't rung?

Chloe reached around my back and grabbed it. "Tall Pines Landing Recreation Center, where fun and fireworks await! Chloe speaking. May I help you?"

"Where fun and fireworks await?" I mouthed.

She covered the phone with one hand and whispered, "Oh, shut up." Then she took her hand away and said, "Yes, the annual July Fourth fireworks on the lake start at nine thirty this Saturday night. Right, on Saturday the sixth, NOT tomorrow. We always celebrate on the Saturday closest to the Fourth. No, it's not rain or shine, but the forecast looks good. Hope to see you there, Mrs. April!"

When Chloe hung up the phone, she said, "For your information, fun and fireworks *do* await. We're going to do something special on Saturday night! After all these rainy days, we can all use some fun, and you need a distraction."

"Okay," I said, "what's the plan?"

"You'll see. Ava and I still have to put some finishing touches on, but it will be super fun. I guarantee you will not be disappointed."

"Well," I said, "what if I am?"

Chloe grabbed my forearm, whipped the friendship bracelet over my wrist, and had it tied in place in two seconds flat. She grinned, her gray eyes flashed, and my knees trembled again. "Come on, Jess. When have you ever been disappointed when you've been with me?"

6. Fun and Fireworks

The Fourth of July fireworks display was one of the two biggest summer celebrations at Tall Pines Landing. (The other was Christmas-in-August.) Everybody gathered at the beaches around Hemlock Lake with sparklers, and all the people whose houses were on the lake lit flares at exactly nine thirty p.m. Then a team of pyrotechnical "experts," led by Larry from the rec center, shot off about a million fireworks over the water. Little kids usually went with their families, but Chloe, Ava, and I had been begging our parents for as long as I could remember to let us be alone together for the big show. When we were maybe eight or nine, that just meant sitting on a separate blanket together on the beach. After that, there were years when we stayed back home and watched from the little deck outside Ava's treehouse, years when we skipped the festivities because we felt like we were too grown-up and cool, and one very memorable year when Chloe got me and Ava to sneak out onto the fifteenth hole of the local private golf course, which was amazing because it was right next to the water. The amazingness faded a bit the next morning, when we all woke up covered in poison ivy, but hey, sometimes adventure comes with a price tag, right?

I had spent three days dying to know what the special event was going to be this time around, but neither Chloe nor Ava had dropped even the slightest hint. All they said was to show up with swim shorts at nine at the rec center, on the far side of the lake from the fireworks beach. They also said not to drive, because I wouldn't want to have my car at the end of the adventure. Oh, and they told me to douse myself liberally in bug spray.

All that really told me was that we'd be somewhere in Tall Pines Landing. Which I already knew.

But of course I could never say no to any of Chloe's plans, so I found myself trudging up to the dark, abandoned parking lot of the rec center, hoping that my big surprise wasn't that I was going to be ritually murdered by Satan worshippers. I'd never seen the rec center so dead. I mean, literally every single living person in the entire community would be at the beach by this point.

Then I saw car headlights coming around from behind the trees in the distance. Fortunately, I didn't spiral into panic. Well, there's a chance I might have spiraled a bit. *This is it*, I thought. *The Satanists have come. Maybe they'll just harvest one of my kidneys and my spleen and leave me in a bathtub somewhere. That wouldn't be so bad. Chloe, how could you do this to me?*

The car pulled up right next to me. I forced myself not

to run away or squeal like an extremely alarmed piglet. Which turned out to be a wise call, because it was Leah and Jake, dropping off Chloe and Ava. As the girls got out and hugged me, Jake said, "Have fun!" and Leah said, "Be careful, okay?"

Having fun isn't that challenging. Being careful isn't that challenging. But doing both at the same time? The struggle, as they say, is real.

Both girls were wearing sweatshirts and shorts, but I could see they had their swimsuits on underneath. And they both reeked of bug spray. Plus, Chloe was carrying a long, powerful-looking flashlight. Whatever this caper was, it was definitely *on*.

I raised an eyebrow, but before I could even ask, Chloe said, "Here's the deal. We're going to take the catamaran out."

I was stunned. A catamaran is a special kind of sailboat that doesn't have a normal hull. Instead, it looks like a trampoline on big, fat water skis. It's just two pontoons, with a canvas "deck" stretched on a framework a couple of feet above the water between them and a sail flying in front and above. The stunning part was that, while the rec center had like ten canoes, seven paddleboats, and three little two-person sailboats, it only had one catamaran. That catamaran was Larry's baby, his pride and joy. He would personally take it out and do little sunset cruises for his favorite residents on weekends, and he spent hours lovingly polishing the fiberglass of the pontoons when we pulled the boats out for winter storage. He wouldn't even let underage staff members look at that boat during daylight hours, much less at night. And at night while there were fireworks shooting off all over the place?

I turned to Ava. "She's joking, right? What are we really doing?"

Ava said, "She's serious. We're taking the catamaran out! How *cool* is this? We're gonna watch the show from *on the lake*! No parents, no problems, no crowd, no poison ivy. Just the three of us, lying on the hammock-y thing and enjoying our front-row seats. That's our cheer-up gift to you, J."

This still seemed too good to be true. I had to ask. "And Larry said yes to this?"

"Well," Chloe said, "he didn't tell us no."

Suddenly, my palms felt sweaty. "What does that mean?"

"It means I told him how much we all love the show every year, and what an amazing job he always does. Then I asked him if we could take out a boat, and he said yes, as long as we wore life jackets and stayed on the far side of the swim buoys—or, as he put it, 'far, far from the awesome flames of freedom and destruction.' He was kind of into it. You know, he loves showing off on the Fourth."

I couldn't believe it. Chloe had flirted with Larry—an ancient crusty dude who was also her boss—to get the boat! I was both impressed and deeply horrified. Also, I'd

42

noticed that she'd asked to take out "a boat," not "the catamaran."

Ava elbowed me. "Whaddya say, J? We can't just stand here. The clock's ticking. Plus, I'm pretty sure a mosquito just flew up my shorts."

I shrugged, even though it was too dark for anybody to see the gesture. "Oh, what the hell. And don't worry, when we get arrested for sailboat theft, I promise I won't testify against you guys."

Chloe smiled and said, "Yay!"

Ava said, "Wow, J, you smooth talker! Girls love a dude who won't rat them out to the cops. And don't worry. I bet you'll look hot in black-and-white stripes."

We walked around the back of the community center, down the little gravel path that led to the lake, and onto the aluminum dock. Chloe turned on her flashlight, and we grabbed three life jackets from the rack, plus two paddles to use just in case something went wrong with the sailing part of the mission. Then we walked all the way out to the end of the dock, where the catamaran was tied.

The girls climbed on first. Chloe started to raise the sail while Ava lowered the rudder into the water. Meanwhile, I undid the knots that kept the boat attached to the dock and pushed us gently away. The wind filled the sail with a soft thwapping sound, and we glided out toward the center of the lake.

There was only a thin crescent of moon in the sky, but

between that and all the flares burning around the shoreline, I could see pretty well. The swimming beach was maybe half a mile straight ahead of us, and there was a little cluster of rowboats and canoes arrayed just before the ropes and buoys that separated the swimming area from the rest of the lake. Aside from that, our boat seemed to be the only thing moving. I hadn't brought my phone, because I had a serious fear of accidentally drowning it, but I knew Ava never went anywhere without hers. I asked what time it was, and she said it was 9:24.

Perfect.

After a few more minutes, we lowered the sail and let the boat drift. We were a few hundred yards farther out than the other boats, which was good because we didn't want to be seen and we definitely didn't want to drift into either another boat or the rocks around the shore.

"Relaxation time, kids!" Chloe said. The boat had been sailing straight toward the beach, and the wind was blowing softly at a ninety-degree angle to our path, so I figured we would slowly drift sideways, but the front of the boat would basically remain pointed toward the fireworks. We arranged ourselves on our backs in our usual pattern, with Chloe on my right and Ava on my left, shoulder to shoulder. It had been warm all day, but the slight breeze across my bare legs made me shiver a bit.

Relaxation time? I was between two girls who both tormented my dreams, waiting for fireworks to explode suddenly out of the dark almost directly overhead, on a boat that we had essentially stolen. It wasn't exactly relaxing.

I will say this, though: It definitely distracted me from my family problems.

"What time is it now?" Chloe asked.

"Two minutes!" Ava said. "Make a wish, guys! New rule: Any wish you make on July Fourth fireworks will come true."

"Is that a thing?" I asked.

"It is now!" she replied. "Hurry up and wish! It only counts if you make the wish before the first firework goes off."

I closed my eyes. I didn't know what to wish for. I pictured myself kissing Chloe. I pictured myself kissing Ava. I pictured my parents jumping on a plane to Spain, holding hands and chatting happily. I pictured myself plugging my bass into a brand-new, super-high-tech amplifier. *Oh, wait,* I thought. *Maybe I should wish for good PSAT scores. Or for world peace. Or for Ava's mom to be okay. Or—*

BOOM! A tremendous red starburst lit up the sky over our heads. Ava's hand found mine, and Chloe gripped my arm. My heart skipped erratically. For a jumpy kid like me, that first firework was always pretty shocking. As the next volley of three blue pinwheels whistled overhead, so close I could actually feel the heat on my skin, I thought, *Great, I blew my wish. So much for world peace.*

But then Chloe said, "This feels nice, right?" And I realized that maybe I was living my wish already in that exact moment, if I could just lie back and let it flow over me.

Ava held up her phone—which was a bit daring because we were lying on our backs on a boat—and said, "Smile!" She took a series of selfies in burst mode as a red, white, and blue pinwheel whizzed overhead. I wanted to look at the photos, but I also didn't want to do anything that would take me out of the moment.

It felt like the display went on for hours. By the end, the smell of gunpowder was so strong that I couldn't detect even a whiff of bug spray. Also, I was at least half-deaf, and my night vision was absolutely shot. Still, I felt totally blissful.

"Oh, shit," Chloe said. "Guys, I think one of the flares on the shore just burned out. If they all go, we're not going to know where the rec center is!"

I squinted and looked around at the shoreline. I wasn't 100 percent certain, but it did seem like maybe there were fewer flares going than there had been at the beginning of the festivities. "Let's go!" I said. "I've got the sail. Ava, can you steer again?"

While Ava crawled toward the stern and grabbed the tiller, I pulled on the rope to raise the sail back up. Chloe said, "I've got my flashlight, but I don't want to use it unless we really have to. As soon as I turn it on, anybody who looks out will be able to see we're out here with the catamaran. And it will blow our night vision even more than the fireworks have already."

"I think it's okay," I said. "I'm pretty sure the long dark strip on our right is the golf course. So then the rec center dock should be straight ahead. As long as some of those flares on the left stay lit, I think we'll be fine."

We were not fine. The wind died down to the barest whisper, and within moments, we were just inching across the surface of the lake. It was so quiet we could clearly hear the little *pfft* sound as each flare burned itself out. In the end, we had to lower the sail and bust out the paddles. Ava pulled the rudder out of the water. Then she paddled on one side and I paddled on the other while Chloe shined the light straight forward.

For what it's worth, what we saw was that we would only have missed the dock by about fifty feet, which wasn't bad under the circumstances. However, when we corrected our course and got the boat pointed in the direction of the dock, the circumstances got much worse. A whole bunch of lights clicked on, going all the way from the rec center down to the edge of the dock. Then at least three flashlights came bobbing onto the dock itself.

"Uh, guys?" Ava said.

"I see them," Chloe replied.

"What do we do?"

"What are we going to do, make a run for it?" I said. "Because I hate to break it to you, but the Canadian border is pretty far."

"Jess..." Chloe said. Well, I use the word *said*, but actually, she kind of growled. I wasn't sure I'd ever really heard a girl who wasn't a mom growl before.

"I'm kidding. This is fine. We're fine. It's all fine. No worries. It's probably just the Independence Day Welcoming Committee, bringing us a complimentary cheese tray. Let's just dock and say hi. I hope they have some nice gouda. I sure do love me some gouda!"

Sometimes I ramble when I'm petrified. It's probably not endearing.

Ava laughed. "Not helping," Chloe mumbled.

"Or perhaps a warm brie with crackers."

"Still not helping," Chloe mumbled.

We pulled aside the dock with the lightest bump imaginable. I mean, it was really just a top-notch sailing performance, especially when you factor in how much my hands had started to shake. I looked around and tried to see who was there. It was hard to tell from all the crisscrossing beams of the flashlights, which were also reflecting off the bobbing aluminum dock, but I didn't see anyone who looked like a uniformed law enforcement officer. I took that for a good sign.

Then I saw my sister and Jake at the back of the group.

Traitors, I thought.

In front of them was my dad. And at the very front, holding out the mooring line to Chloe, was a grim-faced Larry.

As soon as Chloe took the rope from his hand, she started to apologize. "We're not here for you, Chloe," Larry said. "Ava, honey, can you come onto the dock?"

Ava crawled past me and stepped off the boat. As she stood up, everyone except me and Chloe crowded around her. I was behind her, but I heard her say quietly, "What's—"

Then my father said, "Ava, your father asked me to find you. I'm afraid I have some terrible news. It's about your mother."

7. The Price of Adventure

The funeral for Ava and Annie's mom was held two days later, in Florida, so Ava and Annie were both gone for the next week. Chloe and I spent that whole time at the rec center. When we weren't working our own shifts, we were either doing all the menial jobs at the pool to make up for the fact that the lifeguards were short-staffed without Ava or doing extra work down at the dock for Larry. He hadn't exactly yelled at us for taking the catamaran out. All he'd said was that we owed him one.

So far, it felt like that one had turned into about five. On the other hand, we were making a ton of extra money in overtime at the pool, which was kind of nice, and staying busy was good because it kept my mind off all the bad stuff that was going on.

My parents had even started noticing me again. They were both texting me multiple times a day to see how I was doing.

I was pretty sure our best friend's major life tragedy wasn't supposed to be this rewarding.

. . . .

On the third day of that week, Larry was supervising as Chloe and I pulled the catamaran onto the sand for its annual polishing. He had warned us to wear ratty old clothing, so I was in stained workout shorts and an ancient, ripped Ramones shirt I'd gotten at a street market near my high school in downtown Manhattan. Chloe was wearing gym shorts, too, along with flip-flops and an old, small T-shirt bearing the Tall Pines Landing motto: THE REAL WORLD ISN'T REAL!

"Heave!" Larry shouted at us. "Heave!"

I was like, *Thank you, Captain Hook.* He was so happy, it was ridiculous. Chloe bit her lip to keep herself from laughing. Usually, when she did that, all I could think about was kissing her. But with Ava gone for the reason she was gone, that felt weird.

With the help of some guys from the lawn-maintenance crew, we got the boat up onto a couple of sawhorses. Then the lawn dudes left and Larry spent another excruciating twenty minutes giving Chloe and me blow-by-blow instructions for how to wipe the industrial-strength cleaning solution onto the hulls, how to hose it back off, how to carefully hand-dry every square inch of the hulls, and then how to use fresh rags to apply the sealing wax.

After this long-winded speech, he asked, "Do you have any questions? Because I'm going to go inside now, and then it will be a whole big hassle to make me come out here again."

Chloe said, "Don't worry, Larry. I'm pretty sure we can read the directions on the cans if we have to. And if we get really stuck, we can always just look for how-to videos online. We're fine out here."

"Well, I'm sure *you* will be fine out here. You have a good head on your shoulders—except when you're stealing my boat. Just keep an eye on Science Boy over here. God knows how much damage he can do without supervision."

Chloe smirked at me. "I won't let him out of my sight for a second. I promise."

"Okay," Larry said, "you're responsible for this project, Chloe. Now get to work!"

Fifteen minutes later, I was on my back under one of the so-called hulls, scrubbing it down with cleaning solution. Chloe was standing up, wiping the same hull from the top. She prodded me softly with one sandaled foot. "Don't let this stuff drip down into your eyes, okay?" she said. "It's probably super toxic, and you have such pretty eyes."

Hey, I thought, *I have pretty eyes. But wait. Is that good? Should I have handsome eyes? Powerfully built eyes? Fine-hunk-o'-man eyes?* Whatever kind of eyes I had, they were having a hard time avoiding the view up the bottom of her shirt.

"Besides," she added, "you don't want to be staring straight up, anyway. You'll hurt yourself if you look right at the sun, and the only other thing up here is my midriff."

I turned my head away from her so fast, there's a chance she heard my vertebrae cracking.

"That's a funny word, isn't it?" she said. "Midriff. Midriff. Mid-RIFF. *Mid*-riff. It kind of sounds made-up."

I coughed. The paint-thinner smell of the cleaning fluid was making me lightheaded. Yeah, that had to be it.

"Try saying it," she said. "I'm serious."

I felt ridiculous, but you know—this was a direct order from Chloe. "Uh, midriff? Midriff. Midriff!"

"Am I right?" she asked. "Doesn't it sound totally fake?"

"Completely fake," I said. "Like birds. Or pandas. Or the moon landing."

Chloe nudged me again with her foot, a bit harder than the first time. "Laugh all you want, but you know I'm right. It's a weird mutant word. By the way, I got dress-coded in school for wearing this shirt. Can you believe it? It's not even that short. See? Look!"

I looked. I was definitely lightheaded. Freaking cleaning fluid. Freaking Larry. This was a hazardous work environment. I was lucky to be alive.

Also, the shirt looked pretty short to me. Maybe it was just the angle.

"Um . . ." I said.

"And, you know, I love wearing this shirt when I'm on Long Island. Do you remember when I got it?

We were twelve, and they were having a sale after Christmas-in-August. You bought the hoodie version the same day, and Ava got the same shirt, but in pink. Anyway, wearing it at school comforts me. Then, when I get upset about some stupid drama there, I can just close my eyes and tell myself, *The real world isn't real.*"

I was relieved to have a change of subject. "Yeah, I do that, too, with my hoodie," I said. "I did it a lot more in middle school. Leah used to laugh at me before she left for college. She was like, *You wear that thing every day,* but I don't know. It calmed me down when I needed it. Now I don't wear the hoodie as often."

"Why not?" Chloe asked.

"Well," I replied, "now I have your friendship bracelets."

Suddenly, her foot was touching my side again, but this wasn't a kick or anything. It was like some kind of hug. "Aww," she said. "That might honestly be the nicest thing you've ever said to me."

"Well, you know," I said, "I'm nice. I'm *famously* nice. Why, just last year, at the International Niceness Finals in Lisbon, Portugal, I scored a near-perfect nine-point-nine-three in the 'Endearing Comments Triathlon' event, and—"

She knelt down next to me and put two fingers over my lips. "Don't spoil the moment, Jess," she said. Unfortunately, her fingers were wet and gritty.

I gagged. I couldn't help it. "You . . . have . . . boat . . . cleaner . . . on . . . your . . . fingers," I gasped.

"Moment officially spoiled," she said. "Come on, sweet talker, let's get you a drink."

Luckily, there's an outdoor water fountain near the back door of the rec center, so we didn't have to go inside and explain to Larry why we weren't working. I had to splash a whole bunch of handfuls of water on my face, rub my lips with wet fingers for about thirty seconds, and then swish about ten swigs around my mouth before the toilet-cleanser taste and gritty consistency were all gone. When I stood back up, my shirt was soaked and completely plastered to my body.

Chloe flicked a finger against my chest. "Maybe we should dress-code *you*," she said, smirking.

"Uh, sorry," I said, "but we don't really get dress-coded at my school. You know, it's Manhattan, so as long as we're not, like, actively getting our nipples pierced in the middle of homeroom, it's pretty much anything goes. Plus, I mean, it's a math-and-science magnet school. The teachers don't really care what we wear, as long as we keep solving linear equations and winning National Merit Scholarships."

"Huh," Chloe said. "I never really thought about it, but the girls there must be really different. So . . . city-ish and, I don't know, intellectual. Is there anybody at school you, uh, like?"

I pretended to think about it for a minute as we strolled back down to the dock, but of course there wasn't. I had friends at school, but Chloe and Ava had always been pretty much the only two girls who mattered to me. "Nah," I said. "I mean, there are some interesting girls at school. Some are really sophisticated. And they're all smart. But."

"But what?" she asked, leaning toward me.

"But, you know. The real world isn't real. *This* is."

We picked up our rags and the cleaning fluid, and scrubbed the entire second hull in silence while I worked up the nerve to ask the question I'd been dying to ask for months. I'd even stalked Chloe's social media to try to figure it out, but honestly, she was so popular at home, and was tagged in so many different people's photos, that there was no way to figure out anything for certain.

"How about you, Chloe?" I finally croaked. "Sorry," I said, "I guess I still had some of the boat cleaner down my throat."

"What?"

"The boat cleaner. You know, from when you put your fingers on my—"

"Yeah, I remember the boat cleaner. Just because I don't go to some brainiac high school doesn't mean I can't recall whose lips I touched last. I mean, what was your question?"

"Oh, uh . . . is there anybody special for you? At school, I mean?"

Chloe bit her lip and turned halfway away. "I don't know," she said. "Kinda. But . . ."

"But what?"

She turned back toward me. "The real world isn't real."

As we dragged a hose over to rinse all the cleaning fluid off the hulls, Chloe said, "By the way, your dad was pretty great with Ava the other night."

I had noticed that, too. My father was generally the quietest member of my family in social situations, and he had been nearly silent in the weeks since my mom had dropped the big Europe-cancellation bomb. But he was a psychiatrist, and most of his patients were either kids or very elderly people, so it made sense that he would know how to talk to Ava in an emergency, especially when the emergency involved death.

"Yeah," I said. "You know, it's weird. Psychiatrists always do everything they can to hide their work from their families, so I've never really seen him dealing with anything like that. Once in a while, we'll run into someone who might be a patient of his when we're at a store or something, and he rushes us away like he's fleeing a fire. Then when we ask who the person was, he'll only say, 'Oh, that's just someone I know.' But I have to admit, he *was* pretty impressive. I feel guilty saying this, but I was almost surprised."

"You shouldn't be," Chloe said.

"Why not?"

"Because watching him with Ava the other night was like watching *you*."

That was a pretty mind-blowing thought, for a couple of reasons. First of all, it hadn't occurred to me that I was anything like my dad. And second of all, if my dad was so good at the calming thing, why was my mom suddenly so furious all the time?

8. See? Everything's Fine!

All week, I kept wondering how Ava and Annie were doing. When I texted Ava to ask, all she wrote back was very cryptic stuff like *Not good* or *Super awk*, or my personal favorite, *Tell you when I see you*. And I didn't know how much I was supposed to intrude. I couldn't imagine what they were going through. I had only gotten to give Annie one quick hug the night the news came, and she hadn't even looked like herself. Her eyes were red, haunted, and empty.

Half of me wished I could actually fly to Florida and be there for them, but the other half was relieved I didn't have to. I was super afraid I'd say the wrong thing.

Of course, I had my own family to worry about. My mom had been at the house all week, and then left just hours before my dad arrived for the weekend late Friday night. Neither of them had said a word about the timing. I'd been hoping that maybe they would overlap for dinner on Sunday before my father headed back to the city for the workweek, but then things got really weird.

My dad's favorite thing about the summer house was

the Sunday-morning pickup softball game. He never, ever missed that, unless he absolutely couldn't because he was on call at the hospital. (He even dragged me along sometimes, which, though I hated to admit it, was actually fun.) My mom loved all sorts of things about being at the house: She liked shopping for decorations, and going into the little towns nearby to look for antiques and gifts, and suntanning by the pool or the lake, and paddleboating, and taking long walks with her friends, and inviting people from the city up for the weekend. For my dad, though, the big attractions were basically grilling and softball.

So, as soon as he got home from the game that Sunday, he took a shower, got dressed, and then casually announced, "Okay, guys, I'm heading out! I hope you have a great week. Leah, you're in charge of your brother, okay?"

Leah wasn't even awake yet, even though it was almost lunchtime, so she just mumbled something from her loft upstairs. I jumped up from the couch by the door and said, "Wait a second. What do you mean, Leah's in charge? Isn't Mom coming up?"

Dad didn't look me in the eye. He just rushed around grabbing his duffel bag and a mug of coffee for the road. "No," he muttered. "Mom's, uh, staying on the island for a few days. Don't worry. I trust you and your sister. I talked it over with her last night. Just call or text if you need anything, or if you want to talk about Ava's situation."

I tried to think of something to say as my father

stepped around me and out the door, but for every question I could think of, there were several answers I didn't think I wanted to hear. So I didn't ask, our inordinately loud screen door slammed, the gravel of our driveway crunched, and he was gone.

I shuffled over to the kitchen table, feeling kind of numb in the pit of my stomach. I knew something was really wrong with my family, but it didn't seem like there was anything I could do about it. On top of that, Ava had texted early that morning to say she was back in New York from Florida, and that her dad was going to bring her and Annie up to their house by dinnertime.

I had to deal with my own weird family drama and get it out of the way so I could be there for her. Because no matter what was happening with my parents, I told myself it was nothing compared to what her week had been like.

My parents had never just left us in the mountains before. I know it sounds stupid, and a lot of teenagers would have been thrilled by the sudden freedom, but I was stunned. I felt like they had just forgotten us or something—like we didn't exist to them. Like suddenly, they were both in the real world, and we weren't, and *we were the part that wasn't real.*

Leah came stumbling downstairs, banged around the kitchen for a couple of moments, and then groaned, "You . . . finished . . . coffee?"

"Yeah, but—"

"Jess, don't. Can't talk yet. Coffee."

Ever since she'd left for college, my sister had been like some weird cross between a vampire and a caveman. She was basically nocturnal, and she couldn't say a complete sentence before noon unless she had drunk at least one huge mug of coffee. So I sat there biting my tongue as she slowly started a fresh pot and made her breakfast.

Meanwhile, I just wanted to scream at her, *How are you not panicking? Can't you see what's going on here?* It was like we were both in the back seat of a car that was headed for the edge of a cliff, but I was the only one awake.

I needed to calm down or I was going to have a heart attack right there at the table. I took out my phone, opened up my music player, and put on my all-time favorite album: *Plans*, by Death Cab for Cutie. I know it's kind of a weird choice, because it came out when I was two years old. But for some reason, it was one of the albums my dad always played when we were driving to the summer house, so it meant a lot to me. Plus, I love the bass parts. In a way, they're incredibly simple. They aren't flashy. Nobody's going to give the bass player a medal for his musical virtuosity or anything, but every note supports the rest of the song perfectly. The bass player holds everything together.

For five songs, I hummed the bass parts while the music filled the kitchen. By the time Leah's eyes were fully open and the scent of coffee had stopped being completely nauseating to me, I felt composed enough to speak.

"So, you . . . uh, you caught the part about Mom not coming up, right?"

Leah took a sip from her mug, swallowed a bite of the bagel she'd been working on, and said, "Yeah. No problem, right? You're working every day, I'm working at the day care center every day. We can do take-out dinners, or maybe we can even try to figure out something to cook one night. Just promise me I won't come home and find you on the couch in some kind of crazy situation with Chloe or Ava. Or both."

"Really? *That's* your big concern? Also, eww."

"Well, if I'm going to be responsible for your moral upbringing this week, I don't want to be raising some kind of irresponsible pig, that's all. So treat the women with respect, that's all I'm saying. Or go to their houses, and let their parents deal with you."

"My moral upbringing? Please. You've been in charge of me for what, thirty seconds? Besides, what kind of example have you and Jake been setting for me for the past year and a half? I've walked in on you fooling around, getting high, fooling around *while* getting high—"

"For the record, Jake and I are adults. You and your friends are children. Besides, Jake and I are an actual couple. It's natural for us to do actual couple things. If—and I am not saying this is ever even going to happen—but *if* you and Chloe or you and Ava become a legit couple, then it would be different."

"I'm not doing anything with Chloe or Ava!"

"I didn't say you were. Chill!"

"And that's not even my point. I wanted to say that—"

"By the way, I'm totally Team Chloe. In case you're keeping score. Jake's Team Ava, but he's an idiot. So yeah, don't take girl advice from Jake, whatever you do. Because I promise, the time *will* come when he will offer it."

I blinked. I thought, *Yeah, like I'm just lining up to beg for dating advice from a dude who would be attracted to you.*

But Leah, in her very special, annoying big-sister way, was getting me sidetracked. With a little mental apology to Death Cab's bassist, Nick Harmer, I turned off the music and took a deep breath. "Forget about my non-existent and totally imaginary love life for a minute, okay? Aren't you at all concerned that our parents have stopped speaking to each other? Or that they're never up here at the same time anymore? Or that NOBODY EXCEPT ME IS EVEN TRYING TO TALK ABOUT THIS?"

"Oh, that's why you're all worked up? Is this about the little Europe squabble they had?"

I blinked again. It sometimes felt to me as though Leah and I spoke two completely different languages that, by some wild coincidence, were made up of words that all sounded identical, yet had completely different meanings. *Squabble?* How could she be serious? From everything I could tell, our parents were waging some kind of silent cold war.

64

"Leah, this doesn't feel like a squabble. Mom and Dad had that trip planned for a year. Mom embarrassed Dad in front of their friends. She wouldn't even tell him why she canceled. And you don't get your money back when you pull out of a trip at the last minute like that. Nobody does that unless there's a really big problem."

Leah tipped her chair onto its two back legs. I hated when she did that. I always thought she was going to fall backward, crack her head open, and die.

"Jess," she said, "you have to understand. Mom and Dad have done this before, and it all turned out fine. Do you remember the bathroom tile fiasco when we were little?"

I had no idea what she was talking about, so I shook my head.

"Okay, do you remember when we moved into the house on Weston Avenue, it had that awful 1970s wall-paper in the upstairs bathroom, with the pink-and-green tile floor?"

"I don't know," I said. "Maybe? Were there cats?"

"Yes! There were little black-and-white cats between the vanity and the mirror. They were just the right height to be at eye level for the little step stool you stood on to reach the sink. When you brushed your teeth, it looked like the cats were staring at you. When we first moved in, you were too scared to brush your teeth alone because you said they looked like they were angry."

"Okay, yeah. That sounds familiar. So?"

"Well, Mom wanted to get the bathroom redone right away because you were freaking out. So Dad reluctantly agreed. But the tile she liked for the floor was really expensive. I mean, I was pretty young, obviously, but I remember Dad saying over and over, 'Why does it have to be a special order for a kid's bathroom? What child needs custom tile?'"

I had no memory of this at all, but I had to admit, it did sound like something my father would say. He didn't like spending extra money on anything, and our mom really, really liked fancy stuff. "So the gray tile we have in there now is . . . ?"

"I'm getting there, Jess. Mom listened to Dad and ordered some kind of cheaper tile. But I guess our bathroom floor is, like, an irregular size or something? So the builder guys had to cut the tile? And when they tried to cut it, a bunch of the pieces shattered. So then, Mom and Dad had to buy some kind of more expensive tile after all, which is the gray floor we have now. Which means we ended up spending even more money than if Dad had just let Mom get what she wanted in the first place, but Mom still got stuck with a floor that wasn't the one she wanted. Mom didn't talk to Dad for *weeks*."

"Well, what ended the fight? What made them start talking again?"

"*You* did. It was the day of your fourth birthday party, and you threw a fit. You started screaming because

Grandpa Art was trying to take a picture and you noticed Mom wasn't holding Dad's hand. You pointed right at Mom and started shouting this hand-holding song you knew from day care. Do you remember the one?"

With a bit of a shock, I realized I did know the song. A bit hesitantly, I started singing, "I hold your hand, you hold my hand. We sing, we play, and we don't . . . let . . . go!"

"Yup. You were shouting the words, and you grabbed Mom's hand and Dad's hand, and you pushed them together. Then you started yelling, 'SING!' at the top of your lungs. They looked at each other, and I don't think either one of them knew what to do."

"Wait, I kind of remember this. Did Grandma Jean say something?"

"Uh-huh. She was putting the candles on your birthday cake. I was on her lap. She pointed a candle at Mom and said, 'Far be it from me to tell my grown daughter what to do, but my grandchild is crying on his birthday. So maybe you might consider holding hands and singing for his sake?' So then Mom and Dad stood there holding hands and singing the song. It was the most awkward thing I've ever seen in my life. To this day. And that includes your many, many excruciating interactions with Chloe and Ava."

"Thanks for throwing that in."

"My pleasure. Anyway, after that, they just kind of started talking again. They moved on. Things got back to normal. So, all I'm saying is that Mom and Dad will work this out eventually. Maybe in December for your birthday. Just in case, you might want to practice the hand-holding song. Not gonna lie, you sounded a little rusty there."

I had a totally different thought, though. Our grand-parents, Art and Jean, were still alive and well, though they had retired to Florida. If things between the parents didn't improve, maybe I could invite Grandma and Grandpa up north for a visit.

9. Chloe and *Annie* Make Things Weird

I was too edgy that afternoon to just sit around and do nothing, so I went up to my room and took out my "emergency instrument." I mostly left it in Pennsylvania all summer so I had something to play. It was a Kala U-Bass, which was a ukulele-style bass. Even though it was tiny, had rubber strings, and looked like a toy, if you played it through a half-decent amplifier, it had amazingly deep tone.

And, especially when I was panicking, any bass was a zillion times better than no bass.

A secret benefit of the ukulele bass was that the small size and the soft strings meant I could play for hours without tiring my hands or ripping up my fingers. I played along with several of my favorite albums, and the only times I stopped were for urgent things like eating snacks and checking my phone for Ava arrival updates. She had texted to say her plane had landed in New York, but there hadn't been anything the rest of the afternoon.

Still, when I figured I had less than an hour left, I decided to cue up one of my all-time best mood-changing albums: Stevie Wonder's *Talking Book*, from the 1970s. I loved playing along with it, and the bass parts were insanely good. The nutty thing was, there wasn't even an actual bass player on the record. Stevie Wonder is a piano player, and he played all the bass parts with his left hand on an electric keyboard.

If someone had interrupted me while I was dancing around my room playing along with Stevie's most famous song, "Superstition," that wouldn't have been too terrible. I mean, I would have felt a bit sheepish, because I was rocking out with this tiny instrument, and my back was to the door, so the first sight would have been a bit more booty shaking than strictly necessary. But I sounded good, and the song was undeniably cool.

Sadly, Chloe let herself into my house and crept up the stairs like some kind of ninja four songs later, while the last song on the album was playing. The song, "I Believe," wasn't as funky or as famous as "Superstition," but if you'd held me down and injected me with truth serum, I'd have been forced to admit it was my favorite. The bass line wasn't super flashy, but it had the same kind of perfection I loved in my Death Cab for Cutie songs.

Plus, and I would have never said this out loud unless the whole truth-serum thing happened to me first, the lyrics got to me.

So what Chloe found me doing was not some slightly overdone rock-star act. No, she found me swaying gently, as though caught in a slightly wistful tropical breeze, caressing the notes out of the instrument with the side of my thumb and singing—SINGING!—"I believe when I fall in love with you, it will be forever."

Not once, mind you, but something like seventeen times in a row.

What can I say? The essence of funk is repetition.

And the essence of embarrassment was Chloe, in my doorway, clearing her throat at the end of all that repetition.

I whirled around so fast I nearly smashed the headstock of the bass against the door frame. The only thing that saved the instrument from total destruction was how short it was. As it was, I just lost my balance, got halfway wrapped up in the cord from my bass to my little practice amp, and knocked my phone down.

"Who knew you were so romantic, Jess?" Chloe said.

"It's just a song," I mumbled.

"It's okay," she said quickly. "*I* knew you were romantic. That's one of the things I love about you."

Suddenly, I felt like it was about a thousand degrees in my room. Now, to be fair, it was just a little loft carved out of an attic space, so it *did* get pretty hot up there in the summer.

"So, uh, do we have a plan for when Ava comes?" I asked, unstrapping my bass and wiping the neck down with a rag. (Sweat and wood are a bad combination.) "Because

I'm afraid I'll say something awkward and terrible and scar her for life. And Annie. What am I supposed to say to Annie? She just lost her mom and she's *twelve*."

Then it hit me: Chloe had lost *her* mom when she was twelve. "I mean, I know you were twelve. When your mom . . . Oh, God, I'm sorry. There's no way I'm not going to say the wrong thing. I'm saying the wrong thing *right now*. What did people say to you?"

Chloe sat down on my bed. I turned off my amp, unplugged the bass, zipped it into its soft case, and sat down next to her. My parents never let me be alone with either of the girls in my room, but I figured if they really cared, they wouldn't have both arranged to be two states away at the same time.

Chloe put her hand over mine. "Listen, Jess, you're gonna say the wrong thing. Everybody does. People who love me said absolutely horrible things. They didn't mean to, but honestly, what can you possibly say to a girl who's just woken up from a medically induced coma and found out her mother is dead and she slept through the funeral? It was almost comical. Even the doctors were like, 'We had to remove your spleen, but don't worry! You still have your liver!' Like, *I'm twelve! I didn't even know I had a spleen until five seconds ago, and now it's gone. Thanks a lot!* So, don't worry about being awkward. Just be there for Ava. And for Annie. I mostly don't remember who said what. I remember who showed up."

Chloe stared at the corner of my room, where the steeply sloped ceiling met the floor, for a long time without saying anything. A pile of my dirty laundry was heaped way over there, which my mom would normally never have allowed, but hey—things weren't normal that summer. Anyway, I was squinting at the pile, hoping none of my underwear was near the top, when Chloe said, "You sent me a bunch of cards. Do you remember?"

"Oh, geez." I remembered sending something, but not exactly what it was. Ava and I had spent hours in the treehouse working on one shipment of artwork for the hospital room, but I had no idea what we'd made. Neither of us was exactly a gifted artist, though. "I hope it wasn't anything too awful."

"No, it was sweet. You made me an incredibly childish-looking hemlock tree and a lake. In crayon. With a mangled-looking animal with antlers next to the tree, and a little speech bubble that said, 'I miss you, deer.' As in, *D-E-E-R.*"

That was the corniest thing I'd ever heard. What could I possibly have been thinking? And why hadn't Ava stopped me?

Chloe smiled. "So you see, Mr. Jesse Dienstag, you've been a romantic soul for a long time, and you were there for me. I still have your card. It's in a box under my bed in Long Island, with all of my other favorite things. Now, let's go wait for Ava and Annie. And don't worry. We all love you for a reason." As we stood up to head downstairs, she gestured around the room. "And you can be *sure* it isn't your housekeeping abilities!"

. . . .

Ava's dad's car finally pulled into the cul-de-sac around twilight, just as Chloe and I finished stringing up a bunch of battery-powered white fairy lights all around the inside of the treehouse. I worried it might look a bit too Christmas-in-August-ish, but Chloe insisted Ava would want a warm welcome. She had even downloaded dozens of old movies we had liked from when we were little kids, in case Ava felt like having a mindless marathon instead of talking. We didn't have power or Wi-Fi out there, but Chloe had charged her laptop all the way up to 100 percent.

I looked at Chloe in the fairy light and thought, *See, this is why you are our leader. You think of stuff.*

We ran out from behind the house to meet Ava's family in the driveway. Her stepmom, Tracy, came out the front door just as the girls got out of the car. Annie ran right into her arms, but Ava just kind of stood there. Meanwhile, their dad, Richard, seemed totally oblivious to the drama and headed directly for the trunk to get the luggage.

"Family dynamics, am I right?" I whispered to Chloe.

"You are not *not* right," she whispered back. "Now shut up and let's go hug Ava."

74

Ava was wearing all black. She never wore black. It felt wrong to me. Ava was a red-and-pink kind of person. She liked bright, flashing things, and sunshine, and sparkles. Even in the dead of winter, she wore fluorescent, ski-bunny kinds of colors. Now it was like her light had gone out.

When we put our arms around her, for a split second she stood stiffly with her arms straight at her sides. I almost let go, like we were forcing unwanted physical contact on her. Then, all of a sudden, her knees kind of sagged, her arms came up, and we were supporting her weight as she broke into sobs. I had to let go of her and quickly get my arm under hers and around her waist, or she would have sunk down to the ground.

It was the first time I'd ever felt the literal weight of another person's grief.

By the time we got Ava up to the house, Tracy had set out trays of cookies, some cut-up fruit, and milk. Annie was eating and seemed basically okay. Their dad was sitting next to her, looking concerned. He made eye contact with me, and I was pretty sure he was trying to ask me with his eyes whether Ava was going to pull through.

I gave a little nod that I hoped was vaguely reassuring. Then I grabbed two cookies and a brimming bowl of watermelon chunks. Plus a large serving of milk.

I might have been sad, but I was also a growing boy. My bird chest problem wasn't going to fix itself.

While everybody except Ava ate, Tracy made small talk about the flight, the weather in Florida, and how Chloe and I were enjoying our work at the rec center. I could see Ava's jaw clenching. Even when her mom hadn't just died, Ava had no patience for her stepmother. On the other hand, the woman really knew how to curate a snack assortment. Also, she seemed to be good at engaging Annie, which made me glad.

The instant I put down my milk glass, Ava practically lunged for my arm and said, "Let's go out to the treehouse!" Chloe, who had only eaten maybe a cookie and half a berry, jumped right up and said, "Thanks for the food, Mrs. Green!" Then she turned toward the back screen door as Ava yanked me in that direction. I took a step to follow, but Annie said, "Jesse, wait! Can I talk to you for a second?"

Ava sighed, let go of my arm, and walked out behind Chloe. I started to sit down at the table, but Annie said, "I mean, alone." Then she led me downstairs to a little TV room that was kind of tucked in under their back deck. I saw the fairy lights winking on in the distance as I sat down in a recliner facing Annie, who was perched on the very edge of their couch.

"What's up?" I asked. "Are you okay, Sunshine? I mean, I know you're not *okay* okay, but are you *doing* okay? Can I help? Can I get you something? I don't know. Do you want to hit tennis balls tomorrow?" Annie bit her lip. I was afraid she was going to cry super hard, like her sister had, and I wasn't going to be able to calm her down by myself. "What is it? Do you . . . do you need water?"

Annie surprised me then. She burst out laughing. And I don't mean just a little. I mean, like she laughed until she was doubled over, wheezing. She made sounds I'd never heard a human being make before. It was like I was trapped in a room with a very verbal dolphin that was trying to win a shouting match with a broken set of bagpipes. It got so bad that her dad yelled from the top of the stairs, "Jess, is everything all right down there?"

I said, "Um, I think so. I'm pretty sure Annie is having some kind of weird . . . laughing fit?"

From the kitchen, Tracy chimed in, "Oh, yeah, she'll do that when she's stressed. Just wait it out!"

So I sat there. Three different times, Annie nearly got herself under control, began to sit up straight, held one pointer finger up in the air, looked at me, and then lost it all over again.

This went on for *minutes*. I seriously considered breaking out my phone and timing it. Eventually, though, Annie managed to pull herself together. Then she locked eyes with me and said in a deep, mock-serious voice, "Do you want to hit tennis balls tomorrow? *Do you need water?* Oh my goodness, you are such a dork!"

I was kind of hurt. She must have seen it in my face, because she said, "I love you the absolute most, but come on. Tennis balls and water? I'm fine. Honestly. I knew my mom was going to die, and I got to say goodbye. I'm sad, but I was ready for this."

"Okay," I said. "I'm . . . glad, I guess? But then, why did you want to talk to me?"

"I'm worried about Ava. You know she doesn't get along with Tracy or my dad as well as I do. And at home—I mean, in Connecticut—she doesn't really have close friends. There are a couple of girls, but . . ."

"But what?"

"Well, you know how she is. She gets snappy. She pushes people away sometimes. And then there are the guys."

I felt the hair rise on the back of my neck. I forced myself to keep my voice even and neutral. "What guys?" I asked.

"Okay, you have to swear you won't repeat this to anyone." She stared straight into my eyes and I nodded. "Ava attracts a certain kind of boy. These boys aren't her friends. I don't even think they really like her. They're just hot for her body. But I think she likes the attention."

Wow, I thought. *Somehow, when I wasn't paying attention, my little Sunshine became a thirty-year-old with a psychology degree.* "Well, that doesn't sound ideal," I said.

"It's not," Annie said. "So that's where you come in. You have to promise me you'll be there for Ava this year, no matter what happens. Chloe is really nice, but I think Chloe gets distracted during the year. When she's out in the real world, she doesn't always text Ava back. Or, like, Ava will tag her on social media, but she won't like the posts. I know Chloe loves Ava, but Chloe is so popular wherever she goes. Chloe is the kind of person who loves you *when you're in front of her.*"

"Okay," I said, hoping with at least half my heart that Annie was wrong about Chloe. "So what am I?"

"You're a ride-or-die person. I mean, you're still a dork. But you're a dork who would never, ever use Ava. Or hurt her. She's safe with you. So that's your job: Keep her safe. What do you say?"

I swallowed. My life was getting more and more complicated.

"Fine," I said.

10. Ava's in the Club

As I climbed the wooden ladder up to the treehouse, I could hear that Ava was in the middle of a pretty raging monologue about her trip to Florida, but strangely, she sounded kind of jolly about it. As soon as my head popped up above floor level, I found out why. She was propped up in one corner, holding something small and shiny between two fingers and her thumb. She stopped speaking for an instant, and raised it to her lips.

It was one of those miniature liquor bottles you can buy on an airplane. That wasn't good. As far as I knew, Ava hadn't really had any experience with alcohol before.

"Hi, J," she said after taking a swallow. "Can you believe they just left a whole cart full of these unattended by the bathroom, ALL THE WAY IN THE BACK OF THE PLANE? I wasn't gonna take any, but then I was like, *Who needs it more than me?* So I decided to have myself a little Christmas-in-July action. I don't know how you guys knew to put the lights up in here, but good job. So smart! Ten points to Gryffindor! That's a book joke. Because I am also smart. *Master* thief here. Check my purse, Klo! But gently. That's evidence."

Ava's purse clinked and clanked like someone was throwing chains down a flight of stairs.

"Holy wow, Ava," Chloe said. "This is a lot of evidence."

"Well, it's a lot of *little* evidence. Because, you know, small bottles. In fact, this is my second one, and it's finished already!" She put it down next to her on the wooden plank floor and patted it like a dog. "Thank you, next!"

I laughed. Chloe gave me a dirty look. "What?" I said. "That was funny. It's a song! You know, Ariana Gran—"

"I know it's a song. But don't encourage her."

"So, Ava," I said, "you were telling Chloe about your flight. Was that the flight down, or the flight back up to New York?"

"No, I already *told* her about the flights. That's where I got these!" She held up another two little bottles, and then slid them across the floor toward us. I had to lunge to stop mine from flying over the edge of the treehouse floor and smashing on the stony ground below. "Now we are going to do a toast."

"Uh, why are we going to do a toast, Ava?" Chloe said.

"Because in Florida at the fluneral, I didn't have anyone to toast with." She snorted. "I just said 'fluneral.' Because I'm flunny! Anyway, I wasn't going to get Annie drunk, was I? Plus, I couldn't even if I wanted to, because I got these on the way *home*. But that's not the point. The point is that there was nobody real at the . . . I can't even say it right . . . at the *burial event*. So we are going to conduct the ceremony now."

She looked at Chloe, then at me. "Any questions?"

"Uh—" I said.

"That was rhetorical, J. The correct answer is 'No.' Now, any problems?"

"Well—" Chloe said.

"Right you are, Klo. I can see it in your eyes that you've realized the flaw in my plaw. The flan in my plan. The problem. We can't climb down once we start drinking. And I am already drinking. So—NOBODY LEAVES. I hereby declare a mandatory sleepover! I hope everybody's wearing clean underwear."

Chloe said, "Ava, can you give us just a second? Jess, conference, please?" This was kind of ridiculous, because the whole treehouse was only about eight feet by ten feet. We had two narrow, plastic-covered foam mattresses leaned up against one wall, and when they were laid down side by side, they nearly filled the entire floor. But Chloe crouched next to me by the ladder, which at least meant we weren't within arm's reach of Ava.

"What do you think, Jesse?" she asked.

"YOU KNOW I CAN HEAR YOU!" Ava blurted.

"I think we're doing this. We kind of don't have a choice. She already can't climb down, right? Plus, even if we managed to get her down, her dad and Tracy would kill her."

Chloe bit her lip. "Okay," she said, "but I think someone

has to run inside and tell the Greens we're sleeping over. While I'm in there, I'll grab a couple of bottles of water, too. I can text my dad, and you better let your parents know."

"Don't worry about it," I said quickly.

"Wait," she said. "Won't your mom freak?"

"She's not here. It's just me and Leah."

Chloe raised an eyebrow. She had very expressive eyebrows. "That's unusual. Okay, will you text Leah, then?"

I sighed. My sister was irritating, but she would probably want to know. "Yes."

"Okay. Ava, I'm going into your house for a minute."

"YEAH, I CAUGHT THAT PART."

"Do you want anything from inside?"

"THREE COOKIES AND ... AND ... MY PINK FLASHLIGHT. AND MY PLILLOW. PILLOW! AND ANOTHER COOKIE. AND A HUG. BUT I WANT THE HUG FIRST."

Chloe crawled over and hugged Ava, who whimpered, "I love you."

On her way back past me, Chloe bumped my hip and whispered, "Watch her. It's gonna be a long night."

I told Ava she couldn't open her next drink bottle until Chloe came back. In the meantime, I got her to lean forward and slid one mattress behind her back. Then I got her to stand for a moment and slid the other mattress onto the floor where her butt had been, so we had a sort of homemade couch. When Chloe came back, she found us with our backs to the wall, but cushioned in comfort.

It took her two trips up the ladder, but she hauled in a bag of snacks and water, plus a bag stuffed with pillows and what looked like a big blanket. "I couldn't find your flashlight," she said, "but your dad promised he'd leave the porch lights on."

"Okey-dokey," Ava said. "Now it's toast time."

Chloe sat down so that Ava was between us. "It's toast time, honey. And we're here for it."

Ava handed me a bottle. I couldn't see the label, because even though beams of light were streaming in from the porch, they weren't hitting the side of the bottle that was facing me. When I unscrewed the lid, a strange smell rose up, kind of like a mix of paint thinner and dessert.

"What did you get, J?" Ava asked.

"I have no idea," I said. Honestly, outside of wine at Jewish holidays, I'd had about five sips of alcohol in my life, so it wasn't like I was some great expert.

Chloe reached across, took my bottle, and sniffed it. "Smells like Baileys," she said. "Be careful with that, Jess. It tastes like ice cream, but it's super strong."

I took it back from her. When our hands touched, she took an extra second to squeeze my fingers. She probably meant it as a warning, but I felt it as a thrill. The excitement lasted until Ava opened her mouth.

"So," she said, "lift 'em up! To dead moms!"

Chloe wrapped one arm around Ava's neck and raised her bottle with her free hand. I did the same. "To dead moms!" we repeated. I felt weird saying it, like I didn't have the right. But when you're with your two favorite people and they're toasting, you can't be the only one who doesn't say the toast, right?

Then we drank. Ava downed the contents of her bottle in one gulp. Chloe sipped daintily at hers. I took a mouthwash-ish approach: I swirled maybe half the contents around my mouth before attempting to swallow it. When I did, the effect was basically like what you'd expect if you tossed back a shot of Listerine. I felt like my throat was on fire. I gagged a bit, and I was pretty sure a small yet forceful jet of the stuff had been propelled up into the back of my nose. Ava started pounding me on the back, which wasn't helpful.

Neither was her giggling.

Chloe quickly broke out a water bottle for me. That helped a bit, or at least, it made me feel like my sinuses weren't going to melt and fall off my face.

"Thanks," I gasped.

"No prob," Chloe said.

"Now finish the bottle, J," Ava said. "You have to do it fast before you think about it too much."

That sounded like really good advice—for becoming an instant alcoholic. "Sips, Jess," Chloe said. "We've got all night. Ava, what's the next toast?"

"No, now I have to *talk* about the toast. See, I couldn't talk to anybody in Florida. It was just all these old people we didn't really know, like great-aunts and half uncles—which, I don't even know what a half uncle even *is*—and my mom's creepy, cigarette-smelling *boyfriend*. I didn't even know she had a boyfriend until, like, two months ago. Plus, 'boyfriend,' really? A boyfriend is what you have when you're fifteen. When you're forty-six, you're not supposed to have a boyfriend. You're supposed to have a, I don't know, a husband. Or a companion? And when you're dead, you definitely don't have a boyfriend. I was like, 'Look, my dude, now you are her nothing.' Am I right? Have you ever seen a tombstone that said, 'Survived by her beloved children, her ex-husband, and her boyfriend since last Tuesday'? No, no, you haven't, and there's a reason for that. Jesus, Florida was a whole mood. No wonder I need a drink."

She stopped to distribute more little bottles, and cracked hers open.

"Ava—" I started to say. I had no idea what was going to follow, but I didn't like the sound of "I need a drink" coming out of her mouth. Just like forty-six-year-olds shouldn't say "boyfriend," sixteen-year-olds shouldn't say, "I need a drink." Ava was scaring me.

"Shhh," she said. "That was another thing about the old people. They wouldn't shut up. They were all like, 'I just want you to know, we'll always be here for you!' And

I was like, 'Great! Who are you again, exactly?' Annie kept asking me if there was a family tree somewhere, and I have no freaking clue. Like, our mom's parents are dead. Our mom is dead. Who knows this stuff now? Who's going to tell Annie who everyone *is*?"

Ava paused. Her moods swung fast at normal times. I felt a swing coming on. The hair stood up on the back of my neck.

"So," she said, "we were in the room at the funeral home before the service. And all these dusty-smelling relatives were swarming around us, talking to us. And Annie was crying. I couldn't get them away. And the smoky-smelling guy had his arm around me, and I had this crazy urge to bite him. I mean, literally just bite him and run."

Now Ava didn't seem silly-drunk at all, just totally, brutally honest, and super sad. Reflexively, I unwrapped my arm from around her shoulder. I didn't want to remind her of her mom's boyfriend and freak her out.

"No, J, hold me. I wanted you there. I wanted you there more than anything. You too, Chloe. I felt like we needed bodyguards. Anyway, the . . . I don't know what you call it . . . the lady who was like in charge of the funeral? The funeral boss? Must have seen that we were upset, because she came over and told everybody to leave. She said in this spooky voice, 'It was the will of the deceased that only her daughters see her remains before the interment.' It took me a minute to realize what she was saying, that our mom wanted us to look at her *body* in the *coffin* one last time. After she kind of shooed all the old people out, I asked her, 'Do we have to see her?' I didn't know if I wanted to. I mean, when we saw her in the spring, she already didn't look like her. She was so . . ."

Ava stopped talking, took a few deep breaths, and wiped her eyes. Then she took a sip from her bottle and shuddered. "She was so thin. My mom was *never* thin when we were kids. Cuddling up with her was always comfy. She was *pillowy*, kind of like a plushy toy, you know? And then she lost her hair, and her boobs, and . . . she wasn't even *herself* by the end. She didn't even *sound* like her."

Ava finished the bottle and dropped it on the mattress. It occurred to me that the whole treehouse was going to reek of alcohol in the morning.

"So anyway," Ava said, "I wasn't sure I wanted to see what was left of her. And I wanted to protect Annie. She's usually the happy one, you know. She's the *well-adjusted* Green girl."

Chloe started to protest, but Ava held up a hand. "Come on," she said. "I love you for trying, but you know it's true. Annie's the sweet child in this family and I'm the difficult one. But that's not the point. The point is, she was crying, right? And if I didn't protect her, who would? The lady looked at us and said in that funeral voice, 'It's your choice, of course, but in my experience, most loved ones find closure in seeing the departed one last time.' When she said 'the departed,' I felt Annie's back get all stiff under my hand. I didn't know what to do, but Annie said, 'I want to see her.'"

Ava stared out of the treehouse, over the roofline of her house, into the darkness. "*I'm* the big sister, right? But Annie was the one who made the decision. So then this woman walks us over to the . . . she walks us over to my mom's *coffin*. Which I've been trying really hard to ignore, if I'm being honest. I mean, thank God my mom was Jewish, or I guess the coffin would have been open the whole time, right? And we would have had to be in the room with it for, like, days while everybody in America walked by and *breathed* all over her. Ugh, she could barely stand running into random people when she was *alive*. Where was I? Oh, yeah: the 'closure before the interment.'"

She paused to take a sip. Just to be polite, I finished my bottle. Then I quickly slugged down some water before I could choke again.

"So the lady opens the lid. There are all these little hidden buttons and latches that keep it open. It was surprisingly complicated for something you basically only use once. I thought about how weird it was, like my mom wouldn't care how fancy the coffin was. She didn't even care if her car had working air-conditioning, and she lived in freaking Florida, you know? But anyway, the lid swung up, and there she was. But I felt like that wasn't really her.

It sounds crazy, but I thought, *This is fake. It's a doll. My mother isn't that tiny. And they got the wig color wrong. And her hands are too still. My mother had nervous hands. Plus, who bought that dress? It has lace around the collar. She didn't like lace!* My mind was going about a mile a minute, and my heart was pounding. I wanted to scream, 'Close it up! That's not her!'"

She paused again, and I could see tears running down her cheeks. Chloe was facing me, and she was crying silently, too.

"And then what happened?" I asked softly. I was kind of afraid to make her go on, but it seemed like she needed to get it all out.

"Then Annie said, in this squeaky little voice, 'Goodbye, Mommy.'"

Suddenly, tears were running down my face, too. Without a word, Chloe reached into the snack bag, pulled out a huge wad of loose tissues, and dumped the tissues in Ava's lap. I raised an eyebrow. How had she known?

"Come on, Jess," she said, half laughing and half sniffling. "This isn't my first rodeo."

For about fifteen minutes that felt like about fifteen hours, we all just sat there, occasionally grabbing another tissue or another burning sip. When everybody finally seemed reasonably calm again, I raised my bottle and said, "To Annie."

"To Annie," Chloe and Ava repeated.

We all drank, but slowly.

"To you, Ava," Chloe added.

"Ava!" I said.

"Aw, you guys!" Ava said. For a moment, she looked almost contented. But then she frowned. "Klo," she said, "to *you*. You're like my . . . I don't know, my guide. All of this would be even worse if you hadn't been here to talk me through it ahead of time. Thank you."

Chloe patted Ava's leg. "Yeah, well. Dead moms. It's not a club you *want* to join. The initiation *sucks*. But once you're in, the other members really have your back."

That pretty much ended the toasting portion of the evening's festivities. Chloe declared that it was bedtime. We stood up, making sure that Ava stayed way over by the back wall, and laid the mattresses down. Then we put the pillows down, covered the crack between the mattresses with a blanket, and got Ava settled in over that middle area. Finally, Chloe and I placed ourselves on either side of her, like bookends, so she wouldn't be able to get up or roll without us knowing.

Chloe even took off Ava's shoes.

Ava curled up on her side, facing Chloe and the back wall. She mumbled a couple of "I love yous," and was snoring softly within about a minute.

Chloe and I were on our backs, looking up at the ceiling.

Actually, the way we had placed the mattresses, I was near the edge where the floor met the ladder, so I was looking up at both the ceiling and a slice of the sky.

"Oh, Jess," Chloe said in a quiet, sleepy voice, "I just thought of something! You don't move around a lot when you sleep, do you?"

"Not usually," I said. "Why?"

"Well, it occurs to me that if you roll to your left, you're going to fall out of the tree. And that would be bad."

Truthfully, I never moved around when I was in my normal bed. But then again, Ava tended to toss and turn a lot, like she was burrowing into her bed. In fact, she was already pressing against me with her butt. If she pushed hard enough, I supposed I could end up doing a very brief and unsuccessful impression of a baby bird in its first flight. Also, I realized I was just a tad lightheaded.

"Uh, I hadn't really thought about it, but you're right. I would not be a fan of the midnight tree plunge."

"Don't worry," she said. "I am formulating a plan. You are lucky to have me, I swear."

I sat up. So did she. "I know I'm lucky to have you, Chloe. Believe me. So, uh, what's the plan?"

She held up a finger. "I've got it! We secure you."

"With what?"

"Blanket technology. I've got this. Lie down again."

I did. I could hear Chloe rustling around. I couldn't

really see over Ava's shoulder, but I figured she was getting another blanket out of the bag. Then Chloe's face appeared above me. She was leaning way, way across Ava.

"What are you doing?" I asked.

"Tucking you in. Relax and enjoy it. Now tilt yourself up toward Ava."

I did, and Chloe kind of scooted handfuls of the blanket all along underneath my back from my shoulder to my feet. "Now lie back again."

When I rolled back toward the edge of the mattress, the blanket was beneath me. "See?" Chloe said, still braced on her forearms across Ava's waist. "Now all I have to do is tuck the other edge under me and you'll be anchored in!"

I was dazzled by a combination of Chloe's thinking, the closeness of her face above mine, and—okay—a few assorted shots of alcohol. "Chloe," I said, "can I tell you something?"

"Sure," she whispered from seven inches away. "But hurry. My arms are getting tired in this position."

"Do you know why I never call you 'Klo'?"

"No, I guess I never really thought about it. Why?"

"Because your name is too perfect. I don't want to make it shorter. I want to say the whole ... lovely ... thing."

Chloe stared into my eyes. I was hypnotized. If she

ever wanted a job as a lion tamer, or one of those cobra-charmer people in the circus, I was pretty sure she would be the greatest of all time. I felt my neck straining. Almost involuntarily, my lips were moving closer to hers.

"Good night, sweetest boy on the block," the lion tamer said. She bent down and kissed me, mostly on the cheek, but maybe 20 percent on the edge of my mouth. Then she pushed herself up with a tiny grunt, lined herself up on the other side of Ava, and pulled the blanket tight.

I suddenly felt claustrophobic. Ava arched her back so that now one shoulder blade was digging into my arm, but I couldn't give her any more room. I sighed.

"Chloe," I whispered.

"Yeah, Jess?"

"I'm the *only* boy on the block."

11. Shake It Off

It wasn't just a long night. It was a long summer. I signed up for every shift Larry would give me at the rec center. I was trying to avoid the weirdness of my house, which always felt empty. During the week, my mom was sometimes around, but she always seemed to be staring off into space or disappearing into her bedroom to "take a phone call."

I was pretty sure I had never heard her use that phrase before in my life, but now, suddenly, she was "taking a phone call" every few hours. My mom is a high school French teacher. She was off for the summer. It wasn't like she was constantly getting bombarded with urgent French-verb-conjugation-related inquiries, so who the heck was calling? All I knew was that she had developed a new, super-quiet phone voice, and was getting a whole lot of practice using it.

My dad was often in the house on weekends, but he was distant, too. Meanwhile, Leah was either working with Jake, talking to Jake, talking *about* Jake, or asleep. Or she was at the table, in a semi-coma, waiting for her coffee to brew. Those were pretty much the only options.

In elementary school, I had this really evil principal for

about a year and a half who hated noise, so he installed a sound-measuring device in the cafeteria. It was connected to a traffic light. When the room was quiet, the light was green. When there was a bit of talking, the light went to yellow. When things got noisy, the light turned red, and the principal flipped out and screamed that we all had to be ABSOLUTELY SILENT for the rest of our lunch period.

Well, somehow, I suddenly felt like I was living through The Summer of the Silent Lunch, only it was 24/7.

Ava seemed to be working on the same plan I was. I guess she didn't feel like sitting around and mourning all summer, because she was racking up the overtime, too. We got into a kind of groove. Annie would come by near the end of my shift and I would hit with her for an hour or so. Then we'd stop by the snack stand inside, get three ice creams, and take them to the outdoor pool. Ava would finish whatever her last chores were, like skimming grass out of the water or straightening out the patio chairs, and the three of us would sit with our feet in the water and eat our ice creams.

Then, if Chloe was also working, we would all walk home together.

That was my favorite part of the day. It felt normal. It felt safe. And for the six weeks between our little drunken sleepover and the Christmas-in-August weekend, it felt like it could go on forever.

On Friday, August 23, I made my first big mistake. When I got off work, my mother was on our back deck, watering the plants, which she usually did before leaving. She said that was because "your father wouldn't notice a houseplant if it was on fire. He barely notices the house!" Which was hurtful, but not entirely inaccurate. Anyway, she shouldn't have been watering the plants. It was Christmas! She had to stay for the weekend. There would be presents for everybody, and the big singalong at the rec center, and the bonfire at the beach. Plus, we always had Christmas cookout dinner in the middle of the cul-de-sac with all three families on Sunday afternoon. That was like the official end-of-summer gathering. After that, we'd only have one more week before Labor Day, which meant everybody would be pulling boats out of the water, the summer-only people would be winterizing their houses, and our jobs at the rec center would wind down.

This weekend was important. She couldn't just ruin it. So finally, after months of not saying anything, I asked, "Mom, what are you doing? Aren't you staying for Christmas?"

She didn't even look at me. She just laughed and said, "Honey, we're Jewish."

It was the worst non-answer I had ever heard in my life.

Twenty minutes later, I was playing bass along with the Clash in my room when I heard her call "Jess?" from the bottom of the stairs. But she didn't call very loudly or very many times, and she didn't bother walking up before she muttered, "Okay . . ." I just kept cranking along with the band until I heard our screen door rattle against its frame.

It was kind of funny and kind of sad. The song I was bopping along with was "Should I Stay or Should I Go." It didn't seem like my mom had struggled too hard with the decision.

Leah picked up pizza, and she and I were eating a late dinner in total silence when my dad got to the house. He looked kind of worn out and draggy, but I still had a glimmer of hope that things could feel a bit normal, so I said, "What's the news from the real world?"

My father said, "It's dinner for three, apparently."

Leah muttered, "Ho ho ho."

So that was a fun start to the weekend.

Chloe had texted Ava and me and asked us to meet her in the treehouse when it got dark. I figured it was going to be our favorite Christmas tradition: the joke gift exchange. I had been working in secret on my present for both of them for weeks, but I was nervous to show it to them. Fortunately, it was cool and dry out, or this present would never work. In July, it's hot and sticky after sunset in the mountains, but by late August, it's sweatshirt weather. I went up to my room, threw on a hoodie, grabbed some things from my room, put them in a big, cushioned hiking backpack, strapped it on, and walked over.

Both girls were leaning against one of the big boulders

that separate Ava's back deck from the treehouse. The floodlights on the porch were on, so they were silhouetted in the glare. Chloe was wearing jeans and a Christmas-red sweater, and had matching lipstick on. She looked very grown-up. Sometimes I forgot for a while how intimidatingly beautiful I thought she was, but then she would do something like putting on that lipstick, and suddenly, I would feel like a twelve-year-old meeting Beyoncé. Anyway, she was carrying two big gift boxes. Ava was dressed all in black, and had just one very small box in her hand. She was looking down at the ground, and it appeared as though she might cry at any moment.

Call me crazy, but I thought she looked extra mature and beautiful, too.

Climbing up the ladder is tricky when one is loaded up with gifts, but we all managed. To be fair, Chloe had done it, hungover, with two bags of assorted breakfast snacks and laundry, just weeks before, so this was probably a piece of cake for her. I was a bit nervous because I had unusually precious cargo on my back.

We all put our stuff down, set up the mattresses as a couch, and made ourselves comfortable, relatively speaking. Chloe looked comfortable, Ava looked sorrowful, and if I looked like a nervous dork, that would have been a pretty accurate impression of my inner state. I always dread giving presents. The whole occasion is perfect for spiraling: *Is this thing too expensive? Not expensive enough? Too jokey? Not sufficiently jokey? Does this gift convey thoughtfulness? Does it convey too much thoughtfulness? What if Chloe thinks I like her? What if Ava thinks I like her? What if one of them thinks I like the other one? What if they are both equally right, and my brain finally just explodes all over the treehouse walls from the constant tension and drama?*

Okay, I realize that last bit was oddly specific. Also, graphic. But my point is, I always dreaded giving presents, and this Christmas-in-August, I dreaded it just that extra bit more.

Chloe went first, because of course she did. She handed her first box to Ava, who opened it and proceeded to read the card inside by the light of her phone. Then Ava wiped her eyes with the back of her hand and sniffled before opening the present itself: a sweatshirt (light pink, not black) that read on the front:

I'M WITH HER

AND WITH HIM!

There were arrows next to the words, pointed to both the left and the right, so that if she sat between Chloe and me, the arrows would point to both of us at once.

"I love it," Ava said. She immediately started to yank off her black sweatshirt, and realized when it was about six inches above her waistband that there wasn't a shirt underneath. "Oopsie," she said. "Close your eyes, J."

I did. I also blushed, so I was glad we weren't sitting in daylight. When Ava told me to open my eyes again, she was wearing her present. It was the first time I'd seen her in anything other than black since the fireworks.

"I hope it's okay, sweetie," Chloe said. "The color, I mean. You just always look so pretty in pink."

Ava's voice sounded husky as she said, "No, yeah. It's time, I think. Thank you. Now everybody stop looking at me. You go, J."

Chloe handed me my box, and I opened my card. I tilted it so it caught the light from the porch. There were a few paragraphs in her loopy, super-girly handwriting, all about how much she loved me, how I was the sweetest boy on the block, special times we had shared over the summer, etcetera. She had always written me great cards (which I hoped she didn't know were all saved in a special box under my bed in Staten Island), but this one had one major, major difference that I was sure would keep me awake wondering for months to come.

Instead of her usual "XOXO" at the bottom, this card was sealed with a literal kiss, as in, she had put on lipstick and kissed it under her name. I turned the card slightly away so Ava wouldn't see it, feeling incredibly excited and also incredibly guilty.

Ava kicked the edge of my outstretched foot with

hers. "Well, are you gonna open the box or what?" she said. I felt like there was an edge to the words, but what the heck did I know? I mean, I was right in the middle of having a moment. It wasn't like I was capable of actual thought right then.

My gift was a sweatshirt designed just like Ava's, but in navy blue. The words on mine read:

I'M WITH HER
AND WITH HER!

It was one of those jokes that feel too true for comfort, but I loved the sentiment behind it. I mean, if Ava had given it to me, I would have spent like seventy-five hours in my room, staring at the wall and wondering if the message was a complicated passive-aggressive mind game, like CHOOSE ONE OF US ALREADY! But Chloe wasn't jealous or possessive like that.

I kind of wished she would be, because maybe that would be a sign she liked me the way I liked her. I sighed. It was all so complicated. All I could do was thank her and put it on.

Ava gave her gifts next. She opened her little box, pulled out two rectangular objects wrapped in white tissue paper, and handed one each to Chloe and me. When they were unwrapped, I saw that the gift was a framed photo. I assumed Chloe's held the same picture mine did.

Even in the dim light, I knew immediately when the shot had been captured: during the Independence Day fireworks, while we were all on our backs on the catamaran.

Ava shined her phone light on my frame, and I saw the details. Our faces were all lit up in red, white, and blue. Chloe's hand was on my arm. On the other side of me, Ava's shoulder was pressed against mine. I had an expression of totally dopey bliss on my face. Chloe was looking over at Ava and me, smiling softly. And Ava was absolutely, radiantly beaming.

"I hope you like it," the real-life Ava said.

Chloe and I both stumbled all over ourselves to tell her how much we loved it. And I mean, I did. I thought I looked a bit goofy in it, but it definitely captured us having a moment.

"I look at it on my phone every night before I go to sleep," Ava said, "because it's . . . you know. It was my last *good* time." Then she just *crumpled*.

Crap, I thought. *How did I not see this coming? I've been so wrapped up in my parents bickering that I almost forgot it was Ava's first Christmas without her mom even being alive. I am the worst friend in the world.*

I put my arm around her. "No, it wasn't," I said. "Please don't say that. It might have been your last good time for a while, but it wasn't your last good time ever. And hey, we're not going anywhere, right?"

Chloe leaned in. "Nope, we're not going anywhere, sweetie. I made my dad promise a long time ago that he would never sell our house here. I'll be up here on weekends buying cheesy sweatshirts for your grandchildren."

Ava sniffled and wiped her eyes. "Promise?" she asked.

"Promise."

We sat there for a minute without anybody saying anything. I really didn't want to break up the moment, especially because I was kind of terrified to do my presenting anyway, but then Chloe said, "All righty, then. Jess, you're up!"

"Oh," I said, "I, uh, I didn't actually get you anything this year. Sorry!"

They both looked at me like I was an idiot. "Of course you did, Jess," Chloe said. "We're your favorite people. Now come on!"

"Yeah," Ava said, "come on!"

"I'm serious! I didn't buy you anything. What can I say? It's been a tough year. You know, money's tight. College is just around the corner. And I mean, my parents are making me chip in for gas and car insurance. This stuff adds up. Soooo . . ."

Ava leaned toward me. "What do you mean, 'Soooooooooo?' Soooo what? You better have something for us in that backpack over there, Jesse Dienstag, or I'm taking back your present."

Then Chloe leaned in. All the way in, so I was

overwhelmed with her coconut scent, even in the chilly late-August night air. "She's right. If you didn't bring us something . . ." She paused and smiled in a way I hadn't really seen before. She put her arms around my neck and whispered in my ear, "Then I'm never, ever doing *this* again."

And she nibbled on my earlobe.

Honestly, it is a miracle I didn't faint, fall out of the treehouse, and die. But I did sit there stunned for a while, until Ava said, "Uh, are you okay there, J?"

Chloe giggled.

"Yeah, I'm fine," I said. Which was mostly true. I was shivery, and overwhelmed, and confused, and nervous, and quite possibly delirious. But wow, not in a bad way. "And," I continued, "I might have something in that bag, now that I think about it."

I pulled my backpack over, wiped my suddenly sweaty hands on my jeans, and unzipped the main compartment. I carefully unpacked my laptop computer, my tablet, a portable speaker, and my ukulele bass in its soft case. I felt extremely self-conscious as I fired up the laptop, turned on the speaker and the tablet, opened up the tabs I needed, and took out my bass.

"I was telling the truth, kind of," I said. "I didn't buy you anything. I, uh, I wanted to do something different and I really wanted you to remember it. So I wrote you a song. But, I mean, it's probably stupid. And now that you're both actually sitting in front of me, and you gave me such thoughtful presents and everything, I realize this was a really terrible plan. I'm sorry. I should probably just—"

"Jess," Chloe said, "no."

"What do you mean, no?"

"You're not getting out of this. You know we love you, right?"

I didn't trust myself to speak without my voice cracking. I nodded.

"And we know how talented you are. So just trust yourself, trust us, and play."

I cleared my throat. "Okay, so I have to warn you: It's a little rough. I mean, I've only written a couple of songs so far, so it's not like I really know what I'm doing."

"Jess . . ." Chloe said.

"What? I'm just explaining. Anyway, I kinda just threw this together in GarageBand. Which isn't even a professional recording platform. And I don't have instrument inputs up here, so I have to play the bass part live. Plus, it's hard to play bass and sing at the same time, so I might mess that part up a little. Oh, and there are a couple of harmony vocals that might sound kind of distorted, because I didn't have a microphone, so I had to use the built-in one on my laptop."

"Jess . . ." Chloe said again.

"I know, I know. Shut up and play, right? But I don't want you to expect some great genius epic, like I wrote *Hamilton* or something."

Ava clunked her knee against mine. "Don't worry, J. I thought *Hamilton* was totally overrated." She paused and thought for a minute. "Well, I did like the duel parts. Oh, and the king's song was pretty funny. And I might have cried when his kid died."

"So what you're saying is you basically loved it, but you're trying to make me feel better?"

She grinned. "Yeah. So let's hear what you've got. Don't throw away your shot."

"I see what you did there," I said. "Fine. But just please be nice to me."

"Jess," Chloe said, "who's nicer to you than *us*?"

I sighed, strapped on the bass, and pressed PLAY on the backing tracks I'd prepared. A fast, poppy drumbeat filled the treehouse, and synthesized chords followed: A minor, C, and G, repeating over and over, in what I hoped was a catchy and hypnotic manner. After the sequence had run through once, I started to play and sing:

> *I'm feelin' so alive,*
> *As we begin to drive,*
> *Leave the world behind,*
> *Get the island off my mind,*

Jersey Turnpike then go west,
Feel the weight come off my chest,
Now I am serene,
Here where ev'rything is green,

The real world isn't real,
That's just how I feel,
The real world isn't real,
It isn't real, it isn't real,
It isn't real, it isn't real.

I'm where I want to be,
Where trouble can't find me,
The sky is always blue,
Because I am with you.

The real world isn't real,
That's just how I feel,
The real world isn't real,
It isn't real, it isn't real,
It isn't real, it isn't real.

When I finished, I clicked to stop the backing tracks, and then stared straight down at my legs. I was afraid to see the looks on my friends' faces. But then Chloe and Ava both clapped.

"Aww, that's so sweet!" Chloe said.

"And that's totally what I feel like when I'm on my way out here," Ava added.

"There is one tiny thing I feel I should mention, though," Chloe said.

My heart skipped. "What is it?" I wasn't sure I really wanted to hear this.

She was biting her lip. It looked like she was trying to suppress a smile. "Well, you know the 'Isn't real, isn't real' part?"

"The chorus? Yeah, what about it? Is it bad? Was my singing pitchy? That part is hard, because the bass line and the vocals don't really—"

"No, you sounded great. It's just that . . . well . . . that part kind of sounds like a Taylor Swift song."

This offended me as a musician. "A *Taylor Swift* song? Seriously?"

"Yeah," she said. "I mean, not in a bad way. You know I love Taylor Swift."

"Me too," Ava added. "Like, more than *Hamilton*, even."

I sighed. "I don't know what you're talking about."

"Sing that part, and I'll show you," Chloe said.

"For real?"

"For real."

So, feeling extremely ridiculous and more than a little annoyed, I sang:

> *The real world isn't real,*
> *That's just how I feel,*

The real world isn't real,
It isn't real, it isn't real,
It isn't real, it isn't real.

Just as I got to the second-to-last line, Chloe sang, "Shake it off, shake it off!" Ava joined in for the last line.

Holy crap, I thought. The beat was kind of similar. The chords were the same. The notes were basically the same. Chloe was right. I had ripped off Taylor Swift!

My face felt like it was on fire. "I'm sorry," I mumbled. "I'll make you some freaking friendship bracelets, okay?"

"Oh, J," Ava said, "it's all right. We love the song. And you're super talented. You know that, right?"

"Yeah," Chloe said. "Neither of us can even play an instrument. You play the bass, *and* you sing lead vocals and harmonies, *and* you write songs, *and* you did all the recording parts, too. That's why we have to tease you a little. Otherwise, you'd be all like, 'Look at me, I'm a genius!' all the time."

"Oh, come on. I'm not a genius. I can't write songs, apparently. When I try, all I do is write fake *Taylor Swift* songs."

"But even that's a pretty hard thing to do. Besides, you're literally a genius, J. You go to a literal genius high school," Ava said.

"Yeah," Chloe said. "So thank you and merry

Christmas-in-August. Now, shake it off and give us a group hug!"

"Ha, ha," I said.

"Ooh, too soon?" she asked, raising an eyebrow.

It *was* too soon, but I went in for the hug anyway.

12. Secrets and Coffee

The next night, after the community singalong at the rec center, Ava went home to make s'mores with her family, but Chloe asked me to stay behind when our families were leaving. She was wearing a dorky Christmas sweater with a shiny, goofy gold reindeer on it, but somehow still looked breathtaking to me.

"What's up?" I asked.

"I don't know, I just wanted to spend some time alone with you. Why, do you have a date or something?"

"No!" I said. "I mean, of course not. Not that I couldn't have a date. Because I could. Theoretically. I bet. But I don't. Tonight." Honestly, if Chloe still considered me a genius after hearing the way I spoke when I was alone with her, she wasn't particularly picky about geniuses.

"It's settled, then. Now you're my date," she said, and I could hear that teasing smile in her voice. She took my hand and started tugging me along the path that led down to the dock.

"Are you . . . asking me out?"

"Kinda. It's more like I'm *telling* you out. Because let's face it, the date has already started."

It was darker behind the building than it had been the night of the fireworks, because this time there weren't flares lit up all over the edge of the lake. But then, when we got to the dock, Chloe knelt down and did something I couldn't see. Suddenly, the whole thing was outlined in Christmas lights.

"Ta-DA!" Chloe said.

"Do you ever not have a plan?" I asked.

"Nope, never," she replied, standing back up and facing me. Now I could just barely make out that teasing grin, tinged in the twinkly glow from the lights.

"But what if I'd had plans? What if I'd said no?"

She took my hand again. "Then this would have been the least romantic night of my life. Now come on. I'm cold!"

As Chloe led me out onto the dock, I thought, *She said "romantic." SHE SAID "ROMANTIC!"* That was enough to make me lightheaded. If she hadn't had a good grip on my hand, I'm pretty sure I would have wandered off course, wrapped a foot in the Christmas lights, fallen into the lake, and gotten both drowned and electrocuted. As it was, we made it safely to our destination, which I realized was the only boat left in the water.

The catamaran.

"Oh, no," I said. "No, no, no, no, no. We are not taking the catamaran out. We barely got away with it last time. Nuh-uh. No way."

She giggled. "Oh, Jess. Don't you want to wax this

thing with me one more time? That was kind of fun, wasn't it?"

"Uh," I stammered.

"Relax, I'm kidding. We're not taking it out. We're just going to use it as, like, a hammock. We'll be docked here the whole time. I promise."

She didn't wait for my answer. Like I was even capable of saying no to her. I followed her onto the boat. She crawled around a bit, pulling stuff out of a bag, and I saw that she had set this part up ahead of time, too. There were two life jackets, a big, floppy-looking pillow, and a blanket.

"Wanna watch the stars with me?" Chloe asked. If I had said that, it would have sounded cheesy. Also, to be fair, I probably would have said something more like, "W-w-w-wanna watch the—I mean, if you don't have anything better to . . . not that this means anything, but . . ." She probably would have fallen asleep waiting for me to even get to the "stars" part.

When Chloe said it, though, she didn't sound cheesy, or nervous, or anything. Possibly because she already knew the answer. She laid her head back on the pillow and patted the space next to her on the canvas deck. I placed myself next to her, but left a bit of room between our bodies so it wouldn't be weird or creepy for her.

Immediately, she took the blanket and spread it over us. "I'm cold," she announced, wriggling over so we were completely touching. "Can you put your arm around me?"

I did, and then I tried to just be perfectly still and look up at the stars. I was super aware of every molecule of my body. I felt like the instant I moved, everything about my life would change. I had dreamed of a moment like this about seventeen million times, but now that it seemed to be happening, it was terrifying. This was the most perfectly attractive girl in my universe, completely alone with me, under a blanket. And okay, it was great that she had brought me out here and set up this whole scene, but what if I was still misreading things?

She nibbled your earlobe! a little part of my brain screamed.

That little part of my brain was not wrong. But still, if I blew this, I could destroy my whole life in Tall Pines Landing. Then it occurred to me that even if I didn't blow this—even if it went extremely well—just doing it could destroy my whole life in Tall Pines Landing. *What will this do to Ava?* I thought.

Chloe ran her fingers through my hair and then gently turned my head toward hers. *Ava isn't here,* I thought. It was the last clear thought I had for a while.

. . . .

A text from Ava woke me up early the next morning. All it said was, *I need to see you.* I groaned. I had come stumbling into the house at like one o'clock, and it was barely sun-rise. I texted back, *Treehouse in ten minutes?*, which got an immediate thumbs-up.

Ugh. Apparently, my sudden popularity was going to affect my beauty-sleep regimen. I forced myself to roll out of bed and slouch my way to the bathroom. Peering into the mirror to brush my teeth and comb my hair, I thought I should look different somehow, more experienced and wise. *I'm in love now. I mean, with someone who's in love back. Shouldn't that give me some kind of sheen, some glow, some polish?* But no, all it did was put bags under my eyes and make my lips feel vaguely crushed and oversensitive when the toothpaste hit them.

Downstairs, I wolfed down a bagel and gulped some orange juice. Ouch! Yeah, the lips were definitely chapped, but I felt that was a small price to pay for the night I'd had.

Chloe and me. Me and Chloe.

If I thought about it too long, I was afraid I might actu-ally levitate off the ground. But, eek—how was I going to tell Ava? *Was* I going to tell Ava? Or was that more of a girl-talk thing? *Yeah*, I thought. *Probably that should really come from Chloe. From me, it would just be excruciatingly awkward.*

I looked at the time on my phone and realized the weekly pickup softball game was in only two hours. I'd promised my dad I'd play, which was a really big deal. It was only the second time he'd asked me all summer, so I didn't want to screw it up. I figured I had plenty of time, though. How long could one little treehouse talk take?

Assuming Ava hadn't squirreled away any additional aviation refreshments, I didn't foresee a problem.

Ava was waiting for me behind her house. As soon as we climbed the ladder, she turned to me and said, "I'm really upset about something that happened last night, J. I was up all night thinking about it."

Oh boy, I thought. *How did she find out so fast?*

"I'm sorry," I said. "What can I—"

"You don't have to be sorry. What do you have to be sorry about? We really need to work on your confidence, Jesse. Honestly. I'm just worried about you."

"Um, I'm confused. What happened last night that made you worried about me?"

"Your song, J. It was your song. But really, the song was just the continuation of something you've been saying all summer. You've gotten kind of obsessed with saying that the real world isn't real, that it can't touch you here. I don't know if you've noticed." She stared into my eyes. Ava's stare was always intense, but at dawn on five hours of sleep, I felt like it was burning two holes through to the back of my skull. And not in a good way.

I squirmed. "Well, kind of. I guess."

She grabbed me by the shoulders and literally shook me. "No, not *kind of.* You wrote a freaking song about it. Listen, J. I love this place, too, but it won't magically keep you safe from whatever's going on in the rest of your life. Look at what happened to me the night of the fireworks!" She let go of my arms and wiped one of her eyes with the back of her hand. Then she turned away from me and sniffled.

I didn't know what to do or say, so I put a hand on her shoulder.

When she spoke again, her voice was shaky. "I just don't want you to be surprised when the world reaches you here and hurts you. Because it will."

. . . .

I debated stopping by Chloe's house, but I assumed she had to still be asleep. *Hey, she might be dreaming about me!* I thought. I didn't want to take any chance of disturbing that, so I kept walking.

Which turned out to be my loss.

I got home in time to witness the joys of Leah's coffee ritual, which kind of shocked me. I couldn't believe she was up so early on a Sunday. As soon as she had taken her first sip from her mug, she said, "So, Jess, I guess it's you and Chloe, huh?"

The hair on the back of my neck stood up. "Wh-what do you mean?" I asked. Because I was excellent at acting casual.

"Oh, come on, Slick. Ava got home right when Dad and I did, but I couldn't help but notice that you hung back with Chloe. And then you still weren't home when I went to sleep. Which means . . . you and Chloe! Which also means . . . Jake owes me five bucks!"

"Wait a minute!" I sputtered. "You made a *bet* on my love life?"

She raised an eyebrow. "Ooh, your *love life*. There's a nice little flex to start my morning. I'm thinking it's more like your *puppy* love life, but yeah. I made a small, friendly wager."

"I don't believe this!" Actually, I wasn't sure whether I was outraged or flattered.

"Oh, get over yourself. It's not like I was betting against you. Jake and I were both betting you were going to end up with a girl this summer. Even though I have to admit, you did kind of have me nervous the past week or so. You kind of just brought it in under the wire."

"I still haven't confirmed your ridiculous speculation, Leah."

"But you're blushing. So your face has confirmed my 'ridiculous speculation.' Or my solid investigative reporting work, as I like to call it. Anyway, mazel tov."

"Uh, thanks, I think? But listen, you can't say anything. To anybody. And no social media. Ava has no idea, and I don't want to hurt her. Okay?"

Leah gave me some serious side-eye. "Oh, there's no possible way *this* is going to end badly. But don't worry. Your poorly kept secret is safe with me."

Just then, our father came out of his bedroom, which was around the corner from the kitchen. He was wearing his Sunday-morning softball outfit of dark gray athletic pants and an old black T-shirt from his medical school. "What's the poorly kept secret?" he asked.

"Nothing!" I said, my voice cracking. Because again, acting casual was a definite strength of mine.

Fortunately, my father had other things on his mind. "Is there more coffee?" he asked.

"Yeah, Dad. Why don't you sit down and I'll get you some?" Leah said.

That was unusual. Leah was not generally known for her household attentiveness, but she scrambled around, pouring our father his coffee just the way he liked it, with a heaping spoonful of sugar and about an inch of half-and-half.

Basically, he wanted his coffee to taste like coffee-flavored cotton candy.

As soon as the mug was in front of him, Leah said, "Can I get you something else? A bagel? Toast? I think we might have a muffin I could microwave. Or some cereal? You like cereal. Maybe some eggs?"

Okay, this had definitely crossed over into some bizarre science-fictional territory. My sister had never offered to prepare food for anyone else in the family. Also, what was with the *You like cereal* thing? First of all, that was something you would say to a four-year-old, and second of all, I was fairly sure my father had never eaten a bowl of cereal in his life.

"Thanks," my dad said, "but I'm not hungry. I, uh, I ate before you got up."

I supposed he could have come out after I'd left to meet Ava, eaten something, and then gone back into his room before Leah had come down to make coffee. But then, why hadn't he started the coffee himself? I couldn't handle this much weirdness in one morning.

Fortunately, I figured, there wasn't much room for anything odd to happen during a pickup softball game.

13. "Was I Safe?"

The thing about those late-August days was that even though the mornings started out as sweatshirt weather, it could get scorching hot by noon. At game time, a lot of players were still wearing long sleeves or even hoodies, but by the second or third inning, it was probably in the low eighties, and the sun was brutal. My dad and I were on opposing teams. My team put me at third base, and he was playing right field. The angle of the sun wasn't so terrible from either dugout, but I noticed when I looked out at him in the field that it was pounding down directly in his face.

The thought crossed my mind that it wasn't a good day to be wearing all black out there.

Usually, the game was pretty low-key, and on weekends that weren't the big holidays, players sometimes even had to field for both teams in order to make up for a shortage of players. That was not a problem on the Christmas-in-August weekend, though. We had so many players that there were substitutions going on, and a lot of people who hadn't arrived early had even gone home when they'd seen how crowded the field was already. People were more animated than usual. There was even some trash talking. I distinctly heard an eleven-year-old girl I knew from the tennis courts calling her dad a "slow old man" after he missed catching a pop-up, which horrified me a bit. I couldn't imagine making that kind of joke to my own father.

My dad hit a single in the second inning, and came around to third on a walk and a sacrifice fly. Usually, he was very dedicated when he played, like he would run all out on a ground ball, even if it was super obvious he was going to be out at first. It struck me that he seemed to be jogging a bit from second to third, and I almost said something to him about it, but I didn't want him to think I was trash talking him.

Big mistake.

I didn't think much more about it, and truthfully, my mind mostly just kept cycling back and forth between my night with Chloe, my morning conversation with Ava, and how tired I was. Every once in a while, I would remind myself to focus on the game, because if someone hit a screaming line drive at me while I was remembering the feeling of Chloe's lips against mine, my morning's athletic activities were not going to end well.

A couple of innings later, I was in the dugout (which was really just a rickety old wooden bench behind a rusty fence) after scoring a run. I poured some water over my head to get the sweat out of my eyes, then put my trusty old Mets cap back on. My team had a runner on first, and she took a really big lead, which meant my father was standing right behind her from my angle. He was bobbing from one foot to the other, like a slow-motion boxer avoiding invisible punches. I couldn't figure out what he was doing.

Then I heard the loud TING! of a metal bat, and saw that a high pop-up was headed toward right field. My father shielded his eyes with his non-glove hand, took a couple of steps back, and then seemed to stumble. I wasn't sure whether he had lost the ball in the sun, or whether it was some other problem, but I knew something was really wrong. It unfolded in awful slow motion: my dad staggered to the right. Then he staggered to the left. Then he started spinning around in place, but he only got through about a quarter of one turn before he slumped to a sitting position on the grass.

The ball plopped to the ground beside him, and total chaos broke loose. The other guys on his team hadn't noticed his stumbles before the ball got to him, because their backs had been to him. They started shouting, "Doc, the ball! Get the ball!"

My dad's first name is Martin, but everyone at softball has always called him Doc. In this case, I quickly realized that was terrible, because it probably meant nobody else on his team was a doctor.

I jumped up from the bench and ran around the fence onto the field. "Time!" I shouted. "Time-out! He's hurt!"

Larry, who was there umpiring, called time-out and followed me into right field. By the time I got out there, the guy playing second base was already crouching down next to my dad, saying, "Doc, can you hear me?"

I got down on my knees directly in front of my father and said, "Dad, I'm here."

My father looked very pale. At first, his eyes were closed, but then he opened them when he heard my voice. He looked around, but didn't seem to see or understand what was going on around him. He also didn't say anything in response to the second baseman's question.

The second baseman held two fingers against my dad's wrist, like he was feeling for a pulse. He turned to Larry and said, "Call nine-one-one." Then he gestured toward his team's dugout and shouted, "Can someone bring us some Gatorade, some water, and some towels? And do we have any ice packs?" Finally, he looked around frantically for a moment before turning to the assembled fielders and saying, "And bring me second base."

I just sat there feeling useless while the second baseman took command of the situation. "My name's Tim," he told me. "I'm a volunteer firefighter at home, so I have my

EMT certification. We need to get your father checked out, but I'm going to start treating him for heatstroke. Do you know whether he ate or drank anything this morning? And does he have any health conditions I should know about, like diabetes?"

"He had coffee with cream and sugar." My thoughts flashed back to the weird little scene with Leah at breakfast. "Um, I think that's it. And no, he doesn't have diabetes or anything."

Tim turned back to my dad and started loosening up his clothing. "What's your name, son?"

"Jesse."

"Okay, Jesse, I'm going to try to cool your dad off a bit. Doc, can you drink a sip of this?" He held up a bottle of sports drink to my father's lips. My father didn't respond at all. Tim said, "Okay, I don't think that's going to work." He looked up at all the people standing around and said, "Can a few of you hold some towels or something over Doc to keep the sun off him? And can somebody else put the base down behind his head so we can lay him down? I need to get the ice packs on him. Steph, Pete, can you both go wait in the parking lot for the ambulance? Jesse, help me get your dad's head onto the base."

"Dad," I said, "we're just going to help you lie down, all right?" My father looked toward my voice, but I could tell he still didn't really know what was happening. My heart pounded in my chest.

I got my hands behind his shoulders and eased him backward while Tim guided the back of his head gently onto the base. Then Tim said, "Jesse, take off his shoes and socks, okay?" While I was working on that, Tim started pouring bottles of water all over my dad's clothes. Then he asked two other people to hold my dad's feet up off the ground. He said that would help with circulation.

I scurried back up to be next to my father's head just as two teenagers, a boy and a girl, put down a big cooler full of drinks a few feet away. "Is there ice in there?" Tim asked. The girl nodded. Tim said, "Start wrapping as much of the ice as you can up in a towel, please."

Then he turned to me and said, "Keep talking to your dad. See if you can get him to respond. We want to keep him calm."

As the whole array of people stared down at us and Tim arranged towels full of ice on top of my dad's chest and groin, I said, "Hey, Dad, can you hear me? I'm, uh, I'm just gonna hold your hand, okay?"

Without looking away from his face, I felt around until I found his hand. It was hot and dry under my fingers, like he had a bad fever. We weren't really a hand-holdy kind of father-son duo, but I forced myself to grip his fingers in mine and squeeze.

Suddenly, his eyes locked in on mine. "Dave!" he said excitedly.

For the record, I was 99 percent sure there was

nobody on the field named Dave. And I was 100 percent sure *I* was not named Dave.

"NO, Dad, it's me—Jesse! Your *son*."

His eyes widened. "Jesse!"

I felt a momentary thrill of relief, until he spoke again. "Jesse," he said, "ask Dave!"

I had no idea who Dave could be. There was nobody named Dave on the field. "Ask him what?"

"Was I safe?"

Oh boy, I thought.

I heard the ascending whine of a siren coming on fast. I squeezed his hand again, looked into his eyes, and told him, "Dave says you were safe *by a mile*."

14. Dads on Diets

The ambulance crew worked really fast. The person in charge, a short, red-haired woman named Amy, started an IV while the other person, a tall, thin Latino man named Lino, took my dad's pulse, blood pressure, and temperature.

Apparently, my dad's heart was beating very fast (bad) and his blood pressure was low (also bad), but his temperature was only a hundred and two (not as bad as it could have been).

So this was an emergency, but not a mega-mega-emergency?

Amy and Lino got my dad onto a stretcher and started wheeling him across the field as the players who had stuck around began to drift away. I almost had to trot to stay within my father's sight, although his eyes were still not really staying in focus. Just as the stretcher was being loaded into the ambulance, Larry shouted to me, "Jesse, is there somebody I can call for you?"

It occurred to me that I would have to call my sister. And my *mom*. I slapped at my pockets to make sure I had my phone, which I did. "Thank you, Larry," I yelled back, "but I can do it."

Lino went around the front to drive, and Amy told me how to get buckled into the little bench seat across from her while she continued to work on my father. She strapped heart monitor wires all over his chest, his stomach, his arms, and even his legs. Then she broke out several new cold packs and placed them behind his neck, in his armpits, and around his groin. "These, along with the IV and the air-conditioning in here, should cool your father's body down," she explained. "Watch him. Let me know if he wakes up, all right? We have about a thirty-minute ride, so now might be a good time to make your phone calls." After we'd gone for a few minutes and I realized there really wasn't anything for me to do but watch Dad, I whipped out my phone and called Leah.

Of course, she immediately heard the siren that was wailing three feet above my head.

"Jess, where are you? What's going on?" she asked.

"Dad collapsed at the baseball field. We're in an ambulance. We're going to the hospital in, uh—"

"Honesdale," Amy said.

"Honesdale. Can you come?"

"Of course I'll come. I'm coming. Is he alive? Is he conscious? Did he have a heart attack?"

"He's alive. He's not really, um, with it. They keep saying it's heatstroke. I don't even know what that is," I said.

I didn't want to sound scared and make her feel panicky, especially when she had to drive all alone, but I was scared. No, scratch that: I was terrified.

"I'm coming, Jess," my sister said. "Can you call Mom so I can concentrate on the road?"

"Uh, sure," I said, although the prospect of having to involve my mother in this might have been even more alarming than the event itself. As I got off the phone with Leah, my mind raced through the possibilities: *What if Mom doesn't answer? What if I call her number, but a man answers? What if she refuses to come?*

Just as I was about to call, Dad's eyes popped open. "He's awake!" I yelped.

"Got it!" Amy said. "Thank you." Then she started talking quickly and calmly to my dad. "Sir," she said, "can you hear me? Nod if you understand what I'm saying." He just stared at her. She waited a few seconds, then continued. "I'm Amy, and I'm taking you to Wayne Memorial Hospital in Honesdale. Your son, Jesse, is here, too. They're going to take good care of you, okay?"

My dad stared at her for another moment, and then his eyes flickered shut again. There was a tightness around his mouth. I felt like he looked frightened.

"Can I hold his hand?" I asked Amy.

"Sure, honey," she said. "Just reach under the blanket and grab it. You won't hurt anything. The IV is in his other hand, by me."

I found my father's hand and squeezed it gently. "I'm still here," I said.

He smiled a tiny bit, without opening his eyes. "Jeessssssss," he said. Then his whole body, which had been tensed up, seemed to go limp.

The siren wailed. A tear rolled down my left cheek. My father's breathing slowed down a bit, and he started to snore.

When we got to the hospital, Lino wheeled my dad away to a glassed-in part of the emergency room. I started to follow, but Amy stopped me. "I'm sorry, honey," she said, "but you can't go in there. The docs need room to work, and your dad needs privacy. Let me take you to the family room, okay?"

Before I even really knew what was happening, I was sitting alone in a little lounge. There were two mini couches, a couple of folding chairs with a table between them, and a Keurig with some cups, napkins, and coffee supplies. The table had a lamp and a big box of tissues on it. Amy had told me to sit tight, and that someone would be in soon to check on me.

But what do you do while you're sitting tight? I thought about texting Leah to tell her where to find me, but then I realized I didn't actually know the number of the room, or what floor I was on, or anything. Plus, I didn't want to distract her while she was driving to a strange place in the middle of being scared and alone.

Then I realized I had gotten so distracted in the ambulance that I hadn't called my mother. When I tried to call her, I didn't have enough reception, so the call failed. I tried sending a text instead:

> Dad's in the emergency room in Honesdale, heat-stroke. Can you come?

I thought about trying to write something else to soften the blow or ease into it or whatever. Just then, the door to the lounge banged open, and a lady in a white doctor coat barged in and stood over me. I hit SEND.

The doctor was not playing around. "You're Martin Dienstag's son?" she asked.

"Yes," I said. "My name's Jesse."

"Great, Jeffrey," she said, clicking through a bunch of screens on the laptop she was holding. "Tell me, how long has your father been dieting? And do you know what plan he's on?"

Dieting? What was she talking about? My mom was always on one diet plan or another, even though she always looked perfectly fine to me—but my dad didn't *diet*. He just ate whatever he ate, and then rode the exercise bike every night while he watched the news on TV.

"Um, I think there's been a mistake? Like, my dad's not on a diet?"

"Well," the doctor said, "I can see the notes from

his visit here in May, and at that time, he weighed one hundred seventy-seven pounds. The scale built into his bed has him at one sixty-three, fully clothed and under a cooling blanket. I can see all his blood work from that visit, and everything was perfect, so there's no reason to think there's any underlying illness—but your dad has lost an awful lot of weight in an awfully short period of time. Is your mom in the picture? Might she know something you don't?"

"Well," I said, "she might know something, but she's in New York. I just tried to call her, but I don't have any service in here. I'm telling you, though. My dad doesn't go on diets."

The doctor chewed on her lip. "Okay," she said, turning to leave. "We sent out some blood work. I'll be back when we know more."

I couldn't believe this woman. She had the worst bed-side manner (or couch-side manner, or whatever) of any doctor, ever. Couldn't she see I was a minor? A minor whose father was unconscious? Why wasn't she being nice to me?

And why had my dad gone to the hospital in *Honesdale* in May?

I cleared my throat. "Doctor," I said, "can you please tell me your name? And anything about how my dad is doing? Like, the paramedic person said something about his core temperature?"

She sighed, like I was causing a major hassle. Then she put the laptop down on the table, not very gently. Then she pinched the bridge of her nose, tipped her head back, shook her hair out, and seemed to refocus. "I'm sorry," she said. "We're very short-staffed today, and I've been here since midnight. I'm Dr. Ruddy. Your father is still basically unresponsive, but there is some guarded good news. His core temperature is already down to one hundred and one point nine. We started a second IV line with cool saline, which should help lower it even further, and we're also running cool water down a tube through his nose into his stomach. From what I was told, there was a trained EMT on site when your father took ill, and it sounds as though that person did everything right. That's great, because the real danger threshold with heat emergencies is one hundred and three degrees, and your father's temp is below that. We'll see what we see when his bloods come back, but it could just be that your dad got a bit carried away with the dieting, got himself dehydrated, and then got really lucky with that EMT being nearby."

She scooped up the computer again. "Do you need anything else before I leave, uh, Jeff?"

"No, I guess that's it for now," I said.

She was out the door before I even finished the sentence. I muttered to the empty room, "But it's Jess."

I sat there for a few minutes, trying to gather my thoughts. Then I stepped out into the hall, because I figured I should see whether my mom had gotten my text or responded, and I also needed to have service for when Leah arrived. I turned and took a picture of the lounge doorway so I'd recognize it if I got lost, then walked over to a big nurses' station that was about thirty feet away. I assumed they had to have reception out in the middle of the floor.

I never got there, because Leah came barreling out of a stairwell to my left and grabbed me. "Jess! Where is he?" she shouted. "What's going on? Is Mom on the way?" Then she pushed me away from her so I was at arm's length and asked, "And oh my God, I'm an idiot—are you okay?"

I opened my mouth to speak, and all of a sudden, my throat felt like it was closed off. I couldn't breathe. I shrugged her hands off, bent over, and put my hands on my knees. I wanted to say something, but I was hot all over. Tears filled my eyes. I was lightheaded.

Finally, I choked out, "Dad's in a room over there." I gestured vaguely with one hand, partly because I was afraid I'd fall over if I took the hand off my knee for too long, and partly because I wasn't really sure where my dad's room was in relation to us. Then I filled her in on what had happened and what Dr. Ruddy had said.

When I was done, Leah said, "So, you were talking pretty fast, but I thought you said you talked to a doctor? And she said Dad was dieting?"

"She said it seemed like he had to be, because he wasn't sick in the spring, but he lost all that weight in only a few months. Have you ever heard anything about Dad being on a diet?"

"No, but he's been looking kind of thin and tired all summer. That's why I was trying to get him to eat breakfast this morning. I just thought it might help? I don't know. Maybe Mom will. Which reminds me, is she coming?"

I took out my phone. The text to my mother had sent, and then there had been two missed calls from her. Eek. I showed the phone to Leah and closed my eyes. "Can you call her?" I asked.

"Sure," Leah said. "Let me step outside. *This* ought to be fun."

. . . .

Maybe an hour and a half later, Leah and I were sitting in the little lounge, eating snacks from a vending machine and killing time, when the door to the room came flying open and Dr. Ruddy marched in with her laptop.

"Jeffrey," she said, "your father is awake. Come!"

"Um, excuse me," Leah said. "I'm Leah, *Jesse's* older sister. Who are you? And what's going on with our father?"

"I'm Dr. Ruddy, your father's attending physician. We've gotten your father's core body temp down to one hundred point eight degrees. His bloods came back a little while ago. Red blood cell counts normal, whites normal, enzymes normal, kidney function fine, liver function fine, cholesterol fine, sugar fine, basically everything fine. No signs of a heart attack, which we routinely check for in middle-aged men who collapse. The only thing that was way outside the normal value range was his serum potassium, so we put a bag of that in his IV and he perked right up."

"What does all of that mean?"

"Your dad let himself get really dehydrated and messed up his electrolyte balance. Anyway, do you want to see him? He probably won't be awake for long."

Because the whole front wall of my dad's room was glass, there was a long curtain drawn across to keep people from seeing in. When we got there, Dr. Ruddy held the curtain aside and gestured us in. She didn't follow.

Dad was awake, and someone had tilted the head of his bed so he was half sitting up. When he saw us, he smiled weakly but sincerely. I could tell he knew who we were, which was enough in itself to make my eyes burn.

"Jess! Leah!" he croaked.

Leah rushed past me and crushed him in a bear hug, which stunned me.

My mom had always said I was the "affectionate child" in the family, but apparently parental near-death experiences made Leah all emotional. Dad's machines started beeping like crazy.

"Leah, I'm fine," he gasped, "but I think you just ripped off one of my electrodes."

Sure enough, a nurse came hustling in, presumably to see whether my father was in need of resuscitation. She turned off the alarms, got him wired back up, and left us to our reunion.

"I'm sorry," Leah said. "You really scared us, though."

"I told you, I'm fine," our father said, from the hospital bed in which he was strapped down with tubes up his nose and in both arms, and attached by wires to every monitor known to man. "I think all of this is a bit of an . . . overreaction."

It was amazing how fast my dad could make a person go from being worried about him to wanting to strangle him personally. "An overreaction?" I asked. "Are you kidding me? You toppled over on the softball field in the middle of a play, Dad. Your eyes were rolling around! You didn't know who I was. You were in right field, but you thought you were batting. You thought I was some guy named Dave! Then you passed out completely! The second baseman had to give you emergency first aid. You came here in an ambulance! You were unconscious for hours!"

My dad held up one hand to interrupt. "So I got a little overheated. These things happen. I'm sorry you worried. I'll eat breakfast next time."

Now Leah looked ready to pounce. "Oh, that's another thing. The doctor said you've lost like twenty— *look at me, Dad!*"

But our father was staring past her, because our mother had just pushed aside the curtain. Her hair, which was normally straight and neat, was sticking out in all directions from a disastrous attempt at a ponytail. She had smeared some makeup on her face, apparently while driving at high speeds. With one hand. Over potholes. Most strikingly, she was wearing a gigantically oversized University of Rhode Island T-shirt. Nobody in our family had attended the University of Rhode Island, and my mom was not the random-college-T-shirt-wearing type. I only had about a second and a half to be struck by the visual, though, before my mother took over the room.

"Oh, God, Marty!" she said, her voice cracking. "What were you *thinking?*"

Then she put her head in her hands and wept as Leah took me by the elbow and backed out of the room.

15. The Real World

I wasn't an idiot, okay? I knew all along that the summer was going to end. But I kept thinking I had more time. And then, all of a sudden, when my dad had his emergency, my time was up. He spent just one night in the hospital, but then he and my mom made a super-rare joint decision and said it was time for all of us to head back to the city.

Maybe this was a good thing. Maybe it meant they were going to work on their relationship. Maybe whatever this weird starvation episode was, it had ended up saving my family.

Whatever. I was furious that I was getting ripped away from Chloe. And Ava's and my last week at my job and Annie and the trees and the mountains and the deer and the bears and . . . oh, who was I kidding? All I could think about was Chloe. We'd had one night together. *Part of* one night. I didn't even get to say a private goodbye to her. I'd had a bunch of frantic texts from her, and from Ava, too, during the morning and afternoon of the hospital ordeal, but most of them hadn't come through until the evening.

I'd written back, briefly, to say my dad was going to be all right. I hadn't said anything more, because I was so flooded with feelings that I couldn't even begin to think how I would express them. Mostly, I just wanted to hold Chloe. I wished, more than anything, I could just be on my back, on the catamaran, looking up at the stars, with her in my arms. If I closed my eyes and concentrated, I could almost still feel her body against mine, smell her hair, and taste her lip gloss.

On the other hand, that boat must have been cursed, because by the time my family had piled (or, in my dad's case, hobbled weakly) into my mother's car and driven the forty minutes back to our house, Chloe and her family had already left. Her last text simply said, *So sry, dad has art emergency, more soon*, followed by a few heart emojis.

I was like, *What the heck is an art emergency? Did the gallery run out of runny cheese and cranberries just before a showing? Did Banksy run out of spray paint?* But all that mattered was that the Conti family's cars were gone. Their house was dark. I thought back to my conversation with Ava, which had only been fourteen hours before—even though it felt like about a year and a half. She had been right. The real world had reached into Tall Pines Landing, and it had hurt me.

Because my family had all three of our cars in Pennsylvania, we couldn't all go back to Staten Island together. Leah had to be back at college before Labor Day, so she needed to go home to pack and see her "home" friends. The original plan had been that my mom would spend the last bunch of weekdays with me, but now, *because of your father's health concerns and all*, she said she really needed to be in New York. I argued that I could stay in Pennsylvania alone, and that I didn't even really need a car just to get to the rec center and back each day. I also wanted to point out how weird it was that she suddenly cared about my dad's health, or that anyone cared whether I was supervised.

I wasn't quite angry enough, or nuts enough, to say those things out loud, though. Yet.

So I made an extremely awkward visit to Larry's office on Monday morning while Leah waited for me in the parking lot. As soon as my head came around the corner of his door frame, he gestured to one of the two chairs in front of his desk and said, "Sit!"

I did. I cleared my throat. I mumbled a few *ums* and *ahs*, but I just couldn't bring myself to speak. I didn't want to tell him I had to quit my job a week early, effective immediately. I didn't want to quit. I loved this job. I loved this place. And I didn't want to burn my bridges for the next summer.

"You've gotta go," Larry said.

I nodded. I didn't trust myself to speak.

"It's okay, Jesse. Your mother called me just a few minutes ago. Scary thing, what happened to your dad yesterday. Good guy. Decent right fielder. Great arm. It just goes to show you what I always say . . ."

He just trailed off and looked at me expectantly. I had been working with Larry all summer, and I'd known him practically my whole life. I racked my brain, but I had absolutely no idea what he always said that would relate in any way to my father passing out in the outfield during a pickup softball game and nearly dying. I cleared my throat again. I just had to know. "What do you always say?" I asked.

He slapped his hand down on his desk with a loud bang. I probably jumped about a foot and a half. "HYDRATE!" he barked triumphantly.

Then we sat there staring at each other as my heart slowly settled into something like a normal rhythm again. Finally, he said, "Anyway, we'll miss you around here, Jesse. You're a solid worker. Great with the little kids and the old ladies. That's a rare combination of skills, kid. Besides, your coworkers love you. I mean, they *loooove* you. Plus, you're a promising polisher of boats. I think maybe you could come up a few days early next spring and wax up the whole fleet—whaddya think?"

I looked at him in shock. I'd just walked off my job with no warning, and he was offering to hire me back the next summer for even more hours?

"Okay, fine, twist my arm," he said. "I'll give you a quarter-an-hour raise. And I'll hire your friend Chloe, the Magic Desk Girl, to wax the boats, too. Who knows, maybe she'll even decorate the dock with string lights again!"

I blushed.

"Aha!" he said. "What, you thought I wouldn't notice that? I should *dock* the two of you seven bucks!"

I had no idea what he was talking about. "Seven bucks? Why?"

"I bet you'd end up with Ava the Pool Girl by Labor Day, and I lost. String lights! Who knew Chloe was going to be so . . . whaddya call it? Wily. Anyway, it's fine. Tell your dad I said get well soon. And I'll see you around."

Clearly, I was dismissed. And embarrassed. But hey, also promoted. I got up to leave, but as I reached the door, I turned back, because there was something I couldn't go the whole winter without knowing. "Wait, who bet against you?"

"Annie. Can you believe it? I got sharked by Ava's own little sister."

. . . .

On my way out of the rec center, I got two texts from Ava:

Come back
Say bye

Leah was in a rush to leave, but I begged her to go back to our street. Ava and Annie were already waiting at the bottom of their drive when we pulled in. I said, "Uh . . ."

Ava said, "Don't get all weird on me, J. We'll see each other soon." She grabbed me in a tight hug, then pushed me to arm's distance. "And anyway, we'll stay in touch. Won't we?"

"You know we will."

Then Annie wrapped her arms around me. As we hugged, she got on tiptoe and whispered in my ear, "Ride or die, right?"

I forced myself to put on my most reassuring smile. "Absolutely!"

As my sister slammed the car into reverse and started backing away, Ava's lips moved. It looked like she was saying, "I love you."

. . . .

Forty-five minutes later, I was in the passenger seat on Interstate 80. Kesha was bumping on iTunes. Leah was steering with one hand, sipping from a to-go cup of coffee with the other, and occasionally doing an alarming juggling move in order to take a bite from a corn muffin she had stopped to purchase from Yetter's Diner, our traditional snacking stop on the way home. Being Leah's passenger got kind of hairy at times, because she was a big multitasker. She could be in the middle of a screaming argument with Jake while following directions from her phone's mapping app, and she'd never miss a bite of pizza.

The topic at hand was, of course, our parental crisis (or crises, if you considered our dad's collapse and the summer of not talking to be two separate issues).

"Leah," I said, "you have to see there's a problem in the marriage, right?"

She turned to look at me, taking her eyes completely off the road as we were passing a tractor trailer on the right at seventy-five miles an hour. It would have been a great time to be Catholic so I could have crossed myself. "It's fine now," she said. "Mom cried. They made up. We'll all be back under one happy roof again. Bada bing, bada boom! Happy ending, I go back to school, everybody gets what they wanted. I told you."

"The road!" I squeaked as she casually switched her muffin for her coffee again and a sports car cut us off without signaling. Then I added, "Wait, I didn't get what I wanted. I'm missing my last week of work."

"And your first week of true love," she said. "I'm sorry about that, Romeo. But Chloe will probably be back up soon. Don't they always make it up for Labor Day? And maybe you could visit her in Long Island. You can get there by commuter train from Manhattan."

"Yeah, whatever. Easy for you to say. You'll be back at school, seeing Jake every day. Do you really think Mom and Dad are fine now, though?"

"They will be. It's just the bathroom tile all over again."

I had my doubts. In the back of my head, I was still trying to figure out the mystery of the Rhode Island T-shirt. I changed the subject to something I thought was happier news. "At least Dad's okay. That was scary, huh?"

She took a bite of muffin and said, "Hey, Siri, turn off the music." *Uh-oh*, I thought. *This is serious.* Leah never turned off the music.

"Actually, I wanted to talk to you about that, Jess. I think you're gonna have to keep an eye on Dad's eating for a while."

"Me?" I said. "I'm never with Dad when he's eating. Mom drives me to the seven o'clock ferry in the morning, and then I'm gone all day. I come home and eat dinner at five by myself, or *occasionally* with Mom. Dad eats in the hospital cafeteria, or at the diner on Forest Avenue. About the most I'd be able to do is, like, slip a Slim Jim into his laptop bag. Besides, he *said* he's fine. You heard him."

"Everyone in this family says they're fine. Doesn't mean it's true."

"But he had a whole explanation and everything. You heard him. He's been picking up extra shifts at the nursing home. You know, to save up for my college fund. And he doesn't like the food there. And it's the summer. He said he always loses some weight in the summer."

"Wow," Leah said, "you really drank the Martin Dienstag Kool-Aid, huh?"

I had no idea what she was talking about, but I knew it sounded insulting, so I said, "Well, you really slurped down that Stephanie Dienstag . . . uh, Slurpee!"

She snorted. "Stephanie Dienstag Slurpee?"

"Yeah, because you said 'Martin Dienstag Kool-Aid,'

right? So that's Dad's name, plus a drink. So I said 'Stephanie Dienstag Slurpee,' because that's Mom's name, plus a drink. If yours makes sense, then so does mine."

"Jesse, you're such a dork sometimes," she said, picking up her coffee, taking a sip, and switching lanes without checking for traffic in any perceptible way. "Hey, Siri, play Kesha again. 'Drinking the Kool-Aid' is a saying. 'Slurping down the Slurpee' isn't."

Some random song by Run the Jewels started blasting out of the car stereo. My sister's multitasking, aside from nearly giving me multiple heart attacks and spreading enough cornmeal crumbs to feed a mouse army, had overwhelmed her iPhone's artificial intelligence.

"Hey, Siri, play Kesha," she repeated. "KESHA!"

I had bought a blueberry muffin at the diner, so I unwrapped it and started eating. For the next hour, as one poppy dance song led into the next, I tried to concentrate on nothing but the bass lines.

As we crossed the Goethals Bridge from New Jersey to Staten Island, I felt the jolt of reentering the real world, and I couldn't help but start thinking again. Leah had insisted our parents' marriage was "fine." Then, a minute and a half later, she had said, *Everyone in this family says they're fine. Doesn't mean it's true.*

Not for the first time, or the last, I wished the Goethals Bridge had a U-turn lane.

16. A Visit from the Great Detective

Have you ever been to a party where you knew the birthday girl was really mad at her three best friends? That's what the first few days back at home were like. We had all these family rituals for the post-summer homecoming: the big grilled steak dinner on the back porch, the festive Day of Housecleaning (for which Dad was somehow always magically at work the entire time), the Back-to-School Outlet-Shopping Spree. It was a whole lot of togetherness when everybody was trying to be capital-F Fine all the time. And, this year, not quite pulling it off.

Plus, all I really felt like doing was talking to Chloe and Ava, but texting with them had definitely given me weird vibes all week. Chloe and I hadn't even had a real goodbye, so of course it was strange. You can't spend the best summer of your life with two people and then just suddenly disappear ahead of schedule. I mean, clearly it had happened. But you can't do it without everything being all bizarre afterward.

I was tremendously relieved that Thursday morning,

when my best friend from school, Carson Yang, came over to hang out. He threw himself down in my desk chair and put his feet up on my windowsill, like he always did. Then he said, "So, spill. Tell me all. Because I have completely lost the thread of all this Chloe and Ava stuff. And I can't simply let you manage your romantic affairs on your own. That would be like sending a baby chick out onto the West Side Highway at rush hour."

Carson liked to think he was some kind of love guru just because he'd had a girlfriend since the beginning of sophomore year. Which, granted, seemed like a miraculous feat to me, because I had never even been on an official date. Depending on how you classified the Great Catamaran Incident of 2019.

I'd been texting with Carson all summer, but hadn't updated him since before the big Christmas weekend. Now I did, finishing up with, "So yeah. I think Chloe might be, like, my girlfriend now."

Carson raised an eyebrow. "You *think* she *might* be your girlfriend. I have concerns."

"What do you mean, you have concerns? We were building up to this all summer. Everyone could see it. So now it finally happened. It's great! My first girlfriend. I can show her around the city, bring her to all the ridiculous tourist places, take her on a picnic in Central Park. And then she'll see that I can make a romantic plan, too."

"Not so fast. Did she *say* she's your girlfriend?"

"Well, no, but—"

"Did *you* say she's your girlfriend, and then she nodded? Or showed agreement in any manner, verbal or nonverbal?"

"Well, not exactly, no. But we—"

"I'm thinking maybe you just had one really great night. She set it up for the very end of the summer, when she knew you were leaving. She wanted it, and she knew you wanted it. Everyone knew you wanted it. I mean, it sounds like even the *elks* and the *mooses* knew you wanted it. But now you're both back home. So all I'm saying is, maybe you just made an extremely nice memory."

"You don't understand the connection Chloe and I have." I was super frustrated. I wished I could somehow show him. Then it hit me. "Look!" I nearly shouted, waving my arm in his face. "Look at all the bracelets she made me!"

Carson smirked. "And what are those bracelets called, Jesse?"

"Friendship bracelets," I said.

"I rest my case," he said.

"You can't just go around resting your case. I'm not done arguing with you about this. Listen, when she and I tell everyone about it, then you'll have to believe me, right?"

Carson shook his head in disappointment, like a kindergarten teacher whose students had all just accidentally glued their Thanksgiving hand turkeys to their own fingers. "Oh, *there* it is," he said.

"There what is?" I sputtered.

"She hasn't told anybody about you. She hasn't posted on social media about it. She certainly hasn't changed her relationship status. She hasn't posted a picture of you with little hearts all around it. She hasn't *claimed* you as her territory."

"It's only been a few days," I said. "Plus, it's kind of awkward because Ava doesn't know."

He did the raised-eyebrow thing again. "You mean, you *think* Ava doesn't know. But she does. Girls always know. Think about it. If the antelopes and wildebeests of the forest were settling up their bets, do you really think the girl across the freaking *street* didn't notice the two of you slinking home in the dark of night? See, Ava knows, but Chloe doesn't want to make it openly awkward by announcing it right in Ava's face."

"What are you, a detective?" I snarled. Suddenly, I was feeling quite snarly.

"I do seem to have rather a knack for it, don't I?" he said, buffing his fingernails against his chest and grinning.

Just then, my phone started buzzing. It was a string of texts from Ava:

I'm bored

at work

indoor pool

all alone

its drizzling

video call?

I started to type back that Carson was at my house, but Ava must have been *really* bored, because the call came in before I could even compose the message. I ran a hand through my hair, then swiped to answer.

"Hey," she said. Her face filled the foreground of the screen, and behind her I could see the blue-tiled wall of the pool area. I was overcome by a wave of emotion. I missed the rec center. I was supposed to *be* at the rec center.

"Hey," I replied. "Uh, just so you know, I'm here with—"

"Tracy took Annie and me swimsuit shopping yesterday. I think she probably only wanted to take Annie, but my dad made her take me, too. Anyway, she loves the end-of-summer bargain sales. Wanna see what I got?"

"Wait," I said, "I'm not alone!" But Ava had already taken her phone away from her face and leaned it against her chair. For a moment, all I could see was the surface of the pool, with the far wall in the background. Then Ava stepped back into the frame and started posing like a model.

"Wow," Carson whispered. "You're an idiot."

I didn't think I was an idiot. I was in love with Chloe. Ava *did* look incredible, though. The suit was one of her usual pink shades, in this case a very pale bubble-gum color. It was shiny, and high-cut and low-cut at the same time. Basically, someone had just really gone to town cutting away a whole lot of it.

"What do you think?" Ava asked, turning sideways to the camera and putting a hand on her hip. "Tracy says it's too flirty for work. I told her I thought the four-year-olds in kickboard lesson class could handle the distraction."

Carson shouldered his way into view next to me. "Hi, Ava. I'm Carson. I'm pretty sure we once chatted before, like, freshman year. Anyway, just wanted to say, *I* can't handle the distraction. Please put on a parka. Immediately."

Ava looked mildly embarrassed for a second, but then recovered and laughed. "Ooh, I *like* him," she said to me. She walked over, picked up her phone, and squinted at the screen. "Carson, I remember you! But you used to be, like, short and scrawny. When did you get all filled out?"

She was right. Carson had gotten buff. He had asked his parents for weights for Christmas the year before, and they'd said he could have them on the condition that lifting wouldn't interfere with his piano practice. Carson was kind of a musical prodigy and went every Saturday to a super-famous school in Manhattan called Juilliard to study piano, plus music theory and composition. He was so gifted that he had picked up the ability to play marimba and vibraphone just by fooling around with the mallet instruments in a spare practice room during his breaks at the music school.

Apparently, he'd managed to balance the lifting with the practicing, because he'd turned into a bit of a beast.

He flexed a bicep, and it actually popped up like a freaking cartoon. I wanted to barf.

"Oh, you mean *this*?" he said casually. "It's no big deal. I've just been living right. You know, putting in my time in the weight room."

"Well, keep doing it. And maybe drag Jesse down there with you."

Oh no, I thought. *She did not just say that.*

"I'll try," Carson said, "but you'd be surprised. Jesse is stealth strong. He's lean and wiry. Like a panther. Or maybe a puma. A cheetah? Definitely one of the sleek kinds, but not the one with the disproportionately tiny head." I sighed. I wished Carson had just cut himself off after the word *panther*.

I heard a booming, echoey male voice saying something I couldn't make out. It sounded like an *irritated* Larry.

"Oops," Ava said, "busted! Gotta go." She kissed the screen, which then went dark.

"Told ya," Carson said. "She knows."

"What is it about that conversation that could possibly have led you to that conclusion?"

"One: She was flirting with you. Like, crazily, over-the-top flirting with you. She knows you fooled around with Chloe, so she wants to hit on you until you are forced to admit it. She's *so* smart. Frankly, I am amazed that you have a summer house on a street with only three houses, and the other two houses have girls our exact same age, and both of them have so much *game*. And then there's you. It's kind of uncanny. First of all, what are the odds? And second of all, what *chance* do you have? You're like this little tiny Nemo fish swimming with two really hot piranhas."

"I thought I was a panther."

"I *said* you were a panther. But come on. Take a good, hard, honest look at yourself. Are you more of a sleek, predatory jungle cat, or more of a Nemo?"

"I'm just going to ignore that entire line of questioning. Back to the main, and entirely wrong, part of your argument. If she was flirting with me because she knows about Chloe, then why did she start flirting with you? See, it just doesn't make sense. She flirts with everybody. That's just Ava."

Carson whipped a protein bar out of one of the pockets in his baggy shorts, opened it, and started munching thoughtfully. "Sorry," he said. "It takes a lot of amino acids to get all swole like this. Anyway, as I was saying, she was flirting with me to make you jealous. See, she knows about Chloe, but she still wants to end up with you. I might still be wrong that Chloe just wanted you for a little end-of-summer fling. Okay, forget I said that. I'm not wrong. But, I mean, I could be, theoretically. Although I don't think I am."

"Ahem," I interjected. "Your point?"

"My point is, Ava knows. And Ava really, actually likes you. Also, holy moly, I'm no stylist, but pink is *seriously* her color. I mean, wow. I'd play in her treehouse any day."

"Shut up," I said. But I had a feeling he was right: Ava probably knew.

17. The Longest Month of My Life

I thought I'd see Chloe for Labor Day, but she texted that her dad's business was still in crisis mode. I wanted to question this, like *What can your dad and your stepmother possibly be doing to fix a so-called art crisis on a holiday weekend?*, but I realized that probably wasn't going to get me any kind of desirable result, so I just texted back that I would miss her. She sent back a crying-face emoji and a hug emoji, neither of which exactly reeked of blazing passion.

It crossed my mind that Carson might be right.

Then each of my parents individually came to me and made a painfully awkward display of explaining why they couldn't take me to Pennsylvania for the weekend anyway, which made the whole issue irrelevant.

Except for one small catch: Ava and Annie went up with their dad and stepmom, so then Ava ended up being annoyed with me. I texted, *What about Chloe? Why aren't you annoyed with her?*

She wrote back:

Chloe always ditches me
during the year
you never did b4
whats different now

I wrote back, *My parents have gone insane now, which is new.* She never responded.

I didn't hear from Chloe until the middle of that week, when she sent me a long private message on social media, late at night when I was asleep. This only ever happened a few times a year. It always seemed to mean she was in a kind of wistful, sad mood, and maybe missing me a little.

The message said, *Hey, Jess. I can't sleep. This was the strangest weekend. Partly, it was the stuff with the gallery, which I hope I can tell you about in person someday. Partly, it was not being in Pennsylvania. I felt so strongly that we were all in the wrong place by not being together. I hope you know what I mean. But the biggest thing was that this boy Adam, who's been my friend at school since kindergarten, asked me to come out with his family on their sailboat. There's this race of sailing ships on the Long Island Sound for Labor Day, and I've never seen it because we're always away, so I was curious. I hope this isn't weird for you. Anyway, we watched all the ships, and all the adults drank champagne, and they gave each of us some. Then the sun went down, and it got kind of chilly, and Adam put his arm around me. It didn't mean anything to me,*

160

but I was cold. I swear, he didn't try to do anything else, but I think he wanted to. And I just wished so much that it was your arm around me, making me feel safe and secure. And warm. I honestly don't know what I'm trying to convey, except that I miss you. Do you think your parents will take you to PA for Columbus Day weekend? I really hope so.

I read the message in a daze on the seven o'clock ferry to school. Carson asked to see it. When he read it, all he said was, "You *really* need to find a way to keep this girl away from boats."

"Or I need to jump overboard right now, swim to Long Island, and surprise her."

He looked out across the choppy gray waves of New York Harbor, the tugboats, the gigantic container ships off in the distance past the Verrazzano-Narrows Bridge. "I'm pretty sure that's about twenty-five miles of ocean swimming," he said. "So you'd definitely surprise her. Mostly by surviving."

"It would be a romantic gesture, though."

"True. On the other hand, if I'm late to jazz band because the ferry crew has to stop and try to fish you out of the bay, the school might send a robocall to my house. And then my mom might start asking me questions about jazz band. And then she might find out I'm playing the vibraphone instead of the piano."

"Why would she care if you're playing the vibraphone?"

"Oh, you sweet summer child. She'd care because it

would mean I wasn't *fully concentrating on my piano studies.* Frankly, the consequences of that are too terrifying for me to contemplate at 7:12 in the morning. So . . . my vote is for the not-jumping-overboard choice."

"Which is?"

"Literally anything else you could possibly decide to do."

. . . .

The first three weeks of school were a blur. I thought my classwork would distract me from both my family problems and my possibly nonexistent love life, but the reverse turned out to be true. I daydreamed through every period, alternately obsessing over my parents and wishing I were with Chloe. Finally, I couldn't take it anymore. I texted Chloe: *Can I come see you?*

I got back a one-word reply: *Yes!!!*

And that's how, three weeks later, I ended up on a Saturday morning Long Island Rail Road commuter train from Manhattan, carrying a duffel bag full of clothes, with a dozen red roses nestled as gently as possible between my spare jeans and my best black sweater.

When I walked out of the station, I looked around and saw Chloe's stepmom, Caroline, standing at the curb next to their family's old four-wheel drive SUV. "Over here, Jesse!" she shouted, popping the back hatch.

"Hi, Mrs. Conti," I yelled back, and walked over. As I placed the duffel in the space behind the back seats, I couldn't help but notice there was no passenger in the vehicle. I was like, *What the heck, Chloe?* But I didn't say anything. "Come sit up front," Caroline said. "It's so good to see you!"

As I climbed into the shotgun seat, she said, "Look at you, Mr. City Boy, all dressed in black! It's funny. I'm so used to seeing you in the country, but I guess now you're in New York musician mode, huh?"

I couldn't help gazing down at myself. It was true. I was wearing black jeans and a black T-shirt. Carson had advised me to wear black. His exact words had been, *Show her you're the cool New York City kid. You want to have the upper hand.*

I was like, *A. I never have the upper hand with Chloe, and B. Cool New York City kid? Gimme a break, we're from Staten Island.* But in the end, I'd thrown on the black clothes because they were pretty much my standard uniform during the year. Plus, I had no idea where Chloe and I might be going or what we'd be doing, and I figured black was right for basically anything. And, as a bonus, they were clean.

Of course, now that Caroline had said something, I started second-guessing myself. It was bad enough that Chloe hadn't even come to get me, but now I was going to be all worked up into a sweaty panic before I even saw her.

Chloe's stepmother had apparently read my mind, because she said, "Chloe wanted to come with me, but she was making you a surprise, and at the last minute, it wasn't ready yet. She's been so busy with the whole business thing . . . the hotels and all. It's exciting, but we've all had so much work! And she's been *such* a big part of it. I don't know what we'll do when she heads off to college, honestly. But she's so excited already about the business scholarships the counselors want her to apply for next fall. And then there's student council—isn't it crazy that she got elected president *again*? As a *junior*? And she's so humble about it, with such a sense of humor. Just the other day, she was joking around, and she said, 'Not bad for a girl with no spleen, huh?' But I'm sure I don't have to tell you how remarkable she is. I mean, since you're her closest confidant and all."

Am I? I thought. *Because I have absolutely no idea what you're talking about. Hotels? Student council? President? Again???* Chloe was my favorite person in the world, but I didn't seem to know much about her real life.

"Yeah," I said, "she's remarkable."

Chloe's house was only a block from the ocean, which was pretty awesome. Aside from that, it was a normal-looking suburban dwelling. The main thing that struck me when I walked in was that it smelled amazing, like frosting and cinnamon and chocolate and the sweet innocence of childhood joy. Chloe was in the kitchen, wearing big mitten things. She had just taken something out of the oven. Naturally, she looked stunning. She wasn't dressed up or anything: She was just wearing faded jeans and a cute, cartoonish T-shirt with a kitten on it. She even had a bit of flour on the side of her face, but that didn't matter. If you set off her fire alarm at three a.m. and took a flash photo of her as she stumbled across her lawn in a ratty bathrobe, half-asleep, she would still look adorable to me.

"Hi, Jess!" she said. "I made you cupcakes. The second batch isn't decorated, but come see the first ones!"

This was weird. Our usual greeting was a running, full-body hug. This had always included a fairly grand display of cheek kissing in the past, and this time, I'd hoped there might be something more. But no hug? That was unfathomable. I followed her over to the dining room table.

"Look closely," she said. "Bass guitars!" Sure enough, each cupcake had what looked like chocolate frosting on it, and then on top of *that*, there was a blobby design that, if you tilted your head a bit and used your imagination, kind of resembled my ukulele bass.

Admittedly, a couple of them looked a bit more like crossbows. Or sperm whales. But the concept was clear. "Awesome," I said. "And they smell great, too. Thanks, Klo!"

Oh, yikes, I thought. *As if this weren't already weird enough, now I just had to go ahead and call her "Klo" for the first time ever. Swell!*

She realized I was still lugging my bag around, so she said, "Come on, I'll show you where to put your stuff."

She led me down a hallway and stepped sideways into a darkened doorway. "Come here," she murmured.

I followed her into the room and put my bag on the bed. I thought I could salvage the day if I could just find a way to produce the flowers smoothly, so I stood with my back to the bed and started trying to work the bag's zipper open with one hand. Just then, Chloe stepped into my arms and gave me the hug I'd been dreaming of since we'd parted in her driveway in the early-morning hours of Christmas-in-August. Her cheek was crushed against mine. I clutched her to me with my free arm and breathed in deeply. I wanted to inhale every molecule of this moment so I could replay it forever.

Strangely, I noticed that Chloe didn't smell like coconuts. On Long Island, her hair had more of a minty scent.

She pulled away slightly and looked into my eyes, which were starting to adjust to the gloom. "I need to see something, okay?" she said.

"Mmmmm," I responded, partly because she had me hypnotized, as usual, and partly because I was still working on getting the flowers out of the bag. I had opened the zipper a few inches, and now I was fishing around with my hand, trying to get a grip on the flowers and slip the whole bouquet out through the opening.

"Here goes," she whispered, and kissed me gently on the lips, just as my fingers closed around the stems. I know this sounds crazy, but I swear, I saw fireworks. She held the kiss for a few seconds, just long enough for my knees to get weak. Instinctively, my hand clenched around the flowers, hard.

A thorn impaled my palm and my whole body must have tensed up noticeably, because Chloe broke the kiss. "I knew it!" she said. "That was weird, right? You felt it, too."

Actually, I had felt like choirs of angels were lifting me to the heavens while eternal echoes of hallelujahs billowed up all around, thrilling every nerve ending in my body—at least until the whole hand-stabby thing had happened. But what was I supposed to say? It was just too humiliating.

"Oh, yeah," I said. "Totally. *So* weird."

She sighed, put a hand on my chest, and leaned against me. "I'm so relieved," she said. "Now we can just be best friends again. I've been so worried about this. You have absolutely no idea."

No, I thought. *You have absolutely no idea.*

And then . . . *Did she just dump me?*

"So," my best friend said, "are you ready for a cupcake?"

I wiped my bloody palm against my spare jeans and slid my hand out of the bag. As I followed her back down the hall in my all-black outfit, sucking on my puncture wound, I felt like the world's saddest vampire.

18. The Chain

Depression set in. It started the following Monday, when I got my first-ever F, on a major calculus test. No, on second thought, it started before that, when I accidentally got a glimpse of my mom's awful secret. On third thought, maybe it started even earlier, when I had to beg my father to eat his dinner instead of starving himself.

Aw, who am I kidding? It started before any of that, on the ferry ride home from Chloe's.

In my defense, it's easy to get depressed in the fall in New York City, even when your father isn't depressed already and the girl of your dreams hasn't just crushed your heart. I found myself standing on the upper deck of the boat, staring down into the churning waters, thinking, *What's the point of all this? I get up every morning before six, just so I can commute an hour and a half each way to school. I leave my house in darkness. I get back home in darkness. I take all these advanced courses, plus SAT prep on Saturday mornings. Every day is getting colder and colder. I mean, I know junior year is supposed to be hard, but does it have to be this hard?*

Besides, why do I spend all this time working, and trying, and caring, if I don't even get the girl in the end anyway?

Also, where the hell is Mom?

I was on the 5:30 ferry that Sunday night. I'd told myself I was going to use the ride time to do all the sample problems for my upcoming calculus test in the online chapter review. But when I called my mom's cell and asked her to pick me up on the Staten Island side of the ferry, the call went right to voice mail.

This was odd, because my mother had known she was supposed to pick me up, and whatever other distractions she had going on, she was always the one who did the ferry runs.

I could have taken the bus home, but I decided to try my dad first. He answered right away, and jumped on the chance to pick me up. When I hoisted my bag into the back seat and then slumped in front next to him, I noticed he had that drained look, so I asked if he was hungry. He didn't answer directly.

Shocker.

He just said, "Do you need something to eat?"

I said yes, so we went to a diner. I purposely chose one my father had always loved. I ordered fried chicken in the basket, which had been my comfort food since I was little. I also thought that maybe the smell of fried food might stimulate his appetite. He ordered a roast turkey dinner, which seemed weird to me. Like, what person who is not a senior citizen orders the roast turkey dinner when it isn't Thanksgiving?

My dad had always been a particularly intent listener, which probably made him a great psychiatrist, but which sometimes unnerved Leah and me when he focused his skills on us. This night, though, when he asked how my weekend with Chloe had gone, I had the feeling he was barely with me. You know the feeling you have when you're spilling your deepest emotions to someone and they keep checking their phone? This felt kind of like that, although I completely glossed over all the emotional parts of my weekend fiasco and his phone was nowhere in sight. It was more that his eyes were glazed over, or he was just staring down into the depths of his water glass as though he was considering drowning himself in it.

I tried to get him to talk about his weekend, or where my mom was, but all I could get from him was single syllables. He. had. gone. to. see. his. patients. at. the. hospital. and. the. old. people's. home.

Period.

When the food came, I devoured mine, but he just kind of pecked around at his. Like, he was literally just pushing peas around his plate. He actually hid a few under the edge of his mashed potatoes, much in the manner of a three-year-old kid. I couldn't stand it. "Dad," I said, "you have to eat."

He gazed at me blankly.

"Please," I added. He sighed, took a forkful of lumpy-looking potatoes, and shoved the beige mass into his mouth.

By the time we got out of there, it was after nine. We pulled into the driveway of our house ten minutes later, and I noticed all the lights inside were off. Where the heck was my mother? I went up to my room and unpacked. I had chucked the droopy, half-crushed roses in a trash can at the train station as soon as Chloe's stepmom's car had pulled away from the curb, but they had oozed onto my clothes. Also, there was the matter of the bloodstains from my palm wound.

I went down to the basement and started a load of laundry.

Even then, I thought I'd try to do a couple of problems before bed, but as I sat down at my desk, all I could think about was my defeated dad, my missing mom, and the bottomless well of mystery that was Chloe, my presidential business-mogul crush. What had I done wrong? Who bakes cupcakes for a guy, pulls him into a darkened bedroom, kisses him, dumps him, and then spends the rest of the weekend hanging out with him like everything is normal?

I couldn't concentrate on calculus problems. I had too many actual *problem* problems.

I was still sitting there with my head in my hands when the faint beep of the washing machine startled me almost an hour later. By then, my parents' bedroom door was closed, though I hadn't heard the front door open. I assumed that my dad had gone to sleep, but my mom was still missing in action. I tiptoed to the basement and started the dryer.

As I reached the top of the stairs, I was blinded by headlights. A car had pulled into our driveway to turn around. I ducked down, and the instant the lights stopped shining directly on me, I rushed to the big bay window at the front of our house. My mom was just stepping out of the passenger side of a sports car. As she turned, I saw she had a huge smile on her face. The car was pulled up to the curb directly in front of our post light, so I could see it pretty clearly. In the car's rear passenger window, there was a sticker proclaiming P ROUD URI DAD!

It took me a second, but when I figured it out, I gasped. URI. The University of Rhode Island. Like the T-shirt.

You would have failed your calc test, too.

. . . .

On the way home from school that Tuesday, I stepped out onto the front deck of the ferry, put in my earbuds, and made an SOS call to my grandparents in Florida. Three days later, they flew up to New York for a visit. Boy, were my parents surprised! I wouldn't say they were necessarily delighted, but I hadn't known what else to do. The situation in my house kind of felt like an "in case of emergency, break glass" deal.

We all had a tense dinner on Friday . . . and by "tense," I mean that everybody acted like the meal was a cross between a job interview and a high-level nuclear missile treaty negotiation. Then, while I was at my SAT course on Saturday morning, things must have gotten to a whole other level, because when I came home from that, my parents were both out, my Grandma Jean was standing at the kitchen counter cutting up vegetables and crying quietly, and my Grandpa Art was waiting for me by the door.

"What's happening?" I said.

"We're taking a walk, honey," he said. That in itself was super odd, because he hadn't called me *honey* since I was tiny. He was serious about the walk part, clearly. He was already wearing his old-guy New Balance sneakers, a windbreaker, and his VIETNAM VETERAN baseball cap. Before I could even respond, he was up and headed for the door.

I said, "Uh, bye, Grandma," and followed him. The block was a dead end that branched off another dead end. The street at the top of ours used to continue through a major intersection around the corner, but it was a very steep hill, and cars kept skidding off the road and into the living room of one of the houses there, so the city installed three heavy metal poles in the ground and ran a thick chain across the whole street. Grandpa Art turned right and headed up the hill toward the chain. Within fifty feet, he was huffing and puffing too hard to talk. He had never told us the details, but I knew he had gotten hit in the chest with pieces of a grenade in Vietnam. Once when I was in grade school, he had pretended to chase me across the parking lot of his condominium complex, and when I let him grab me, he'd said, "Not bad for a guy with half a lung, huh, Champ?"

All of which is to say, I had about a block and a half to wonder nervously what the point of this walk was. Then we got to the chain and my grandfather leaned against one of the poles to catch his breath. After a couple of minutes, he turned to me, put a hand on my shoulder, and said, "J, you were right to call."

I didn't say anything. My grandfather was the person I respected most in the world. It sometimes took a while for him to gather his thoughts, but I always waited him out.

"Your grandmother and I—no, scratch that. *I* should have seen this coming. From what I can gather . . . oh, hell, J. There's no easy way to say this. I wish there were. Or I wish either of your parents were in good enough emotional condition to tell it to you themselves."

Okay, now I was terrified. My grandfather's speeches were usually a lot more eloquent than this one. Also, they didn't generally have this one's distinctive doomsday quality.

174

"Jesse, I hope I'm wrong, but I think your parents are breaking up. They aren't ready to admit it yet, and neither of them is willing to tell us what's really going on, but I just don't see a way forward."

I looked down at the sidewalk.

"J," he continued, "listen. I've never been through this before, but I'd imagine that at some point over the next several months, you're going to want to get out of here for a while. If you get to that point, I don't care if it's day or night. I want you to call me, okay? I'll get you a plane ticket, no questions asked." He reached out with his other arm so he was holding me by both shoulders, which forced me to look into his eyes. "You got that? Day or night."

I nodded.

He pulled me in for a very strong bear hug. My grandfather was about five inches shorter than I was, and he was a seventy-six-year-old who may or may not have been missing half a lung, but he had always been a powerful man. In my ear, he rasped, "Your parents are a goddamn mess right now, J, but remember, you have your own life to live. Okay? Please don't forget that. You have your own life to live."

Then he released me and I followed him home.

19. The Matzo Balls of Doom, Part One

"Wait a minute," Ava said in my earbuds. I was in bed, in the dark, and my parents were asleep downstairs. "Your grandmother did *what*?"

"She made me, like, a hundred gallons of matzo ball soup. That was her solution to the impending divorce crisis. She stood there all day and into the night, using all four burners of the stove and every inch of counter space. And you know those pint containers the soup comes in when you order Chinese food? And the tubs that soft butter comes in? Well, my mom always stacks those up in the basement, but she never uses them. She always said they'd come in handy one day, and the day finally came! My grandma ladled out two matzo balls, two baby carrots, and a piece of celery into each and every container we owned, and she filled our refrigerator. Next, she filled the upstairs freezer. When that was full, she filled our entire downstairs freezer. I tried like five times throughout the day to ask her what she was doing, but she kept shushing me and shooing me away. Finally, at the end, she slumped down at the table, so I brought her some water and got the whole question out. She said, 'What, I'm just supposed to let my grandchild starve?' Then she talked me through how to defrost soup."

"Aww, J, that's sweet."

"What's sweet about it? Why would I starve? My parents are getting divorced, not dropping me off at Miss Hannigan's orphanage."

"Think about it. Does your father cook?"

For some reason, I felt the need to defend the honor of my male lineage, even though my father honestly didn't know how to boil water. "He grills."

"So that's a no, then. And your grandmother probably figures your mom is going to move out at some point, so she wants you to feel taken care of. She's showing *care* through *food*. It's classic. You should see how many people sent us gift cards for dinners after our mother died. So, did you thank your grandma?"

"Yeah, I thanked her. I'm not an idiot. Plus, my parents work late like half the time as it is. You know that 'Body By DoorDash' T-shirt Carson got me? It's not as funny to me as it is to him. I'm not sure how different it's really going to be if my mom is gone. Come to think of it, maybe I should just tell my mom that."

Ava didn't say anything for an uncomfortably long time. "Oh, shit," I said, "I'm sorry. I'm an idiot. I realize it's going to be different. I'm just talking about food. And I know your mom is really *gone* gone. I'm just super mad at my mother right now."

Ava let out a long, slow breath. "J, I get it. Your mom might be cheating on your dad. But listen. My mom had an affair. Ugh, I hate that word. But she did. I don't know what went on between Chloe's parents, but I can tell you this: It doesn't matter now. So don't say anything to your mom you can't take back, okay?"

I was in a terrible mood. That's my only excuse. I said, "That's easy for you to say. You snap at people all the time."

Ava said, "That's how I know. I said about eleven things to my mom that I can never, ever unsay. Anyway, I have to go."

At some point, we had gotten into the habit of nervously saying "I love you" at the end of conversations. It didn't feel quite natural to say that, but having Ava hang up *without* saying it was a slap in the face. I was so desperate to feel loved that I tiptoed down to the kitchen and ate my first tub of matzo ball soup, cold.

If I'd known this was the last supply of my Grandma Jean's matzo balls on earth, I might have held off for a while.

. . . .

The lead-up to Thanksgiving was rough. I couldn't bring myself to tell Carson what was happening at home. I desperately wanted to tell Leah that our parents were about to split up, but doing it by text seemed like a horrible thing to do, and every time I called her, all she wanted to know was whether our dad was eating. As soon as I said yes, she was like, *Okay, gotta go. Love you, buddy!*

Then there were Chloe and Ava. Talking with Chloe was super hard, because I didn't want to hear about her triumphant Long Island life, and she seemed pretty reluctant to listen to my woeful tales of bitterness and microwaved soup. If I even started texting about my parents, she stopped responding. It hurt, like she had gotten *disengaged* from me. I tried hard to stay away from her social media, but I couldn't help noticing she kept getting tagged in pictures that also featured this Adam dude. I tried to console myself with the fact that the photos all seemed to have been taken on dry land, but that wasn't a whole lot of comfort.

Ava was willing to text and talk, but clearly, I couldn't complain anymore about my parents to her, because her situation was a million times worse than mine. Plus, I couldn't talk at all about Chloe, so that was like a big elephant in the room. It got so bad that I almost wished I could be one of those ladies in the park who walk around with a tiny dog in their purse and talk to it like it's a person, because at least then there would be some living thing that knew what was going on in my life.

Then, the day before the holiday, I woke up before sunrise in a panic. At first, I had no idea what had disturbed me, and in fact, I was still half-submerged in a nightmare. It sounds insane and ridiculous now, but I was convinced that my pillow was breathing. As in, it was alive and moving. I couldn't move, though. I knew—I mean, I absolutely and with great certainty *knew*—that the pillow was evil, and it was right under my head, alive and breathing. I couldn't get away.

I'd had some bad dreams before, but this was some Edgar Allan Poe–level horror.

Gradually, I became more conscious and realized my T-shirt and hair were completely soaked through with sweat. I also became aware of what had really woken me up: My parents were shouting at each other downstairs. For months, they had ignored each other, done a terrible job of pretending nothing was wrong, or, at most, hissed at each other in stage whispers when they thought I was out of hearing range. Out-and-out yelling was new. I was alarmed.

The more I lay there listening, though, the more I realized I wasn't *only* alarmed. I was also furious. My parents had gotten up before dawn *on a day I didn't have school* just to fight. Why? Had they set their alarm just for this? What was so important that they couldn't have screamed it three hours later, over a nice steaming latte? I already couldn't concentrate in school. Did they really need to screw up my only sleeping-in morning to sneak some extra abuse time?

And that's when the crazy urge came over me. The door to my bedroom closet was open a crack, and it occurred to me that my aluminum bat from Little League baseball was in there. Suddenly, all I wanted was to grab that bat, run downstairs, and start smashing all the windows of the house so that everyone in the whole neighborhood would have to wake up and see what the crazy people in the crazy house were doing.

That phrase kept racing through my head: *See the crazy people in the crazy house. See the crazy people in the crazy house. See the crazy people in the crazy house.*

I had just enough self-control left to grip the edge of my bed, resist the impulse, and take a few deep breaths. I really, really wanted to break those windows, especially the huge picture window that overlooked our slate-floored front porch. I closed my eyes, and I could hear all that glass tinkling down on the flagstones. I wanted that explosion of noise. I wanted the reaction. I wanted my parents to be the ones panicking. I wanted them to be the embarrassed ones who had to hide different little pieces of their lives from everybody.

No, we all already were the embarrassed ones who had to hide our secrets. I wanted to force all of us to stop.

I grabbed my phone from the shelf at the head of my bed and called Leah.

Of course, that went right to voice mail. She probably had me on DO NOT DISTURB. Well, too late. I was disturbed.

I called Ava. She answered right away, sounding sleepy. "J?" she asked. "What's wrong?"

She didn't sound annoyed or anything. She simply asked me what was wrong.

"My parents are downstairs fighting," I said. "They *woke up* just to fight. I just want to go downstairs and smash all the windows. I can't be here, Ava. I don't know what to do." Then my voice broke, and I was sobbing uncontrollably into the phone.

"We've got to get your ass on a train, J," Ava said.

. . . .

My parents didn't like it, but an hour later, I was packing my duffel bag again. I had a train ticket and a plan: I was spending Thanksgiving with Ava's family in Connecticut. Leah was staying up at school, so my parents had a few days to figure out how to make things peaceful at home. If I came back on Sunday and they still couldn't be civil, I was going to leave again.

I wasn't sure where in the world I would go, but I knew anything was better than living with my parents while they were being like this until I lost control of myself.

My mother insisted on driving me to the train station in Manhattan. When she pulled over to let me out, she reached across the front seat and put a hand on my arm. "I hope you know your father and I both love you, Jesse," she said, her eyes twinkling with warm sincerity, slanting late-morning sunlight, and unshed tears.

She looked so sad! If I had known any University of Rhode Island spirit cheers, I might have broken out singing one to improve her mood, but I didn't, so I just said, "Then you need to work on your shit this week." I flinched away from her grip, got out, and walked away.

I hated feeling like the bad guy. I hated *her* for making me feel like I was the bad guy for making her cry. I hated my dad for letting things get this far. I couldn't help thinking that maybe if my parents hadn't pretended everything was fine for months and months, it wouldn't have gotten so explosively ugly.

But then again, what did I know about relationships? I had only ever been in one for about four hours total, and apparently, it hadn't gone nearly as well as I'd thought at the time. Maybe my dad was going through what I was, except in his case, the four hours was more like twenty-two years.

I looked down at the still-visible mark on my right palm where the thorn from the rose had plunged into me, and tried to imagine how much more pain my father might be in. Maybe enough pain to make a guy stop eating, or collapse in the middle of a softball field. And then spend months trying not to feel anything at all.

It's hard trying to see your parents as people, because

then you might have to realize they are not doing the world's best job of people-ing.

These were the thoughts swirling around my head as I got on the Metro-North to Greenwich, Connecticut. As soon as I found a seat, I put in my earbuds and tried to drown out my consciousness with a Rush playlist. Usually, the interplay of their aggressive bassist and monster drummer could distract me from just about anything, but somehow, I still couldn't tune out the clack-clack-clack of the train's motion. Or the sound of my own voice, in perfect time with the train's wheels, saying, "Work on your shit, work on your shit, work on your shit."

According to the timetable, the ride was only fifty-four minutes long. According to the click-clack soundtrack of my inner demons, it was about seventeen hundred shits' worth. It was also enough time for Leah to text, *Did you literally just run away from home!?!???*

I wrote back, *No, I just figuratively ran away from home. I literally am taking the train to Ava's. Plus, M&D know where I'm going, so don't get dramatic. Kisses!*

It was kind of like, *Oh, now you're concerned?*

Unlike a certain Long Island girl I knew, Ava was actually waiting for me on the platform when I got off the train. She also hugged me right away. It was tricky with my duffel in one hand and my U-Bass in its soft case strapped over the opposite shoulder, but I held on to her like she was a life preserver. Honestly, that's kind of what it felt

184

like. Plus, I wanted to breathe her in. Even amid the random smells of the train station—coffee, cleaning fluids, a hint of burning oil—her hair still smelled like it always did.

"Thank you," I mumbled into her skull, just above her left ear.

"For what?"

"Just . . . thank you."

She pushed me away a bit and peered into my eyes. "You know we're going to get you through this, right?" she said. "Now come on. My dad's waiting in the car, and I think he's nervous about this whole deal."

"Why?" I asked as she started to walk in front of me up the stairs and out of the station.

"Well, I get the weird feeling he thinks it might be some kind of, like, boyfriend-girlfriend situation."

"But—but—it's—" I sputtered uselessly.

"I know, J. Dads gonna dad, though. So just don't, uh, grope me in the back seat or anything."

I blushed. "Why do you have to make everything weird?"

She stopped suddenly in the middle of the station's waiting room. So suddenly, in fact, that I bumped into her from behind. She turned and grinned. "Everything already *is* weird, J. I just think it's a little bit fun to tease you about it once in a while. Now come on!" She grabbed my hand and started walking again.

As I hustled to keep up and my armpits began to sweat,

I was struck by one great thing about Ava: She was more distracting than the heaviest of heavy rhythm sections.

I slid into the back seat of the car, thanking Mr. Green profusely, and Ava got in on the other side. Annie was in the front passenger seat. In the summer, her hair had been long, but now it was cut shoulder-length, and she had gotten it dyed a light cotton-candy purple. "Hey, Sunshine!" I said, realizing as the words left my mouth how happy I felt to see her. I reached diagonally between the front seats to touch her arm. "New look, huh?"

She turned halfway toward me, and I saw that she was frowning. "What?" she said. "Do you hate it?"

I tried to smile reassuringly. "Oh, come on, kid," I said. "How could I ever hate your hair? You are officially the cutest girl on the planet."

"Oh, barf," Ava said.

"Okay, you are officially the cutest girl on the planet, front-seat division. But I'm serious. I love it. But enough with the hair. How are you?"

Annie grinned weakly. "I'm all right, I guess," she said. Then she turned and faced straight forward again. I looked at Ava and raised my eyebrows. Ava shrugged. I made a mental note to try to talk with Annie alone at some point if I could. I had no idea how it felt to be having a first Thanksgiving after losing a parent, and she wasn't even thirteen years old yet.

Her birthday was in the beginning of December. It

hit me that she was also about to have her first birthday without a mom, and then her first Hanukkah and New Year's Eve.

All of that made me feel like a whiner for running away just because my parents were squabbling.

Ava's house was a sprawling four-bedroom colonial on a huge wooded plot. When we first got inside, I put my bags by the front door. Then Ava and Annie gave me the tour. The parental bedroom suite was on the first floor, along with the kitchen, living room, dining room, and "mudroom," whatever that was. There was also an enclosed back porch connected to an unenclosed side porch.

I was amazed by how much *space* people could afford outside the city. I mean, Ava's dad was an internal auditor at a big accounting firm, and her stepmom, Tracy, was a scientific researcher, so I was sure they made good money. Still, though, nobody in Staten Island had porches that led to other porches.

The tour continued upstairs, with Ava's very-pink bedroom, Annie's purple-and-white one, and the guest bedroom in between, which was connected to Ava's by a shared bathroom. Ava pointed to the door of the guest room and said, "J, you can sleep here," at which point, her father's voice boomed out from the bottom of the stairs, "And by 'here,' she means 'on the couch in the basement'!"

Annie giggled. Ava did not.

When I took my stuff downstairs, I saw that the basement was a pretty sweet setup. There was a full bathroom, a multi-couch area set up around a gigantic TV screen mounted on a wall, a Ping-Pong table, a bar area, a separate weight room with a treadmill and an exercise bike, and two glass doors that led out to a patio.

Ava came down, saw I was looking out through the double doors, and said, "As long as you don't think about kidnappers watching you sleep from the tree line, you'll love it down here."

"Why would you say that?" I asked.

"Oh, stop crying, you big baby," she said. "You'll be fine. Just shout if you get scared. Richard and Tracy are going to be watching you like hawks all week. I'm sure they'll come running!"

At that exact moment, Ava's stepmom called down, "Ava, honey, can you come help me in the kitchen for a sec?"

"What did I tell you?" Ava said. "Like hawks!"

I took a step toward the stairs, but Ava put a hand on my arm. "Wait, J. I have to ask you something. Have you talked to Chloe lately? About what's going on with your parents and everything?"

"No. I've tried, but she's never around."

"That's weird. I thought you guys were getting really close at the end of the summer."

"Yeah, well, don't believe everything you think."

. . . .

That night I had a dream where I was hugging Chloe. We were looking soulfully into each other's eyes, and I could feel that we were about to kiss. *This time*, I thought, *it's going to be perfect. This time it's going to Mean Something.*

I looked down at what Chloe was wearing and could feel myself starting to smile. This was so perfect! It was a hoodie I recognized. There were two lines of text across her chest. The first said THE REAL WORLD IS . . . I had a split second to process that the "is" should have said "isn't." Then she pushed herself a bit farther away from me, and I read the second line: THE UNIVERSITY OF RHODE ISLAND!

. . . .

We spent all Thursday morning helping Tracy with dinner. This was new to me, because my mom had never accepted help in the kitchen. She actively chased Leah and me out of the room, and then complained afterward about how she never had any help. Tracy was nothing like that. Her kitchen was like an assembly line. Ava had always complained that Tracy hated her, but that wasn't the feeling I got at all. Tracy was demanding, but I thought she was appreciative.

And it was shockingly fun. Annie was Tracy's right-hand girl, because she seemed to know what to do without being told. She was like a little chopping, slicing, and dicing machine. Ava and I required a lot more supervision, because Ava didn't seem to have had as much practice, and I was basically a novice. Our first big task was tearing up bread for stuffing.

It turned out I have a gift for destruction. Ava was right there with me. There were two large bakery loaves, and we laid into those things.

Bread was flying everywhere. We might have even gotten into a very minor bread-chunk-flinging fight. But in short order, both loaves were absolutely shredded, and all the pieces were in the big plastic bowl on the dining room table in front of us. We looked at each other and smiled. That was when I noticed Ava had a fairly major crumb in her hair, just above her left eye.

"Stay still," I said. I reached out and gently pinched the crumb between my thumb and first finger.

"What is it?" she said.

"Just a crumb."

She held her hand out, palm up, and I deposited the crumb in it. Her fingers closed around mine. I shivered. Suddenly, the dining room felt very warm.

"Ava, Jesse! How long does it take to tear up some bread?" Tracy barked from the kitchen. "I need you to wash the cutting boards and the knives!"

Okay, Ava, I thought, *your stepmom might hate you a little.*

Late in the morning, we ran out of celery, which was apparently a major crisis, so Ava and I got sent to the extremely high-class grocery store. It was a mob scene. As we were walking in, Ava dug her fingernails into my arm and hissed, "Don't look, but two horrible girls from my school are here." She kind of tilted her chin in the direction of two girls our age. They both had ridiculous fake-blonde hair. Their heads were pressed together like they were whispering to each other, and they were glancing in our direction. "What are you doing?" Ava asked. "I said don't look! They're going to talk to me. I know it. And they're going to try to make me look stupid in front of you."

I used my free hand to unclasp her fingers from my arm. "It's okay, Ava," I said. "They're nobody, right? They can't change how I feel about you." Then an idea came to me. "In fact, why don't we mess with them?"

A few minutes later, we were headed out of the produce aisle with a family-sized pack of celery sticks clutched triumphantly in hand when Ava's classmates rounded the corner in front of us. "Hey, Ava," one said in a grating voice. "Yeah, hey, girl," the other chimed in. They were just oozing fake friendliness.

"Hi," Ava said, without enthusiasm.

"Who's your *friend*?" one girl asked.

"Oh, him? This is just my, uh, my Swedish exchange student."

"Does he have a name?"

No, I thought. *In Sweden, we haven't invented names yet. You clever, clever Americans!*

"Yes," Ava said. "It's Sven."

I burst into actor mode. "Yess!" I exclaimed cheerfully. "I am Sven! Sven Svenlagen! From Svalbard. In Sveden. Because I am Svedish!"

"Hi," one of the girls said. "I'm Britney, and this is Whitney!"

"Hi, Breeny!" I shouted ecstatically. "Hi, Weenie!"

Ava couldn't hold back a little laugh. Whitney glared at her.

"Your friend seems very, um, enthusiastic," Britney said.

"Oh, he is," Ava said. "He doesn't speak much English, but, uh, his enthusiasm allows us to *communicate* in other ways. Right, Sven?" She squeezed my hand and pulled me toward her.

I pulled her in, turned her face toward me, and kissed her on the lips. I meant for it to just be a quick peck, but somehow the contact lasted. And lasted. In fact, I don't know how this happened, or who started it, but I was pretty sure there was a brief flash of tongues. I gasped. Ava smacked me on the arm with the celery. "Sven!" she said. "You are so *bad*!"

Britney and Whitney looked on, stunned.

"Good seeing you, girls. We have to get going. My stepmom really needs this celery. And Sven needs some more communication lessons." She stepped to the side and began to walk around them to the cash registers.

"Uh, bye," Britney said.

192

"Happy Thanksgiving," Ava said happily.

"Bye, Breeny!" I shouted. "BYE, WEENIE!"

As we walked away, I heard Whitney whisper, "I didn't realize Swedish guys were so Jewy looking!"

Ava and I giggled all the way home, but my lips didn't stop tingling.

. . . .

After that, Thanksgiving dinner was almost an after-thought. I only remember one moment vividly.

Before the meal, Richard asked everyone to say what we were thankful for. There were two whole families of cousins there, so the whole thing took a while and, I admit, I zoned out for some of it. I tuned in when I heard Annie's voice saying, "I'm grateful for everybody around this table. This has been the worst year of my life. I mean, duh." People smiled at the "duh" part, but looking around, I saw that the whole table was riveted to see what pain-ful thing Annie might say next, about death or whatever. That wasn't where she went with it, though. "I'm espe-cially grateful to have Jesse here with us," she said, and all the heads swiveled in my direction. I felt myself turn red. I couldn't imagine what I could possibly have done that was worth inclusion in Annie's speech, but she wasn't done. "Jess," she said, looking right at me, "I know you don't know this, but over the summer, my tennis lessons were the only thing that got me out of bed most days. Everyone else kept bugging me, trying to get me to say I was happy all the time, but you just let me be sad when I had to be. You *listened* to me. I know Ava's your best friend and I'm, like, the bonus little sister, but when I was losing my mother, you showed me that other people in the world still cared about me. So yeah, that's what I'm thankful for."

I stood up, walked halfway around the table, knelt by Annie's seat, and hugged her head to my shoulder. I didn't have any idea what to say. "I've got you, Sunshine," I whispered into her hair. She threw her arms around me, and we stayed that way for an awkwardly long amount of time while everybody else just sat in silence.

The whole thing was probably some major breach of Thanksgiving protocol, but hey, we do things differently in Sweden.

When I got back to my seat next to Ava, she took my hand under the table and squeezed it. "I love you, J," she said. And she didn't say it in a flirty way. It was just matter-of-fact. *Ava loved me.*

"I love you, too," I said in my singsongy Swedish voice.

"Oh, nice," she said. "Way to ruin the moment." But she squeezed my hand again. For a second, I felt like everything in my world was all right. I felt thankful.

It wasn't until the train ride home that I started to freak out again. I could feel my thoughts spiraling: *I kissed Ava! I liked kissing Ava! I'm a pig. I betrayed Chloe! No, I* betrayed Ava by not telling her about my sad mini-relationship with Chloe! No, I betrayed both of them.

That kiss can never, ever be repeated!

But it felt good!

See? I am a pig.

I decided to take a nap. Just before I fell asleep, I had one more disquieting thought: I hadn't gotten the chance to check in one-on-one with Annie.

20. More Matzo!
More Doom!

My parents were on their best behavior the next few weeks. I concentrated on raising my grades and on getting my dad to eat as much as possible before Leah came home for winter break. Carson kept asking me to go out on Friday and Saturday nights, to movies with groups of people, or to go see the Christmas lights in Manhattan with him and his girlfriend. It was honestly kind of suspicious, like he thought I needed looking after. So of course, when I kept having to say no in order to stay home and eat with my father, but couldn't tell Carson why, that probably only made things worse.

I guess I should clarify what my parents' "best behavior" meant at that point: They didn't fight. My mom cooked dinner sometimes, and other times she texted me and told me to order for my dad and myself. Once or twice a week, all three of us even sat down and ate together, which was kind of the worst, because then the only safe topic was my life. And "safe topic" was a relative term, too, because we couldn't talk about my emotions, plus I had to skim over how I was actually doing in school, or how I was barely surviving the devastation of trying to text with Chloe as "friends" while secretly poring over her social media for any sign of the dreaded Adam.

Most of all, as Leah's arrival approached, I wanted to jump up from the table and shout, "WHO'S GONNA TELL HER?" On the rare occasions when I managed to get Leah on the phone, her only questions were still about our father's weight and health, so it was clear she was still in complete denial about our parents' breakup-in-progress.

As opposed to the rest of us, who were only in maybe 87 percent denial.

Leah got home on Friday, December 20, just a couple of days before Hanukkah. Both parents managed to be home and at the table for dinner that night, although it was only take-out pizza. They grilled Leah nonstop about her life, which was a lovely break for me. She'd had a great semester. Yes, being the social chair of her sorority was *super* fun! She *loved* her little! ("Don't you mean your 'little sister'?" our mom asked. "In this century, we just call them 'littles,' Mom!") Yes, things with Jake were *great*! Was it okay if he came and slept over from Christmas through New Year's Day?

Something was odd with Leah, though. Even as she was raving about her fabulous campus experiences, she kept glancing at our dad's plate. Plus, as soon as she put down the single slice of pizza she'd taken, she started gnawing on her nails. I was pretty sure I'd never seen her do that before. Also, her phone was face down on the table, and it kept vibrating every few minutes. Then she would snatch it up, fire off an extremely brief reply in her lap, and kind of ease it back into place.

Just as the parents were finally beginning to run out of questions, Leah asked, "Do we have any dessert?" and jumped up from the table. When she opened the freezer, she started pulling out tub after tub of our grandma's matzo ball soup. "What the hell is this?" she asked.

"Uh," my dad said.

"Well," my mom said.

Both of them looked down at their plates. Our mother fiddled with her napkin.

"Jess?" Leah asked, looking at me with a mixture of confusion and something like hurt in her eyes.

"It's . . . well . . . it's soup. From Grandma. Because . . ."

I couldn't. Literally, my throat was closing up. I couldn't even breathe.

"Wait, Grandma was here?" Leah asked, her voice rising in pitch and volume. "When was Grandma here? *Why* was Grandma here?"

I got up and ran out of the room. I felt like if I didn't, I was going to keel over and choke. Plus, this was a golden opportunity for our parents to take some freaking responsibility and communicate truthfully with one of their children.

As if.

I charged up the stairs with the goal of getting into my own bed, putting in earbuds, blocking out the world, and isolating myself until all the damage had been done downstairs. Before I even reached the top of the stairs, though, I heard Leah's feet hitting the steps behind me. "Jesse, wait!" she called out. "What did I say? Are you all right? Jess!"

Distantly, from the kitchen, I heard our father say, "Oh, great! Excellent! Are you happy now?"

I flung myself onto my bed, facing the wall, and wrapped my blanket around myself so only a bit of my face was showing. I realized I was gasping for air. I heard my sister come hurtling into the room. She slowed down and made her way over to the bed. "Jess, what's going on?" she said, much more quietly. "You're scaring me."

I wanted to talk.

But I was crying too hard. I hadn't even realized I was crying until it hit me that I desperately needed to blow my nose. For once in her life, my sister didn't either flee or get more hysterical. She just put her hand on my shoulder and waited. After about a thousand years, she asked if I wanted a tissue.

I still couldn't talk, but I nodded.

Her hand disappeared and her weight lifted off the bed. Her footsteps receded. A moment later, she came back in, and I heard her close and lock the door behind her. She pressed a wad of tissues into my hand and waited for me to blow.

Finally, I felt as composed as I was going to be. I still didn't think I could turn over and face her, though.

"They're getting a divorce," I mumbled.

"What?" she said.

"Mom and Dad. They're getting a divorce."

"That's crazy. Who told you that?"

"Grandpa. Listen. Grandma and Grandpa came up here in September. He told me it looked like Mom and Dad were going to break up, and Grandma made all the matzo ball soup you saw in the freezer because she was worried about what I was going to eat when . . . you know."

"Like, when Mom moves out?"

"Yeah."

"If all of this is true, why didn't they tell *me*?"

"I don't know. Maybe they didn't want to do it over the phone? Or they didn't want to ruin your semester? Or maybe they thought Mom and Dad should be the ones to tell you?"

She sat down on my bed again and put her hand back on my shoulder. "Oh, God. Things must have been awful for you here, Jess. Why didn't *you* tell me?"

"I tried. You kept getting off the phone. Or not texting me back."

She sniffled. Once. Twice. "Shit," she said. "Shit. Shit.

I'm so sorry. I really did know something was wrong. I even told Jake I thought something big was going to drop at dinner tonight, which is why he's been texting me non-stop. But I wasn't ready to hear it."

I let her cry, maybe longer than I should have. When the sniffling got to be almost comically gross, I said, "I'd offer you a tissue, but, well, mine are pretty moist."

She laughed, which was bad news for my sheets.

But in a way, it was good news that the secret wasn't a secret between us anymore.

Leah didn't confront the parents about what I'd told her. I don't know why. It was like there was a force field around the topic. The parents must have been feeling pretty guilty, though, because when Hanukkah rolled around a couple of days later, they lavished us with gifts like it was the last holiday ever.

Which, in retrospect, was true in multiple ways.

The first couple of nights were fairly normal. The gift giving traditionally began with a gift exchange between Leah and me. I gave her a gift basket of different kinds of coffee beans, plus a mug that said DON'T TALK TO ME YET. Before I unwrapped her gift, I could instantly feel that it was a picture in a frame. As soon as I tore off a corner of the paper, I knew exactly what the picture was. She had captured, and then enlarged, the moment when Chloe, Ava, and I had just jumped off the Ledgedale Bridge, probably about a tenth of a second before our hands came apart.

I blinked hard. My eyes stung. "Thanks, Leah," I whispered.

For a few seconds, I was back on the bridge, smelling coconut sunscreen and feeling hot fingers interlaced with my own. I wished I could see where Chloe and Ava were in that moment. Was Chloe with Adam, the boat guy? Was Ava lighting candles and wishing for her mom?

Did they miss that moment as strongly as I did?

I couldn't linger on this thought because it was now the parents' turn for presents. We had chipped in to get our dad a couple of different psychiatry-related joke gifts, like we always did. (I'm not trying to brag, but I'm pretty sure the Dr. Martin Dienstag Collection contained the finest privately held assortment of Sigmund Freud plush toys on the East Coast.) I had also gotten him a gift card to a bakery and coffee shop near the hospital, because I thought that might encourage him to pick up high-calorie snacks from time to time. We got our mother some French-themed decor for her classroom, plus French chocolates to bring in for her students.

Our parents got us clothes on those nights. It was on the third night that they went wild with the spending.

Leah got two tickets to *Hamilton* on Broadway, so she and Jake could go during their spring break in late March. It was for a matinee, and our parents even included a gift card for dinner at a restaurant after the show. At first, I was like, *Oh, come on! This is so transparent! They're bribing her! There's no way Leah's gonna just let herself be bought off like that.* But then she squealed, threw her arms around each parent's neck—one by one, because of course they weren't standing close together—and thanked them profusely.

Half of me was disgusted by my parents' blatant pandering, and the other half was like, *Okay, now it's time to buy me!*

Then *that* half was disgusted with *itself.*

I stared at my parents expectantly. My dad looked at my mom. She hissed, "Marty, you have to carry it up from the . . . you know. *The place!*"

Ah, so it was a large gift. Which meant it was in the laundry room, in the corner, behind the boiler. Where our parents had been hiding things like bikes and other oversized presents since we were little, and we had been pretending not to notice the massive boxes peeking out from behind the pipes.

Not a bad metaphor for the family communication system as a whole, really.

Dad stomped off down the steps, and came clunking up a minute later with a five-foot-tall rectangular box. My heart jumped. It couldn't be! The only thing I might want that was shaped remotely like that would be a bass guitar, but my parents had never bought me an instrument before. It was more than enough that they paid for my lessons. Besides, I already had my Fender Precision and my U-Bass. The only other bass I'd ever mentioned wanting was a fretless Fender Jazz Bass, but that was just a pipe dream. I mean, sure, it would be amazing for jazz band. And sure, I had cut out pictures of fretless electric basses and made a collage of them on my wall next to my bed. But I hadn't bugged my parents about it or anything.

Honestly, I hadn't even talked about music at all with them for months. Because that would have involved, well, talking.

My dad set the box down in front of me with a grunt. Clearly, it was heavy enough to be a bass. "Go ahead," my mom said. "Open it."

I tore off the wrapping paper. Music notes. Clever.

The box was from a major online music store, but it had clearly been used several times, because there were crossed-out address stickers all over it. It was fastened shut with layer after layer of packing tape, so I grabbed my dad's Swiss Army knife out of the junk drawer and carefully slid it under the tape at one end. I pulled open the flaps. I peered inside. I could see the end of a beautiful, slightly scuffed, tweed-covered hard-shell instrument case. I pulled the case out of the box and laid it flat on the ground. I opened the clasps.

I gasped.

I couldn't believe what I was seeing. I was pretty sure my parents, who knew less than nothing about music, had somehow managed to track down a used, but genuine, fretless Fender Jazz Bass. It looked remarkably like the iconic one that Jaco Pastorius, the most legendary fretless bass player ever, had played. In fact, it was even cooler than Jaco's bass, because on this one, the original lined neck had been replaced with an unlined fretless one, so it was smooth and unmarked, like the fingerboard of an upright bass. I wasn't sure whether my parents had bought my love, but they had surprised the heck out of me.

"How . . . ?" I managed to utter before trailing off.

"I hope it's all right," my father said. "We asked your bass teacher for advice, and he told us not to bother with a new one. He kept an eye out for used listings. When he saw this one, he said it was the best deal he had ever come across. I know a new one would be shinier, but . . ."

I ran my fingers reverently over the instrument. I couldn't believe something so historic was really for me. "Dad, it's perfect," I said. "I love it. Thank you. And thank you, Mom." I forced myself to look my mother in the eyes, which made me realize I hadn't done that in a very long time. Maybe it was the flickering light of the Hanukkah candles, but her cheekbones looked more prominent than usual, and her eye sockets seemed deeper. She looked older and more fragile. And were there tears in her eyes?

I looked away.

My dad said, "Why don't you go ahead downstairs

and try it out?" I basically bolted out of the room, and of course I spent hours learning my way around the instrument. My dad eventually came down to listen, but my mom stayed away. It wasn't until much later that I realized: I'd said *I love it*, and I'd said *Thank you*, but I'd never connected those two concepts and said *I love you*.

21. Don't Worry, Be Happy?

My parents were going out to a New Year's Eve party together. The Medical Society had a big gala every year, so I think they probably felt like they couldn't get out of going without just getting it over with and splitting up officially. For one thing, they had a collection of every party's souvenir New Year's Eve champagne flute dating back to the year before Leah's birth. Watching them get all dressed up for a night out was bizarre. My mom came downstairs wearing diamond earrings and holding a strand of pearls, and my dad was in black tie.

Leah, Jake, and I were sitting at the kitchen table. My mom held out her necklace and asked, "Leah, can you do this clasp for me?"

Which was just super-duper awkward with our father standing three feet away.

Leah looked at our dad, who announced, "I'm going to start the car," and then stomped out. Then she looked at me in a panic. I shrugged. I was used to being stuck in the middle of their sad little struggles, but she wasn't. Jake shrugged, too. Leah liked to call him an idiot, but he wasn't enough of an idiot to get involved in this scene.

Meanwhile, our mother was still standing there, pearls in hand, pretending this wasn't a whole big nightmare.

Leah did the necklace, although I noticed she wasn't incredibly careful when it came to holding our mom's hair out of the way. I might have even heard a muttered "Ow!" from the patient.

As soon as the parents had left, Leah asked, "Okay, what was *that* about?"

"Welcome to the real world," I muttered.

Fifteen minutes later, Leah and Jake were out the door. They were headed to some college friend's house in New Jersey for a party. I had lied to everyone and said that Carson and I were going to be Uber-ing to another friend's house for dinner and then to hang out and maybe go in the hot tub. My mom had asked whether girls were going to be there, and I'd just raised an eyebrow and walked away.

Well, I'd half lied. Carson *was* taking an Uber, but he was going to his girlfriend's house. He had *also* lied, and told his parents he was spending the night with me. Come to think of it, even Carson's girlfriend had lied, because her parents were out of town, and they thought she was spending a quiet night at home alone. This way, theoretically, everyone got what they wanted. My family got to leave me all alone without having to feel guilty about it; Carson got to spend a whole night with his girlfriend; I got to be alone in my basement feeling sorry for myself.

I had my whole bass-playing area set up for recording.

I had been meaning to do a song as a thank-you to Ava ever since Thanksgiving, but I hadn't been feeling thankful enough in general to get the vibe right. I'd meant to try and force myself to do the project while I had the whole house to myself, but when I sat down, all I could think about was how sad my dad must be, having to fake being happy in front of all the other doctors and their spouses.

I decided to record a song just for him. For some reason, he had always loved this semi-dorky song from the 1980s called "Don't Worry, Be Happy," which also seemed fitting for the situation. In fact, I distinctly remembered him singing me to sleep with it when I was a tiny toddler in a stroller.

The fretless bass is a very good melody instrument, because it has a kind of wow-wow tonal quality that sounds a lot like a human voice, so I decided to record him an instrumental version of the song, using the fretless in place of the lead vocal part.

This took me hours. First, I had to build up the perfect drum and percussion parts in the recording software on my laptop (even though the original version was a cappella), which meant plotting out exactly how long the song was going to be, how many measures the intro was going to be, how many measures each verse and each chorus would be, and how the song was going to end. Then I had to arrange all the different bass parts. The song had lots of harmonies, so that took a while.

Finally, I had to record each instrument part live, one by

one. I started with the actual bass part, played on my U-Bass. Then I played the chords of the song, using my Precision Bass like a big guitar. Finally, I recorded three different passes of the new fretless, so it sounded like three vocalists in harmony.

When I finally got everything done, I decided I could wait until after I'd slept on it to mix down the parts to stereo, which is the last step to making a song sound "real." I emailed all the files to myself and also saved them on my phone, because I am totally paranoid about losing a song. Then I clicked out of full-screen mode, and was shocked to find it was after one in the morning.

Happy 2020, I thought.

I went upstairs, found I was still the only one home, and made myself a bowl of ice cream. Fortunately, my sister had stocked up once she'd absorbed the horror of seeing two freezers full of nothing but matzo ball soup, so I had my choice of flavors. Leah had even bought sprinkles and whipped cream, so I broke out those, too. I figured if my first meal of 2020 was going to be a lonely dessert, it might as well be a well-crafted lonely dessert. When I was ready to eat, I took out my phone, which I'd muted while I was recording. I had a fairly generic text from Chloe (*Happy New Year, sweetie!*) and a very nice, but cryptic, text from Ava (*Maybe 2020 will be our year*).

I really felt like hearing Ava's voice but I wasn't sure what she was doing, and if I'd be interrupting. So I texted her back instead, *Happy New Year! I hope you are doing something great. Annie, too.*

She wrote back almost instantly.

> *Nothing great*
> *Just at home*
> *After i wrote before, Annie said this is the first year*
> *mom won't see*
> *So I'm trying to do some sister cuddle therapy*
> *How did I not think of that though*

I replied, *I don't think it's bad that you were trying to be positive about the new year. Anyway, please hug Annie for me, and please tell her to hug you. I wish I could be there. Here kind of sucks, too.*

Thirty-seven minutes later, the front door opened and my mother stormed in, clutching the 2020 souvenir champagne glass in one clenched fist and her keys in the other. "Martin," she whispered harshly, looking over her shoulder, "don't make such a big deal out of this. I went to your event just like I said I would."

My father came slumping in wearily behind her. He hated staying up late, and being emotionally stomped on by his wife couldn't have been helping. "I know," he said. "I'm sorry. I just thought . . . with the dinner, and the dancing . . . it might have felt like *something* to you."

Her voice softened. "Marty, it was a nice night. But that's all it was. It doesn't change anything."

I didn't need to witness this scene. I especially didn't need for my father to have me witness this scene. I cleared my throat.

My mother whirled around, and the champagne glass flew out of her hand. It shattered into about a thousand shards all over our entryway. "Jesse," she said, trying and failing to compose her face into something like a bright smile. "Happy New Year, sweetheart!"

"Jesus," my father muttered disgustedly, closing the front door behind him and stepping around her. "I'll grab a dustpan."

It's always nice when a year starts off well.

22. The Cold, Harsh Light of a New Year's Day

The morning came too soon. I shuffled around as quietly as I could. I had to wear sneakers downstairs in case my parents had missed any shards of the champagne glass. I got myself a bowl of cereal and slumped down in my dad's plush recliner in the corner. I ate in a daze and then gently placed the bowl on the floor.

Two hours later, I was still in that chair, scrolling through social media with one hand while eating a second helping of cereal, when my mom came out of her bedroom. "Jesse," she said, "where was Carson last night?"

"What do you mean?" I asked.

"Was he at . . . I don't know . . . a girl's house?"

"Uh . . ."

Suddenly, my mom's face was right up in mine. "Don't lie to me, Jesse! *The Yangs were at the party with us!*"

I swallowed. I felt like I was going to throw up. I was pretty sure I had an entire oat stuck on the back of my tongue. "What did they say?" I asked.

"They asked what you and Carson were up to at our house."

"And what did you say?"

"I said I wasn't really sure. Don't worry, I didn't blow your friend's alibi."

I exhaled slowly. I had been holding my breath without even realizing it. "That was quick thinking. Thank you."

That was when she exploded. "You made me a liar, Jesse! And I do not appreciate it!"

Carefully, I put my bowl down. I wiped my face. I took a couple of calming breaths, which failed to produce any noticeable calming effect. Then *I* exploded. "No, Mom, *you* made you a liar. Months ago. Maybe years ago. And then you made Dad a liar, because he had to live in your lie and pretend it wasn't happening. And then you and Dad both made me a liar, because you made me live in your bullshit world, too. So, thanks for helping my friend. But don't pretend you've made some great moral sacrifice for me."

She took two quick steps backward and closed her eyes. "Oh, Jesse," she said, and it sounded almost like a groan. "You have no idea what marriage is like."

"Yeah," I said, "that appears to be true."

· ·

Leah and Jake didn't stick around long after New Year's, but after I'd told her about what had happened post-midnight, Leah made me promise to call or text her if things got really bad. She even said she'd answer this time. I promised, but I wasn't sure I was telling the truth. First of all, what was she going to do to help me from several hours away, and second of all, why should both of us suffer? If she was lucky enough to have an escape, it seemed like it would be cruel of me to ruin it.

It would be nice for our family to end up with one undamaged kid at the end of all this. Maybe even one with some kind of diploma!

. . . .

I scraped through my final exams in January, but it was a very, very close call. When the second semester started and my schedule got all switched around, I realized I couldn't concentrate in my new classes at all. I didn't want to look ahead and imagine college. I didn't want to think about finals, or the coming summer. I couldn't picture midterms. I couldn't even bring myself to believe that I'd be taking in-class quizzes until my teachers slapped them down in front of me.

At least my parents weren't getting on my case about it. My mother wasn't speaking to me, and my father was too depressed to notice. I had given up on monitoring his food intake, but fortunately, he was now too sad to exercise. That seemed to make up for his lack of appetite. In fact, it might have been my imagination, but he might even have been starting to look a bit flabby.

So, yay? That was what counted as a victory for me in winter 2020.

I was so overwhelmed, I just wanted the whole world to stop. Every change that happened made things worse, so I wanted all the changes to cease. When I was in my room, I spent hours staring at the framed photo of Chloe, Ava, and me falling through the air, wishing with all my heart and soul that I could somehow rewind to that moment. I felt like if I had the chance for a do-over, maybe I could keep the train of my life on the rails.

I came to precisely one decision. The New York City public schools were closed for the week after Presidents' Day, and I needed to get away for a while. I would get Chloe and Ava to come to Pennsylvania for Presidents' Day weekend! Then I would try to make everything right with Chloe. We would talk honestly and openly about our feelings. At the same time, I could see how Annie was doing, and show my appreciation to the Green family again for the whole Thanksgiving rescue. And I could make sure Ava knew that even though I loved her, the grocery-store kiss was just a crazy little fluke.

It would be good for all of us! Plus, it was ridiculous that we hadn't all been there together since the summer. That had never happened before, and I hated it.

Ava was psyched, and her parents agreed right away. Chloe went back and forth, but in the end, she said she'd be there. I didn't even bother asking my mom, even though she would have the following week off from teaching, because being with her wouldn't feel like a break for me. I went straight to my father, and when I told him how important I thought the weekend would be for my sanity, he agreed to take me. I knew what a big deal that was for him, because he would have to flex his work schedule.

He loathed doing that, but he must have sensed my desperation, because he agreed to it.

That's when things started to get weird, almost like the trip was jinxed. First, Chloe started texting about how she was worried that "the new virus in China" was going to mess up her family's hotel business, just when things were going well. I couldn't ask for details, because I hadn't been paying attention for months when she'd been mentioning the "family hotel business," and I had no idea what that had to do with her father's art galleries, or with her, and I especially had no idea how a virus in China was going to affect any of it.

Then Ava told me her stepmom, Tracy, was worried about the virus. I knew Tracy did something in science research, and I had always wanted to ask Tracy more about her job, but I never had, because I thought it might annoy Ava. It turned out that she worked for Yale University, keeping track of breakouts of illness around the world. Ava said that, according to Tracy, President Trump had cut the funding for most of America's early virus response systems around the world. Tracy thought it was too late to contain this thing. She said it was going to become a worldwide pandemic, like something out of a science fiction movie.

I mentioned all of this to Carson, and he said, "Yeah, my parents are starting to get pretty freaked out. Our relatives in Taiwan are saying the news that's leaking out of China is terrible. They say everyone on the streets there is wearing medical masks. My dad even said he wouldn't be surprised if people started pulling their kids out of school soon, even over here."

He paused. "This could do considerable damage to my love life, man."

As for me, I couldn't bring myself to care much about whether the world ended. It just didn't seem real to me, and honestly, if it was going to happen, I basically just wanted it to wait until after my big weekend with Chloe and Ava.

A couple of days before we were supposed to leave, it started sleeting in the middle of the morning. After school, when I got off the ferry, all the buses were delayed. I decided to walk up the steep hill from the terminal to the high school where my mom worked and see whether she could drive me home. She had been working really late most days, so I knew she'd still be there. I thought about texting, but my hands were all bundled up in ski gloves, and it was too loud on the bus platform for speech-to-text to work, so I just set out through the thick slush.

The trek was miserable. I had my massive math textbook in my backpack, along with my laptop. As if that weren't enough to carry, I was also lugging my Precision Bass, which meant I was tilted over to one side by the shoulder strap of the soft bag it came in. Oh, and I was wearing tennis shoes, which got soaked through almost instantly. As an added bonus, tennis shoes have zero traction in winter conditions, so I was practically skating along.

I was in a not-optimal mood when I crested the hill and started scanning the parked cars. I didn't see my mom's SUV, but something else caught my eye. There was a very flashy red BMW sports car in the principal's reserved spot. Even under its coating of ice, the car's paint job gleamed. As I walked around the vehicle to approach the front doors of the school, I saw that, because of the way the wind was blowing, the driver's side was almost completely ice-free.

That gave me a crystal-clear view of the University of Rhode Island sticker in the side window of the back seat.

So my mom was having an affair with her principal? It was such a cliché. I was kind of embarrassed for her. I pictured him making an announcement over the intercom: *Mrs. Dienstag, please come to the main office. I need to show you something.* And then I pictured all the students snickering. I imagined everyone in the whole school knowing what was going on.

I couldn't go in there. My feet numb, my eyes burning,

I turned around to walk back down to the ferry. The body of my bass whacked the mirror of Mr. Rhode Island's BMW. Not hard enough, but it was better than nothing.

I got home an hour and a half late, but nobody was there to notice. I took one of my grandmother's soup containers out of the freezer and plopped it into a saucepan of warm water to start defrosting. Then I took a hot shower. By the time I headed back down to the kitchen, emptied the soup out into the saucepan, and turned on the stove, I could basically feel my toes again. I sat down to eat, flipping through the day's news reports on my phone. The virus was spreading around the world. Even though travel from Asia to America had been restricted for a couple of weeks, cases were now spreading from person to person in the US.

The disease even had a new official name: COVID-19. Somehow, naming it made it seem more real to me.

By the end of my sad dinner, I knew I wasn't going to Pennsylvania for the weekend. Between the confirmation of what was going on with my mom and the accelerating virus crisis, I needed to see my grandparents before it became too late to see them. I called my grandfather and asked for a ticket to Florida.

Then I texted Chloe and Ava to cancel. Ava was sad, but Chloe actually expressed relief. *Whew*, she wrote. *OF COURSE I wanted to see you guys. But my dad was freaking. He said we have to start being really careful abt travel.*

Apparently, girls with no spleen can't fight viruses as well. Fun times.

A little shock ran up my spine. All the news reports were saying this disease was mostly killing old people. That was one of the reasons I wanted to see my grandparents before it really hit. But now I had to worry about Chloe dying. Dying!

Then, because I was a jerk, another shock hit me. Chloe had wanted to see "you guys." Now I was just lumped in with Ava. I wasn't just friend-zoned. I was genderless-friend-zoned. What was she going to compare me to next? Maybe she could make a nice online post like, *I really miss Jesse, and my pet goldfish, and this one really great bran muffin I once had? Well, the muffin was slightly stale, but IDK, it had just the right amount of butter. :)*

My father walked in holding a Subway sandwich and a large drink just as I finished eating. As he sat down to his cold, late meal, I told him about the change of plans. He wasn't thrilled, and tried to argue that it wasn't a great time for me to be traveling by air, but when I told him I had to see my grandparents one more time in case we were about to end up in some crazy end-of-the-world lockdown scenario, he didn't laugh me off or anything. He thought for a second, rubbed the stubble on his chin, and said, "That's a valid point. Maybe when you're down there you could go shopping with them. Get them stocked up on some essentials. You know, prescriptions, vitamins. Staple foods. I'm fairly concerned about how they're going to do with all of this. I've considered calling your grandfather to discuss it, but I'm afraid he won't want to take a call from me at the moment because of . . . well, you know."

My dad had always been close with my mom's father. It made me sad to think they weren't talking. But I was even more concerned that he thought my grandparents might need to stock up on supplies. The hair on my arms stood up. "Dad," I said, "are you thinking this is going to get bad, too?"

"Jess, I'm not going to lie to you," he said. "There's a lot of concern at the hospital. I don't think this COVID-19 thing is going to kill everybody in the world or anything, but I do think there's the potential for a whole lot of chaos and disruption. And some people *are* going to die."

"Well," I said, "we were having a pretty boring year, so it's probably good something came along to shake things up."

He tried to give me a smile. I appreciated the effort. That was when I had a thought. "Hey," I said, "I totally forgot. I made something for you on New Year's Eve. Everything got so crazy when you came home that it slipped my mind."

"Ah, wow," he said. "You know, I never even asked what you did all alone in the house that whole evening. I'm sorry. I've been so wrapped up in my own issues . . ."

"It's okay, Dad," I said, even though nothing was really

okay. "I just . . . I wanted to cheer you up, so I recorded a song for you. I used the new Jazz Bass. It sounds so great, and it's so easy to play. Do you want to hear it while you eat?"

He did, so I ran downstairs to get my Bluetooth speakers.

He listened to the entirety of "Don't Worry, Be Happy" in total silence. Well, aside from the rhythmic munching of his SunChips. Dad had always been a big, big fan of the SunChips. I hadn't listened to the song in a few weeks, since I'd finished mixing it down a couple of days after the initial recording. I had to admit, it sounded almost professional.

At the end, he said, "Thank you," very softly. He sounded kind of choked up.

I couldn't handle that kind of emotion, so I rushed to say, "Oh, it was no big deal. I just wanted to show my appreciation. The bass was such a perfect gift. So thought-ful! You didn't have to get me something so extravagant. And I mean, it was like you read my mind. There's literally nothing in the world I would have liked better." I knew I was rambling, but I thought maybe if I just rushed to say enough words, it would get us past the weird mushy moment.

Instead, it made my dad emit an odd half laugh. Then he looked incredibly embarrassed. "This is very awkward, Jess," he said, "because I would love to take credit for the idea, but I can't. As much as I hate to say it, especially right now for a, um, for a wide variety of reasons, your mother was the one who picked it out. You know I, uh, love you and all, but I've never had the knack for gift giving. That was all your mom. She's quite attuned to your interests. I really hate to say this, but you should probably thank her."

He grimaced at the very thought of that, took a gulp of his soda, and continued, "By the way, what song was that? It sounded so familiar!"

23. Big Moves

That Thursday, I came rushing home after school to pack for my Florida trip. My flight was scheduled for Friday evening, so everything would have to be ready to go as soon as I walked in the door. My mom's car was already in the driveway, but when I opened the front door, all the lights were off downstairs.

"Mom?" I called out.

Nothing.

I made my way through the gloom to the stairs. My room light was on.

As I went up the stairs, I heard a snuffling sound. My mom was sitting on my bed with her head down, crying. She looked up and wiped her eyes when I reached the doorway. In her lap, she was cradling a framed piece of abstract "art" I had made in preschool. It was a bunch of smudgy, rectangular red ovals on white paper. I had no recollection of making it, but she had told me a million times that I had, apparently by pressing the cut edge of a half potato into paint and then onto the paper.

"I remember when you gave me this," she said, her voice sounding hoarse and ragged. "You had paint all over your shirt, and there was even a dab of it in your *hair*. You held the painting out to me with both hands, and I wasn't sure where to touch it, because it was still wet. But I had to take it. You were so proud of yourself. You said, 'I do this, Mommy. I do *art*!'"

I just stood there. What does one say to that? *Thanks for the bass, but enough with the principal, already?*

The awkwardness grew and grew. My phone buzzed in my pocket. Hers dinged twice in a row. Neither of us reached to check, which was something.

Finally, she took a breath and asked, very quietly, "Jess . . . would you hate me if I moved out?"

At some level, I'd known all year that this had to be coming, but it still felt like a physical punch in my stomach. Not just like someone had knocked the wind out of me, but like someone had somehow reached down my throat and *ripped* all the wind out, along with my lungs. And some gory, dripping chunks of my heart.

I'd been so, so mad at this woman all year. I had avoided talking to her. I'd avoided being near her whenever I could. This was the person who was hurting my dad. But somehow, I'd built up a kind of invisible ice wall inside me that allowed me to forget she was also *my mom*. My mom, who wasn't happy.

I sat down on the bed next to her, so close that we were almost touching. Tears were streaming down my face. "Mom," I said, "I think I'd hate you if you *stayed*."

226

She sobbed. So did I. She put her hand over mine. A part of me wanted desperately to pull away, and another part wanted to bury my head in her shoulder. I split the difference, kept my hand still, and let her fingers close around my wrist.

. . . .

At the airport the next day, even though the government was officially telling everyone that face masks shouldn't be worn by the general public, I noticed that several passengers were wearing them. The whole plane reeked of chemical cleaners, too. I had bought Chinese food in the terminal and brought it on board, but when I went to eat it, the smell in the air was so strong that it made the whole meal taste like General Lysol's Chicken.

Things improved a bit when I landed in Florida. Both of my grandparents were waiting for me just past security. My grandfather clasped me briefly, but tightly, in a side-on hug, and then my grandmother clutched me to her like I was a flotation device. "We missed you," she said. "I'm so glad you called! We've been worried."

"I, uh, I've been eating your soup," I replied, in another classic example of the Dienstags' inability to meet direct emotional expression with direct emotional expression.

"Did you check a bag?" my grandfather asked. *Wow, I* thought. *He's not even a Dienstag.*

On Saturday morning, the grandparents insisted on

dragging me to breakfast with a big group of their friends. This always happened, because it was basically the highlight of the Floridian Jewish social calendar when a grandchild came to town. It was absolutely essential that the prized descendant be paraded about for all to admire. Fortunately, knowing this, I had brought a clean shirt with a collar.

It took about an hour and a half to establish that I went to a special math-and-science high school ("A what?" "A MATH-AND-SCIENCE HIGH SCHOOL!"), that I played the bass, that I didn't have a girlfriend but was VERY HANDSOME, and that I was a good boy for visiting my grandmother, "whose friends should be so lucky." After that, I got to go back to their condo complex and sun myself by the pool for a couple of hours, until I got hungry again.

I came inside to find my grandparents arguing at their kitchen table.

"Arthur," my grandmother said, "I'm just saying, we might not want to be in a crowded concert hall a few weeks from now."

"Jeanie, that's ridiculous," my grandfather said. "I want to take you out on the town. It's Sandra McLachlan. You love Sandra McLachlan! She sings that 'When I Remember You' song you like. And we're not going to hide out in our apartment like cave people."

My grandmother replied, "First of all, Arthur, it's Sarah McLachlan, and the song is called 'I *Will* Remember You.'

I do love it. But I don't love it enough to get you killed so I can hear her sing it. I'm just saying we should lie low for a few weeks, until we know a bit more. They're saying people with bad lungs are at high risk. And you don't just have bad lungs. You have *partial* lungs. I just think it's smart to be cautious." She looked at me over his shoulder and said, "Don't you agree, Jesse?"

I shrugged. "I don't know," I said. "I want you to be careful. But I don't want to get in the middle of your fight. I came here to get *away* from fights."

"This isn't a fight," my grandfather said. "It's a discussion. Discussions are what people have so they *don't* end up having fights later."

I thought about that. "Well, in that case, I think we should at least go shopping and stock this house up with basic necessities in case you do end up being stuck in place. My dad was concerned about that."

My grandfather snorted. "Oh, *your dad* was concerned about *us?*"

My grandmother said, "Art, this isn't the time."

He shrugged her off. "Maybe Marty should have tried being concerned about his wife."

"Wait a minute," I said, even though I hated contradicting my grandfather. "That's not fair. Dad's not leaving Mom. *She's* leaving him. He's *been* concerned about her."

My grandpa leaned toward me. "He hasn't showed it, though. If he had, maybe she wouldn't be leaving."

"Grandpa, I love you. But you haven't been in the house to see what's been happening. Dad's been trying. Mom's the one who isn't interested. Please don't ask me for details, but I'm telling you. Plus, Dad truly cares about you. He was, like, medically worried about you and Grandma being alone down here, cut off from help."

My grandfather's eyes flashed. "This discussion isn't over," he said. "But I guess we could do some shopping. Jeanie, do you want to make a list?"

So that was how the three of us spent our second-to-last afternoon together, running around the Super Target, filling up two carts. I sincerely hoped nobody else in South Florida needed any Epsom salt or Sanka decaffeinated instant coffee, because if they did, they were going to be out of luck. This whole endeavor took so long that by the time I'd helped my grandfather carry everything upstairs to their apartment, we didn't even have the energy to go out and get dinner. We ended up having cold cuts on day-old bagels.

I didn't care. I was happy that I'd done something concrete and tangible to make my grandparents' lives a bit safer.

The next morning, my grandfather woke up early to go out and get the Sunday newspapers, but then fell asleep in his big comfy chair while my grandmother and I ate a late breakfast. While I buttered a new, fresh bagel, she said, "Please excuse your grandfather's outburst yesterday. His feelings are hurt."

I was baffled. "Why are his feelings hurt?"

"He loves your father like a son. And now he feels betrayed."

"B-but—" I sputtered.

"I know it doesn't make sense," she said. "But it's how he feels. Your grandfather has strong emotions. He's fiercely loyal to the people he loves, and he doesn't give his love to many people, so this stings for him. You have to give him time to come around. Which reminds me . . ."

She got up from the table and slowly poured herself some orange juice. It felt like she was doing it on purpose to build suspense, but maybe she needed a moment to compose herself. Or maybe she was just thirsty.

"What?" I said.

She took a sip, and then put her glass down. "If anything happens to me, I want you to promise you'll call to check in on him once in a while. I know it's a lot to ask, but what can I say? You're his favorite. You always have been."

My heart skipped in my chest. I didn't want anything to happen to my grandmother. I didn't even want to think about it. And, horribly, I didn't want to be responsible for my grandfather. But he had always taken responsibility for me, just like she had. He was the one who had flown up to break me the news about my parents' breakup, and she was the one who'd made me matzo balls.

"I promise," I said. "But nothing's going to happen to you."

The following morning, my grandmother had a card game, so I said goodbye to her before my grandfather drove me to the airport. "Remember," she whispered in my ear. I hugged her extra hard.

When I got in the car, my grandfather said, "Listen, if anything happens to me, I want you to promise me something."

"I'll stay in touch with Grandma and make sure she's doing okay? Yes, I promise."

He laughed. "Let me guess. Your grandmother gave you the same speech?"

"Yeah. Honestly, it would be a lot easier if you'd just kinda cut out the middleman and take care of each other for a while longer."

As he signaled and pulled out into traffic, he sighed. "We're trying, J," he said. "We're trying."

. . . .

My father picked me up at the airport, and I told him I'd made sure to get the grandparents stocked up. I left out the part about my grandfather being all scornful, because I didn't think it would help anybody. On the flight home, though, I'd thought a lot about it. I wondered what my mom had told my grandpa about my father. I hated to think that she might be saying bad stuff about my dad to her parents, because my dad really did love them.

It was all such a gigantic mess.

My dad seemed super quiet all the way home, but that wasn't so unusual. It wasn't until he pulled the car into our driveway that I suddenly felt a shock of panic. The driveway wasn't my dad's spot.

It was my mom's.

"J," he said, "I don't know how to tell you this."

You know when you're on a roller coaster, and it has just finished clanking its way up the big, steep hill before the first big vertical drop? And you're just waiting for that terrible moment when it feels like your whole insides are going to come flying up your throat?

I swallowed what felt like my whole insides as the downhill plunge began. "You don't have to tell me," my own voice said, sounding strangely far away in my ears. "Mom's gone."

24. Just Two Guys, Hangin'

My mom actually texted to ask whether I wanted her to bring me dinner, which I thought was bizarre. Like, was she going to deliver me a hot meal on a little catering tray while my dad just stood there starving? It just seemed like unnecessary cruelty.

No, thanks, I'm good, I texted back.

I asked my dad whether he was hungry, and he said yes, so I looked in the fridge. Even though I'd only been gone a few days, there was already an accumulation of take-out containers building up, so I yanked out a bunch of them and started pulling off lids. We tried to organize the foods in age order, using a combination of my dad's memory and our senses of smell. In the end, the estimates were pretty rough, but I figured nothing was old enough yet to kill us.

I made up a very strange Mexican/Thai/Italian combo platter for myself, and then encouraged my dad to create his own dinner assortment. When his plate was fully stacked, he said, "Now what?"

I said, "What do you mean? Now we microwave the food."

He pursed his lips impatiently. "No, I mean how?"

"Wait," I said, "you've never used the microwave?" I almost laughed, but thankfully, I bit my lip.

"No," he said sheepishly. "When would I have used the microwave? At the hospital, I just go to the cafeteria. When I'm on the way between the hospital and the nursing home, I go out. And when I'm here, your mother makes the . . . well, your mother made the food. Jesus, I don't know how to do any of this."

I didn't feel like laughing anymore. "Dad," I said as cheerfully as I could, "listen. You know how to cut a human being open and fix their internal organs, right?"

"Well, I haven't done it in twenty years, but sure."

"If you can do that, you can reheat half a burrito and some spare ribs. First you have to make sure there's no tinfoil. That's key."

Seven minutes later, we sat down to a steaming feast. "That wasn't prohibitively hard!" my father exclaimed in amazement.

"You did great, Dad. And now that you've had a taste of success, who knows what *else* you can do? You know what? I'm just gonna say it. Hold on to your hat, for tomorrow, we conquer—the toaster!"

My mom called me three times after dinner, but I didn't answer. Finally, she texted, *When you're ready, I'd love to show you my new place. It isn't fancy, but I got a two-bedroom apartment, because I'd never live anywhere that didn't have a room for you.* She included the address. I looked online and saw that it was only half a mile away. I could walk there if I had to.

But I didn't have to yet.

I texted Chloe and Ava to tell them I'd missed them over the weekend. I also texted Leah to let her know what was happening at home. *I know*, she texted back. *More later—I promise!*

Then I went downstairs. My father was sitting in his big chair, staring at the wall. That didn't seem like a healthy use of his time. He needed a distraction. "Hey, Dad, can I show you something down in the basement?" I asked.

"I'm not sure I'm very exciting company right now, Jess," he said.

"You're my dad. Besides, when was the last time you really watched me play?"

I had this idea that it might be cool to show him how I had recorded the "Don't Worry, Be Happy" song for him, so I had him sit right between the speakers that I used when I was mixing music. Then I played him little bits of each individual instrumental track from my laptop through the speakers, saying things like, "See, this is the fretless bass playing the melody—the part the singer would sing," or, "This is the drum machine. I programmed it to give the song the rhythm I heard in my head."

He was the most attentive he had been since at least before the summer. He even asked me a lot of detailed questions, and when I was done explaining, he said,

"How did you learn to do all this?" like he was honestly impressed with me.

I told him that it was a combination of bass lessons, music classes in school, and the internet.

"You're amazing," he said. His voice sounded thick. "You're so talented. And you're such a good son."

"Dad, it's okay, you don't have to—"

"No," he said sharply. "I *do* have to. You've been a much better son to me this year than I've deserved. I've been barely functional, and *you've* been taking care of *me*. That isn't healthy, and it isn't right. I'm sorry. This is a really rough time for me, but I just want you to know, I'm working on it. I don't want you to feel like I'm your responsibility. Got it?"

I let out a breath I hadn't even realized I was holding. "Got it," I said.

"But Jess," he said, smiling, "you *can* still show me the toaster thing. I mean, if you want to."

25. School's Out

Carson never asked me to sit outside on the ferry unless something was really wrong, so I had a bad feeling when he grabbed me by the sleeve of my puffer coat and yanked me toward the door as we boarded one morning in March.

"This better be good," I said. "It's freezing out here." The temperature was like twenty-five degrees, and that was before the boat started moving. With the wind chill, I was going to be a Popsicle before we finished the twenty-five-minute ride across the harbor. At least I was wearing gloves.

If you let your fingers get all chapped up, playing a bass becomes agonizing. Seriously, at that point, you might as well just go all the way and lubricate the strings with Tabasco sauce.

"Oh, it's good," he said. "And by good, I mean bad."

I looked at him expectantly. His head was burrowed into the turned-up collar of his extremely stylish slim-fit quilted wool jacket. The thing was a total monstrosity. It looked like he was stuffed into a giant oven mitt. Apparently, it also didn't keep him warm, and it smelled alarmingly like a sick sheep when it got wet. But his girlfriend had picked it out for him, so he had bought it with a big chunk of his summer-job money and told her he loved it.

He didn't look at me or say anything for the longest time. It made me uncomfortable. There were a few pigeons eating somebody's spat-out sunflower seed shells near our feet, so I stared at them for so long they got uncomfortable. One of them became indignant, cooed, and hocked up a sunflower shard in my general direction.

"She dumped me," he said. Carson, not the pigeon.

"What?" I sputtered, shocked. Though admittedly, not as shocked as I would have been if the pigeon had said it.

"We were texting last night, like we always do, just before bed. She wasn't replying as fast as usual, so I asked if something was wrong. She said nothing was wrong, but she put a period on there. She never puts a period on the end of her texts, so it was very emphatic, like she was shouting, 'NOTHING'S WRONG' in all caps, with p-e-r-i-o-d-t at the end. So I called her. As soon as I heard her voice, I knew."

He got quiet again, and I didn't know what to say. As we all know, this wasn't my department. Finally, I said, "Did she say why?"

He laughed. "Yeah. She was like, 'We don't communicate. I feel like you never even tell me what you actually want.' Can you believe that?"

I was like, *Hello, Mr. Sheep Coat.* But all I said was, "Uh, I don't know. I'm sorry, though."

239

He said, "You know what the funny part is? I purposely never tell her what I want. That's my freaking *strategy*. Like, I do that to make her *happy*. I just say I like everything she does. I thought, *How could that possibly backfire?*"

I was thinking, *Two words: Sheep. Coat.* But I said, "Didn't the things that bothered you kind of, I don't know, build up? Over time, I mean?"

He thought about it. "Honestly? She bites my lip when she kisses me. I think she probably thinks it's sexy. But it's more like, *Ow.* And she made me watch *The Crown* when I wanted to see *Zombieland.* So I told her I loved it, of course. But ever since then, she's been buying me little mementos about the British royal family. I had to put a little English soldier—the kind with the tall bearskin hat thing—on our Christmas tree. My parents were so confused, you can't even imagine."

"Coulda been worse," I said. "If you'd seen *Zombieland*, you'd have been trying to explain why you were hanging a bloody model Bill Murray corpse next to Rudolph and Santa. So maybe you dodged a bullet there."

"Okay, that's fair," he said. "But still, she's right, in a way. I didn't communicate. But that's because I didn't care about that stuff, mostly. I just liked having her as my girlfriend."

"Did you say that? Because I have a feeling that's a good line."

"No," Carson said. "Honestly, I was too busy whimpering."

I noticed his teeth were chattering. "Hey," I said, "want to go inside and get some incredibly bad coffee?"

"Yes. I'm cold and I want to be warm."

"Look at you. Communicating your needs. I'm so proud!"

. . . .

Just a few days later, on Thursday, March 12, we were in jazz band. The rehearsal felt super strange, because the feeling was definitely in the air that the schools were going to close down because of COVID-19, at least for a couple of weeks. We weren't sure there was even going to be a spring jazz concert, which meant that we didn't know what we were rehearsing for, except that playing music was what we did. More than that, for many of us, it was who we were.

Plus, speaking only for myself, my instrument was something I could control.

Anyway, we were playing a Van Morrison song called "Moondance" when halfway through my solo, a movement caught my eye over the student conductor's shoulder. Carson's mom had just walked in! You have to remember two things. First, our school was on a completely different island from our houses, so our parents didn't just come strolling into the building randomly. In fact, this had never happened before, to either of us. Second, Carson's mom thought he went to jazz band every morning to play the piano, not the vibraphone.

Surprise! I thought.

Truthfully, the surprise was all mine at first. I was so surprised I lost my place in the chords and held a note for too long, until the chord changed and I sounded jarringly out of tune with the piano player, who was the only person besides the drummer playing under my solo. I quickly slid up a half step and tried to recover, but the sheet music slid off my stand and wafted to the floor. The conductor cut us off.

"You okay over there, Dienstag?"

"Yeah, sorry," I said, bending and gathering up the papers. "My music just got, uh, caught in the breeze."

He rolled his eyes, but said, "Okay, let's take the last four bars of Jesse and then go right into Carson's vibraphone solo. Cool? Okay . . . One, two, three, four . . ."

I couldn't help but notice Carson's mother's face as the conductor said "Carson's vibraphone solo." She looked puzzled at first. Then she looked over to my left, where our band room's slightly out-of-tune upright piano was being played by a short, pink-haired Black girl named Trina. That caused a double take. Next, her head panned slowly across the room until it settled on her son, who was on my right, about to burst triumphantly into his solo. I was pretty sure he hadn't spotted her yet.

I finished my solo with a tasteful double-stop slide.

242

Then Carson came in. First, he did the old jazz trick of restating the song's melody, simply and beautifully. After a few bars of that, he started harmonizing with himself, which is tough and super impressive when you're playing with mallets. Then he broke into a single-note melody of his own invention that was so fast I could barely follow the individual notes, before finishing up with two measures of sextuplets, which means he was playing in total counter-rhythm to the rest of the band.

As the horns came in at the end, he grinned.

Carson was always a good musician, but this had been a total clinic. It struck me that he *did* know his mom had walked in. I guess he figured if he was going to get busted, he might as well put on a good show.

We got through our trading-fours section, and then the conductor cut us off because Carson's mom had walked over to stand next to him. "May I help you?" he asked her.

She whispered something, and a minute later, Carson was gone.

The rest of the day felt like one of those early-morning bad dreams, when your sleep is just disturbed enough that you want to wake up, but you can't. School felt like an illusion, but I couldn't make it stop. Some teachers just plowed on ahead like nothing was going on, but a couple talked about contingency plans. In orchestra, the teacher said that anyone who owned their instrument, or who wanted to practice at home, should take their instrument at the end of the day. Thankfully, the huge classical double bass I played in orchestra was the school's, but my Fender Precision was locked in one of the practice rooms.

I decided I would take the Precision home the next day, because several of my teachers had also said to bring home textbooks, and I didn't want to kill my back by carrying everything at once.

Other weird bits of news kept coming in. Chloe texted to say her school district had closed, and Ava's was going to close at the end of the following day. Kids were saying a couple of pro basketball players had the COVID-19 virus, and then the news spread that Tom Hanks and his wife had it. I texted Carson to ask what was going on with him, and he wrote back that his parents had decided he couldn't come back to school.

I didn't know why they had let him leave for school that morning and then grabbed him an hour and a half later, but I figured I'd have to find that out when I wasn't texting under my desk in calc class.

As I was staggering out of the subway train under the weight of my textbooks, a friend on the baseball team texted. Their first game of the season, against a Catholic school, had been canceled. The city's Catholic schools had closed!

This was crazy. On the ferry, I started thinking about what would happen to me if I didn't have school. My dad would still have to work, so I'd be home alone all day. Some of the teachers were saying we'd have online school. Did that mean I'd just be sitting in my room doing my classes on Skype or something? Then it hit me that my mother would be off, too.

She loved her students. Would she go crazy, sitting in her apartment alone all day? Or was her principal spending lots of time there?

I wanted to not care, but I did care. When I thought of her all alone in a strange rented room, my eyes stung. Then, when I imagined the principal's stupid BMW with its stupid college sticker rolling up in front, I found my hands clenching into fists.

My dad got home around eight, while I was at the table eating a slice of room-temperature pizza. He grabbed a slice for himself and sat down.

"J," he said, "we need to talk."

Instantly, my stomach had that reaching-the-top-of-the-roller-coaster feeling. "About what?" I asked.

"This pandemic." I swallowed, with some difficulty. The World Health Organization had announced the day before that COVID-19 was officially a pandemic, but hearing my dad say it out loud made it feel much more serious to me. "Listen," he said, "I'm fairly sure your school is going to be canceled any day now, and then you're going to be in isolation for a while, hopefully until the spread of this thing can be brought under control."

"Okay, that's kind of what I figure is going to happen, too. So?"

"Jess, I work in a hospital and a nursing home. There's no way I'm not going to be exposed to this virus. We need to isolate you from me."

Inside me, the roller coaster went into free fall.

"Dad, what are you saying?"

"I called your mother before I left work. I can't believe I'm saying this, but she and I agree that you have to move in with her for a while. I'll miss you more than you know, but I'm your parent, and it's my job to keep you as safe as I can."

"Dad—" I started to say, but then my throat closed up. My father used his therapist skills, which means he sat there silently, watching me. I hated that trick. "Dad," I finally said again, "you can't do this. *Please!*"

"I'm sorry, J," he said. To his credit, he really did sound incredibly sorry. But I also knew that, once he was in doctor mode, there was no changing his mind. My father would never do anything he thought might harm another person's health.

I took a moment to get control of my face and my voice. "Promise me you'll take care of yourself," I said.

"Don't worry," he said. "I'll be fine. It's not like you're taking the toaster with you."

26. Lockdown

Friday, March 13, was the last in-person day of my junior year. Not much happened. A noticeable number of students stayed home, the hallways smelled like bleach, and there was a weird, day-before-Christmas-if-Christmas-were-a-nuclear-holocaust vibe in the air. The announcement from the city wouldn't come until Sunday afternoon, but everyone pretty much assumed it was a done deal.

Besides, my mind wasn't even on that. My mother was picking me up on Saturday morning, so between rushing home to pack and figuring out what I was going to say to her, I couldn't bring myself to care what was going on in the rest of the world around me. I refused to believe this sleepover was going to be a long-term deal, so I packed like I was going to a weeklong camp.

Well, a weeklong music camp.

I took out my big travel duffel and threw in seven pairs of socks, seven pairs of underwear, two pairs of sneakers, two pairs of jeans, a pair of sweats, a pair of exercise shorts, a bunch of T-shirts, and two sweatshirts. Then I got all my toiletries together. I made sure I had my inhalers and checked how many puffs each one had left, because I realized it would absolutely suck to be marooned in the apocalypse without my asthma meds. Next, I made sure I had my electronics, my chargers, and my school stuff all ready to go. The teachers had said there would be posted directions for how to proceed if school switched to online-only, but I was hoping that would all fall through and we'd just get some kind of extended pseudo-vacation.

Finally, all that was left was deciding how I was going to play bass during my bitter exile. I had my small amp and my Bluetooth speakers. The question was, which instrument should I bring? If I brought all three basses, or even two of them, that was like saying my mom's apartment was a real home—which it was *not*. It was an emergency shelter, and I was being sent there under protest. I also didn't know how much space I would have, or how quiet I would have to be. I mean, my mom was somebody's tenant, and amplified basses make things vibrate. In the end, I decided to take only the U-Bass. It was the smallest and lightest instrument, and it was the only one you could really hear if you played it unamplified.

I looked at my two Fenders on their stands and promised them I'd be back soon.

When I woke up on Saturday morning and went downstairs, I found a note on the breakfast bar from my father. *Rounding on some patients at the nursing home*, it said. *See you as soon as I can. Don't worry about me. Try to get along with your mother. Love you. Dad*

He could have woken me up, but that was my father. He wouldn't want me to miss any sleep just to hug him, even if that's what I would have wanted.

I had just finished eating a bowl of cereal when I heard my mom's car door open and then slam shut in the driveway. I almost put the bowl in the dishwasher, but then had the horrifying realization that I hadn't taught my dad how to wash a load of dishes. Peeking into the machine, I saw that it was about half-full. I debated running the whole thing, but I wasn't sure my dad even knew how to empty it. If I did run it, there was about a fifty-fifty chance he'd just think all the dishes in there had simply disappeared.

If he even noticed they were missing.

I ran to the door and let my mom in without acknowledging her. "Hang on," I said. "I have to do some dishes." She came into the kitchen, sat in her old seat at the table, and watched in silence as I methodically filled the sink with soapy water, took everything out of the dishwasher, washed it all by hand, rinsed each piece, and stood everything up in the dish drainer.

As I dried my hands, she said, "You're so responsible."

"Well, someone has to look out for Dad."

"Dad can take care of himself. He's a fifty-two-year-old medical doctor. He's also incredibly smart."

"Wow, he sounds like quite a catch," I muttered.

"Can we not do this now?" she asked.

I took a deep breath. "Okay," I said. "I guess we have a whole lot of time."

She stood up and looked me over. "I know you're angry, so I've respected your space and stayed away. But I'm so glad to see you. And you look great. My handsome son!"

"Well, you know," I said, "I thrive during divorces and pandemics."

"And you've kept your sense of humor, which is good. I have a feeling we're both going to need it. Are you all packed up?"

Her new place was a dump. As bitter as I was about her leaving, I was almost equally sad to picture what it must have been like for her to leave our house and move into this awkwardly constructed space, all alone. She must have read my thoughts, because she said, "It isn't much to look at, but on the bright side, it's expensive."

I laughed. My mom was funny. I had almost completely forgotten that.

Leah's college was sending all of its students home and going virtual, but she and Jake lived off campus, so they were staying put. That left me and my mother as unlikely roommates. I moved my few belongings into the cheap dresser in the spare bedroom and spent the next few hours lying on top of the covers in the uncomfortable bed, texting my updated whereabouts to my friends. Ava got back to me right away, and her response pretty much summed it all up:

> @ your moms?
> Wow

My mother cooked eggplant parmigiana from scratch for dinner that night, and I realized two things over the course of the meal. First, I was eating freshly prepared food, which had become a novelty. Second, she was paying full attention to me. She wasn't concentrating on ignoring my father, or deflecting my questions about her relationship with him. She wasn't distracted by a constant stream of texts. She was even asking me pertinent questions at all the right moments. I didn't mean to blurt this out, but I did.

"Mom, you're listening to me."

"What do you mean?" she said. "I always listen to you."

"I swear I'm not trying to pick a fight, because I'm glad you're listening to me. But it's just . . . you've been so distracted."

She put down her fork and rubbed her eyes. "Well," she said, "I'm not distracted now."

It was a start.

My mom's phone absolutely blew up with notifications on Sunday when the school district made the closing official. As she and I were talking over how we were going to handle being in quarantine, or lockdown, or whatever this strange new thing was, somebody started coughing really loudly downstairs. The sounds went on and on, constantly, for maybe an hour, until my mom said, "It occurs to me that this house has central heating. If the people downstairs have this virus, we're going to get it, too. Do you think it would be crazy for us to go to the Pennsylvania house for a while?"

"Wait," I said. "Aren't they saying this thing isn't airborne?"

"They're saying a lot of things, honey. But your father thinks it probably is. At least, he told me we should probably be acting as though it is until we know for sure that it isn't."

"Okay, but if we go to Pennsylvania, what about Dad?" I asked. Of course, if I was going to be locked up somewhere, the Pennsylvania house was about a thousand times more appealing to me than my mom's apartment. It seemed wrong to be that far from my father when he was going to be all alone, though.

She thought for a moment. "Well, he's not going to be able to see you indoors no matter where you are, but I promise I'll drive you back to Staten Island if you want to see him outside. Maybe you could take a walk with him, or have a meal at the picnic table in the—in his backyard?"

His backyard. This all still hurt. "And what about . . . what about your principal?"

She flushed. "What are you talking about?"

"I swear again I'm not trying to fight with you, Mom. But won't it be hard for you to be away from your, um, I don't know what to call him. Your boyfriend?"

She sighed. "I don't *have* a boyfriend, Jesse. Look, I have no idea what you think you've figured out, but I . . . things got awkward with a colleague of mine at work for a while. Not much happened, but lines were crossed that shouldn't have been, and I regret it. It wasn't fair to anybody." The coughing downstairs, which had tapered off for a while, revved up again. "Can we maybe pack up the car? I'd much rather discuss this on the way, when we aren't breathing the same air as whoever's making those noises."

Five minutes later, my things were in the back of my mother's SUV. Ten minutes after that, we'd thrown the contents of her refrigerator and her kitchen cabinets into moving boxes, and then loaded the boxes on board. The sun set just as we were driving over the bridge between New York and New Jersey, outbound.

27. Close Enough to Touch

The problem with going to a special math-and-science high school is that, when everybody else was basically getting the whole spring off, my teachers had virtual classes up and running almost immediately. The only good part was that the school made a rule that our end-of-term grades couldn't be lower than whatever our average had been at the time of the shutdown—so, for me, this was basically a chance to rescue myself.

Having very nearly nothing else to do was oddly helpful. Mom and I settled in. For a little while, we still went out just to go to the supermarket, but then cases of the virus started to crop up even out where we were, so my mom switched to having our groceries delivered. At that point, it was almost like being a little kid again. My in-person life became very simple: just me and my mommy.

Every day, we ate breakfast together. We took a walk in the afternoon, when the sun was as warm as it was going to get. When groceries came, we wiped them down together. I even helped her make dinner most nights. Honestly, if she had cut the crusts off my sandwiches and read me a story before bed, I could have been four again.

It was nice. Nobody was out and about. The roads were empty. Everything was so quiet! Birds were coming back for the spring, and their songs filled the air. Deer were walking around more boldly than I had ever seen before. Whole strings of wild turkeys were strutting down the center of the cul-de-sac like they were heading up some kind of poultry parade. One evening, I even saw a bear scratching at the wooden bin that enclosed our garbage cans, which had been a rare occurrence in pre-COVID times.

Life had become kind of simple and basic. There was me, my mother, my schoolwork, and nature.

Online was a different story. Suddenly, everybody was discovering this new app called Zoom. Leah and I started using it to have video chats with our dad every Sunday, which was kind of tough at first, because if talking him through making toast had been challenging, this was basically climbing Everest.

Once he kind of, sort of, very nearly got the hang of it, the calls became a nice part of our routine. My mom observed this in action, and she thought it was so cool, she decided it would be good if we set up a Zoom with her parents. So then we had a regular Saturday call with them and I had a regular Sunday call with my dad. It was weird, but in a way, I was spending more time talking with my family than I had before being locked up away from most of them.

My grades were going up. My family was getting along. I was even tentatively bonding with my mom. But the thing is, you can't get too cozy during a worldwide catastrophe.

The first big shift came in April, when both Ava's family and Chloe and her dad came out to Pennsylvania to stay. There were major outbreaks near both of their hometowns, and Ava's parents and Chloe's dad were all working online, so it made sense. And I should have been thrilled to have months and months of extra time near Chloe and Ava. The change was huge and confusing, though. Our parents made us isolate for the first couple of weeks, and I couldn't decide whether texting and video chatting from across the street was more or less frustrating than being fifty miles away.

I had no idea what to do with my leftover feelings from the summer. With everything that had gone on since then, I almost felt numb to the emotional parts. In their place, I just obsessed over my sheer *attraction* to both girls. Especially knowing that they were so close, yet off-limits, I was driving myself crazy, which made me read way too much into their every sentence. Chloe would text, *I can't wait to hug you*, and my brain would go into overdrive remembering the smell of her hair and the feeling of her fingers against my chest. Then Ava would mention that she was trying on swimsuits, and my brain would go into *double* overdrive.

It got pretty darn frustrating, because I knew—absolutely knew—that I was in love with Chloe. Which meant Ava was off-limits, fantasy-wise. But then again, so was Chloe, because she had rejected me.

Honestly, every single potential girlfriend in the world was off-limits, anyway. Because COVID.

I was just about at the point of renouncing all human contact and becoming a monk. Then the next bomb fell. My dad called my mom. I heard them arguing. She didn't have the phone on speaker or anything, but just from her tone of voice, I knew exactly who was on the other end. She kept saying things like, "What do you want me to do? They don't *want* to come!" and "Am I supposed to drive all the way down there and *kidnap* them?" Near the end of the call, she said, "Don't tell me you love them! They're *my* parents!" Then she slammed her phone down on the kitchen counter.

Normally, I would have stuck to my strict policy of absolute cowardice when it came to interfering in my parents' arguments, but this involved my grandparents, so I semi-casually strolled into the room and asked, "What's wrong with Grandma and Grandpa?"

She scowled. "Nothing's *wrong* with Grandma and Grandpa."

"But . . ." I said, letting the word trail off.

"But your father thinks they'd be safer up here than they are in Florida."

"Why? Are they sick? Is there an outbreak in their complex?"

She looked away from me, out the window, into the woods. "Not right in their complex. Your dad is just getting jumpy."

"Dad doesn't get jumpy for no reason. Something must have happened."

"There's an outbreak . . ." she said. Her voice shook a bit, and she started again. "There's an outbreak at the nursing home. J, patients are dying."

I sat down at the table. My heart was pounding. I heard a rushing sound in my ears. My face felt numb. My mother rushed over, sat down next to me, and put her hands on mine. "Dad isn't sick, Jesse. Okay? He's wearing personal protective equipment every time he goes in or out of there. He said all the staff are being incredibly careful about that, and he hasn't had any symptoms at all. But he said the virus is horrible in the elderly patients, and he doesn't want your grandparents to be so far from family while it's spreading. He even tried to call them and ask them to promise they were self-isolating."

"What happened?" I asked. I knew my grandfather was already annoyed with my dad, and I also knew how stubborn he was.

"Your grandfather laughed. Apparently, he said, 'I'm not going to pay somebody to do my shopping for me. What am I, a millionaire? And *you* try telling your mother-in-law not to play cards with her girlfriends. Let me know how *that* goes.'"

That sounded right. "So now what? We can't just let

them get sick! You have to call them. You and I could drive down there. We'll take turns driving. We could get down there in, like, two days. We could buy a tent and bring sleeping bags. We wouldn't even have to risk a hotel. *Please*, Mom."

She leaned in so her forehead was almost touching mine. "You know your grandparents don't particularly like it out here, right? And that's when we're not all locked in the house twenty-four seven. But I can ask."

You can imagine how well that call went over.

I had to get out of the house. I felt like the walls were closing in on me. I texted Ava and Chloe to ask whether they were willing to take a walk with me if we stood far apart. We had talked about seeing each other in person after the Contis and the Greens had been in their houses for a couple of weeks, and the parents had said they thought it was probably already safe to see one another at a distance outdoors. Ava didn't respond right away, but Chloe said yes instantly.

I threw on a sweatshirt, walked out, and waited in her driveway. It crossed my mind that I should have been all nervous about seeing her, but I was so worked up about my dad and my grandparents that my feelings for Chloe seemed like something from an unimaginably distant past. Or at least, that's what I thought until she stepped out into the spring sunlight and everything came rushing back so hard that I nearly checked my palm for thorns.

She walked toward me with a huge smile on her face, and despite the situation, I felt myself begin to smile and start to open my arms for a hug. Then I realized what I was doing and took a step back. "Uh, hi," I said. "Thanks for coming out. I really needed to see your face. But, well, you know. Distance. I want to keep you safe."

That was true. But I also wanted to bury my face in her hair and hold her for about seventeen hours straight, or until we both passed out due to hunger and exposure.

"Right," she said. "Safety. Totally. Me too. So, let's walk! What's going on, sweetie?"

So I told her about the whole grandparental conversation, which took about a mile. Then I asked her what was going on in her life, and I was amazed. It turned out, I should have been listening all year. Her dad's "upscale art gallery" business had been slowly failing for a long time, so the year before, he had opened up a couple of picture-framing shops on Long Island. Chloe had gotten involved in running the shop in their town, first as a cashier, and then more and more with finding ways to promote the store online. Then she had read an article online in an art journal about the business of selling art to hotels, which gave her an idea. She pitched a plan to her dad: They would sell the art from the artists represented in their galleries to hotels, both as originals and as prints. Her dad did some research and made some connections, and the two

260

of them launched the whole thing—while she was keeping up with her schoolwork and running the student council.

I had this picture of Chloe in our little Pennsylvania world, right? I had always known Chloe was the boss *of us*, but I was so hypnotized by my crush on her that I hadn't seen the whole picture. Chloe was a boss, period.

She was also getting a little sniffly.

"Wait, what's wrong?" I asked.

"It's kind of ironic," she said, wiping her eyes on her sleeve. "I came up with this whole hotel plan to save the family business, and then this stupid virus comes along and closes all the hotels. And the worst part is, I was so distracted this whole year, getting it all up and running. I didn't pay attention to you while your parents were splitting up. I barely even paid attention to your texts. I mean, you must think I'm the worst friend."

I stopped walking and faced her. We were on a two-lane road, but there were no cars anywhere in sight, so I had been walking in the middle of the traffic lanes the whole time in order to maintain our distance. It was almost unbearable to watch her cry without closing that gap and holding her, but I forced myself to do it, no matter what every molecule of my being was telling me.

"Wow," I said. "I thought I was just too depressing. Which I kind of get. Because honestly, I have been really damn depressing. I don't know if I told you this, but my goldfish jumped out of his tank last week. He didn't leave a note, but I'm pretty sure I'm what pushed him over the edge."

"Jess, stop," Chloe said. "No riffing. You aren't too depressing. You were depressed. I'm glad Ava was there for you, because I wasn't. All I can say is I'm sorry, and I'm here now. Socially distanced, but you know. Here. Six feet from you."

I smiled tentatively. So did Chloe. Something in my heart cracked open. We stood there like idiots while I resisted what felt like the tug of a thousand magnets. Then I heard a rustling from the woods over Chloe's shoulder, and a black bear, skinny from the winter, came ambling out onto the roadside grass maybe twenty feet away. It froze when it saw us.

I thought back to a bear-safety speech Larry had once given us at the rec center. "Chloe," I whispered, "there's a bear behind you. Can you step onto the road? Like, toward me? We want to be together so we look bigger. Then I'm going to talk to it in a normal voice, and we're going to back away, okay?"

Chloe's eyes widened. She took a slow, almost gliding step in my direction, like she was skating across the roadside gravel. I tried to watch her and the bear at the same time as she took another step. The bear stayed still as she stepped toward me again. Without thinking about viruses, or really anything else aside from humanity's shaky

262

position on the food chain, I reached out a hand to Chloe. She took my hand, as gently as always, and I pulled her close as I stepped backward across the center line of the road. The bear yawned, which was terrifying, in that black bears have teeth for *days*.

"Easy, buddy," I said, in the most soothing voice I could manage. I was pretty sure I sounded like I was extremely high, but the bear didn't immediately charge, so I kept talking. "How are ya? How was your winter? All good? Family good? Cubs good? I'm Jesse, and this is Chloe. Some people call her Klo. I don't call her Klo, but you know, you *could*. If you talked. But you don't. Talk, I mean. No offense. Maybe you speak bear. In fact, I'd imagine the other bears find you very eloquent. Anyway, we're just gonna keep backing away slowly. Not that you don't seem charming, in a furry, toothy, alarming way. But I'd imagine you have more interesting things to do than just sit there and stare at us, right? Like, go find some nice berries. Or honey. Or a lovely trash mound. Mmmmmmm, sweet moundy trash!"

We reached the far edge of the road and stepped off the pavement into the trees on the other side. We tucked ourselves between a big boulder and the trunk of an enormous hemlock and waited. I was breathing hard. Chloe was leaning back against me, and I felt her rapid, shuddering breaths, too. Her hair was in my face. It smelled like coconut again. Despite the huge predators, I truly did love our life in these woods. Peeking around the tree, we watched as the bear arched its back, looked around, almost seemed to shrug, and then continued on its way until it had walked around a bend in the road and out of sight.

Chloe turned to face me. "Sweet moundy trash," she said in the goofy, fake-deep voice she always used when she was imitating me. Then she said, "I love you," in her own voice. The next thing I knew, her arms were around my neck and she was staring into my eyes from about five inches away.

With one last shred of rational thought, I raised my arms to take hold of her forearms, because I realized we were breathing straight into each other's faces. She shrugged my hands off, murmured, "Family good? Cubs good?" and giggled. Then she laced her fingers together in the hair at the back of my neck and stepped into me until my back was pressed up against the boulder. Finally, inevitably, our lips met.

If you're going to violate pandemic safety restrictions, it might as well be spectacular. In my defense, this was. I don't know how much time passed, but we didn't stop kissing until my knees were weak and my butt was numb from the cold of the boulder. When we came up for air, Chloe ended up next to me, leaning against the rock, snuggled up under my shoulder.

She looked down at her feet and murmured, "You're not going to hurt me again, like you did in the fall, are you?"

Admittedly, I could barely think at that moment, but her words made no sense to me.

"What do you mean?" I asked. I wasn't being a jerk, right? I was honestly baffled.

Apparently, that wasn't how it came across. Chloe pushed off the rock and did a quick quarter-twist so she was facing my side. Then she made a short speech, which she punctuated by repeatedly jabbing her index finger into my shoulder. "You *know* (jab) what I mean! First, I arranged that amazing night we had together in August. I *threw* (jab) myself at you! And I know you had an emergency the next morning, but you didn't even mention it afterward—not to me, not to anybody! You didn't even tell *Ava* (HARD jab!). I kept waiting for you to give me any hint that it *meant* (jab) something to you, that we were in a *relationship*. I even started mentioning other guys to see if it would make you jealous, but you didn't give me any sign. You *hurt* me, Jesse.

"And then when you came to my house—ugh! I baked *cupcakes* for you like it was freaking 1950. That was the first *and last* time I will ever bake cupcakes for a boy. But when you got there, you didn't even put your bag down to *hug* me. And THEN! Then you called me *Klo*!

"So I invited you into the freaking *bedroom*, right? For my one last desperate attempt to, I don't know, get you to show me *something*. I threw my arms around your neck, and you gave me a stupid one-arm hug, like I was your *hockey bro* or something. I felt like you were about half a second away from offering me a high five. And then like an idiot, I kissed you anyway. So what did you do? You jerked away in the middle of the kiss like I was giving you an electric shock. What the *hell*, Jess?"

"Oh, God," I said, rubbing my upper arm. "Chloe. All these months, I was mad at *you* for hurting *me*."

"What?" she said, her face flushed.

"Well, first you didn't say anything after our night together. Then you started mentioning other boys. So I went to see you in Long Island. And I was so nervous about it, you have no idea. I bought you a dozen roses and everything. But then you didn't come with Caroline to get me at the station. And then when I got to your house, you didn't hug me right away, and I felt weird because I was holding my duffel bag. But I didn't want to put it down because I was afraid I'd crush the flowers, and I didn't want to just bust out with the flowers in case you, like, didn't want them.

"Then you told me to follow you to the guest room and I thought that would be my big chance. So I reached behind me into the bag to get the flowers. And I mean, I don't know what I'm doing, okay? I've never given a girl flowers before."

"Never?" Chloe asked.

I had been staring down at the ground, but I looked at her. She didn't look so furious anymore. In fact, she was almost smiling. "Never," I said.

"Okay, I admit I didn't know about the flowers. But then, why didn't you give them to me?"

"I couldn't! Because then you kind of grabbed me, and I couldn't get my hand out of the bag. And when you kissed me, I got so, uh, overwhelmed that my hand kind of clenched shut. On the stems. And a thorn stabbed me in the hand."

She put a hand over her mouth. "Oh, Jesse, you got stabbed in the hand? And that's why you pulled away when I kissed you?"

"Well . . . yeah. There was blood and everything."

"Why didn't you say something?"

Now I was a bit irritated. "Because you said, and I quote, 'I knew it! That was weird, right?'"

"AND YOU AGREED!"

"I kind of had to," I said. "Plus, I was distracted. Like, by all the kissing and bleeding."

Chloe put her hand on my arm, right on the spot she had been punching, and gave me the softest of rubs. "Were you really overwhelmed by that kiss?"

"Yes," I said. "I was completely overwhelmed by that kiss. I'm completely overwhelmed by *you*. Um, how about you? Did you like it, too?"

"I'm not sure," she said, grinning. "My memory is kind of fuzzy. It was such a long time ago. Let me see . . . give me your hand."

She reached out, took the hand that I had impaled on

the thorn, and kissed the palm. I swear, a shock traveled up through my wrist and electrified every nerve ending in my body. Then she laced her fingers through mine, leaned in, and kissed me on the lips again until I thought I might pass out.

"I'd say that was a solid seven point five out of ten, but with lots of room for growth. If you're willing to practice with me. I mean, a lot. What do you say, Jess? I'm warning you, I expect dedication."

"I guess I might as well give it a shot. I mean, I should probably start training now if I want to be in shape for the summer catamaran season, right?"

"Don't get ahead of yourself, buddy boy."

"Oh, come on," I said, pushing off from the boulder and dusting off the backs of my legs. "I'm the guy who saves you from bears."

"SWEET MOUNDY TRASH!" Chloe declared boomingly to the surrounding forests. "It's true," she said. "You are the *cute* guy who saves me from bears. Even if you do have a twig in your hair."

She reached up and carefully plucked a very thin stick out of the increasingly long waves that were beginning to curl over my ears. Then she took my hand and we started the long walk home.

28. The Nine Great Days

And lo, there followed the Nine Great Days. In those Days, which were Nine in Number, all was well in the Mountains, and in the Valley, and likewise in the Cul-de-Sac. Peace fell upon the Mothers, and the Fathers, and upon the Distant Grandparents, and yea, even upon the Older Sisters and their Boyfriends in their Off-Campus Housings.

Plentiful were the foodstuffs in their Cabinets. Reliable was their Wi-Fi. Piled high was the Toilet Paper in their Homes. Supplied were their Chains.

And all in the Several Families were Healthy. And none were blighted by the Unfortunate and Potentially Deadly Plague that had fallen over the Land. None were troubled by the dreaded Three Horsemen of the Coronavirus: the Dry Cough, the Fever, the Shortness of the Breath.

Happy and blessed was Jesse, who had prevailed, even against the mighty and fearsome Bear of the Wood, for in those Nine Great Days Jesse had as his companion the fair and wondrous Chloe.

Far and wide did the two young Lovers walk. Much did they laugh, and kiss, and cuddle, and share the inner-most Secrets of their Hearts. But because the Nine Great

Days, as ordained, were Nine in Number, there came a Tenth Day.

That Tenth Day shall forevermore be known in Pennsylvania as the Day of the Original Treehouse Sin. And lo, over the Mountains and Rivers, off to the East in New York, that Tenth Day shall be recalled in sorrowful whispers as the Day of the Burnt Toast.

29. And on the Tenth Day . . .

Chloe and I had this dumb, romantic idea. We just wanted to re-create the catamaran experience, right? So we thought, *Where can we stay out late into the night? Where's there a soft place to lie down together? That's kind of outdoors? And private-ish?*

We also thought we'd been a lot slicker than we actually had been, as if nobody was going to notice the two of us walking around together at all hours when literally nothing else in the world was moving. I don't know, maybe we hadn't cared. Or maybe we hadn't been thinking at all.

Whatever the process was, I woke up on the tenth day in the treehouse, with my arm around Chloe. I was facing the open side, so I was looking past the top of Chloe's head at the back of Ava's house. At first, I wasn't sure what had woken me up, but I gradually became aware of a soft click-clack sound coming from behind me. I twisted myself around and saw that Ava was hunched over a laptop in the corner, typing. There wasn't much sunlight coming in yet, but in the glow of the computer screen, I could see that she looked intensely sad.

Ava had literally had to climb over our bodies to get

to that corner. I don't know what you get when you multi-ply awkward by heartbreaking, but that's what the current mood was up in the trees of this backyard. Slowly, ever so slowly, I rolled back over so I was facing away from Ava again. I stayed there for the longest time, trying hard not to move or even breathe, because I didn't want Ava to look at me and notice any sign of consciousness. I also wanted Chloe to sleep as long as possible, because the wake-up scene was not something I was eager to experience. My one arm, which was pinned beneath Chloe's neck, was completely numb. I was contorted in some kind of bizarre yoga position that was becoming more cramp-inducing with every second. I also really, really had to pee, but no power on earth could have made me reveal that I was awake.

Until suddenly, Annie's head popped up at the top of the ladder, about six inches from mine. "Eep!" she squeaked, recoiling. For a split second, I thought she was going to fall, but she caught herself. The commotion woke Chloe, who said sleepily, "Hey, Annie." Then, a moment later, I guess she processed this situation a bit more, because she sat partway up and said, "Oh, shit, Annie! Wait, this isn't—we aren't—please don't tell Ava!"

Annie's eyes were so wide she looked like a cartoon. Mine probably were, too. And then Ava's voice rasped from over my shoulder, "Don't tell me *what*, Klo?"

Annie looked around from Ava's face, which must have been a portrait in rage, to mine, to Chloe's. She said meekly, "I have a Zoom with my homeroom, so I think I'm gonna just, um . . ."

Then she descended out of sight.

Chloe sat up fully, straightened her shirt, ran her fingers through her hair, shook her whole head like a cat does when it's gotten wet, glanced at me rather grimly, and angled her body to face Ava. "Okay, sweetie, I guess we need to talk."

Ava's face was all pinched up. I'd seen her in snippy moods before plenty of times, but this went way beyond that. "Yeah, *sweetie*," she said, "I guess we do. So tell me, are you two a couple now?"

I sat up extremely straight. I wanted to hear the answer to this, too.

Chloe took a deep breath. "Well, we're taking it slow, but . . ."

Ava gestured around the treehouse, at the blankets strewn around, at the crooked mattresses, at me with my extremely mussed-up hair and what must have been my most dazed facial expression. "Oh, yeah, I can see you're really taking it slow. And keeping a safe six feet away from each other. So, how long has this been going on? Jesse, were you and Chloe already a *thing* when you kissed me in the supermarket?"

Chloe turned on me so fast that her elbow whacked me in the bladder. I figured there was about a 67 percent chance I was going to wet myself before this all got talked out. Or before someone got hurled bodily out of the treehouse.

"You *kissed* her in the supermarket?" Chloe hissed. I hadn't known Chloe could hiss.

"Well, yeah, but it was a joke. We were just messing with these two mean girls on Thanksgiving. It didn't mean anything."

Now it was Ava's turn to terrify me with alarming new vocal sounds. Her eyes bulged as she said, "It didn't *mean* anything?"

Before I could respond to that, Chloe said, very quietly, "Ava, you *knew* how into Jesse I was. You *knew* how hurt I was at the end of the summer. You knew how sad I was when he came to Long Island and everything just fizzled out. You knew how bad that all made me feel. And then you just, what? You just decided to kiss him? Without telling me?"

"Wait," I said. "Ava, you knew Chloe liked me? You *knew* and you didn't tell me?"

"Oh, come on, J," Ava said scornfully. "How long did you pretend you and Chloe hadn't hooked up last summer? How long have you been flirting with me whenever Chloe wasn't around? Did it ever occur to either of you that it might be tiring for me to be everybody's second choice all the time? Klo, you'll hang out with me unless you have a chance to sneak away with this kid. And J, you spend the whole summer wishing Chloe will fall madly in love with you, but when you need someone to save your life at six in the morning on a holiday, I'm supposed to be the one who picks up the phone every time, right?"

"Wait a minute," I said.

"No, you wait a minute, Jesse. I'm sick of being your safety school. Now you can just cuddle up with Little Miss Early Action over here."

"That's not fair," Chloe said.

"Can we just stop for a second?" I asked. "Please? I love both of you."

"Yeah," Ava said. "That's the problem."

Just then, my phone started clanging in my pocket. I pulled it out and started to push the MUTE button, but then I saw it was a video call from my dad, who never called me that way. I hesitated.

"Seriously?" Chloe said.

"It's my dad," I said. "I have a bad feeling." I turned the phone so all he'd be able to see was my head and Ava's house in the distance, and answered. My father was in his kitchen, half-dressed for work, looking frazzled. Normally, he put on a dress shirt and tie before he came down for breakfast, but his shirt wasn't even buttoned up yet.

"Dad, what's up?"

"Jesse, where are you?"

"I'm, uh, in Ava's treehouse. Why?"

"I've been trying to call your mother, and she isn't answering. It's urgent. Can you go get her?"

"Why? What's happening?"

"Your grandmother just called me from Florida. Your grandfather is on his way to the hospital in an ambulance."

I was vaguely aware of a gasp from either Chloe or Ava. I felt dizzy. My vision narrowed until all I could see was the phone screen. "What . . . what's wrong with him?"

"She said he started coughing yesterday morning and developed a fever overnight. She called me about an hour ago to ask my advice because he was having a severe coughing fit and couldn't catch his breath. I told her to call for the ambulance."

The kitchen looked strangely dark and almost misty on my screen. "I think there might be something wrong with your phone, Dad," I said. "It looks almost like it's cloudy in the house or something."

My father looked around, puzzled. "Hmm," he said, "that's odd. Looks like smoke. I'm making toast, but I don't smell anything burning. Hold on a second, Jess. I'm just going to take a peek in the toaster oven."

My father put down the phone so that all I could see was a rectangle of the kitchen ceiling. Then a piercing shriek almost made me drop my phone.

"Is that your smoke detector?" Chloe asked.

So yeah, on the tenth day, I woke up, lost my two best friends, and found out my grandfather and my dad both had COVID.

30. Zooming Through Ghost World

My dad begged my mom and me not to come to Staten Island, but there was nobody else to buy him supplies and check in on him, so we packed up the car with two weeks' worth of stuff and hit the road. I drove, because my mother was on the phone with my grandmother. "Mom, calm down," she said as I pulled out of our driveway. "Mom, can you take a breath? I can't understand you when you talk this fast," she said as I turned onto the empty main drag of our community. "Mom, please don't cry. I'm sure they're doing everything they can for Dad," she said as I accelerated onto a totally abandoned Interstate 84.

Just as we crossed the bridge into New Jersey, my mother got off the phone. Then she started crying, too. I bit my lip, turned on the radio, and kept us heading east. Neither of us said anything for the longest time, as countryside gradually morphed into towns, which slowly became cityscapes. Near Newark, "Shake It Off" came on, and suddenly I was back in the treehouse the summer before, when my biggest problem was my two lovely friends teasing me about the song I'd written for them.

Now the best I could say about Chloe and Ava was that they seemed to have agreed on a temporary cease-fire during my family's COVID outbreak. And the best I could say about my family was that, well, nobody was dead. Yet.

My mom put her hand on my leg and said, "Jess, watch your speed." I looked at the dashboard and realized I was doing seventy-five. "Oops," I muttered, tapping the brake harder than I meant to. It was hard to judge how fast to go with so few other vehicles around, but really, the problem was how upset Taylor Swift had made me.

I glanced in the rearview mirror and was relieved to see that there were no flashing lights approaching from behind. I wasn't sure how well the Taylor Swift defense would have played with the New Jersey State Police.

I forced myself to take a breath and smile a bit. "So, what's the plan when we get there?" I asked.

"First, we find some kind of drive-through for lunch. Next, we stop at my apartment to wipe down the food containers and eat. Then you stay put while I make a supermarket run for the basics and drop the stuff off at your dad's. I should be back in plenty of time to check in with your grandmother and then make dinner, but maybe you can call the hospital and try to get an update? I mean, if you're up to it?"

"Wait," I said as I exited the New Jersey Turnpike and merged onto the ramp for the Goethals Bridge. "Why can't I come help with the supplies and see Dad? Maybe seeing me will cheer him up. Maybe—" I had to stop talking for a second to swallow, because my voice was all shaky and trembly. "Maybe seeing me will help him get better."

"Oh, Jess," my mom said, squeezing my leg again. "Your father was the one who specifically said you weren't allowed to come over. He didn't even want you to leave Pennsylvania and have the exposure of being in the supermarkets, or the drugstores, or anything."

"But what about you? You're getting exposed to all of it! And COVID is supposed to be worse for people your age than for kids."

My mother gave a short, bitter laugh. "I'm pretty sure your dad is less concerned about my health than he is about yours, bud. And, to be fair, I deserve that. But I'm not going to be face-to-face with him, and I'll be wearing a mask wherever I go. I think the risk to me should be pretty low."

Twenty minutes and a couple of value meals later, my mother was out the door. I spent the afternoon alternately calling my grandmother, listening to the hold music of the hospital patient-information number in West Palm Beach, and texting updates to Leah. In between, I dabbled in halfheartedly playing my bass and staring blankly at an English essay I had no chance of writing that day.

That first week was pretty bad. My mom was basically on standby for my father. He sent her out for a few additional things, like a "pulse oximeter" and a couple of prescription medications. Meanwhile, even though he was sick and feverish himself, my dad was spending his waking hours on the phone with my grandfather's doctors in Florida, telling everyone who would listen about my grandpa's war-related lung injuries, getting updates, and trying to make sure the doctors knew about the latest treatment advances from New York. Apparently, in dealing with the first mass outbreak, the doctors up here had learned that patients with COVID pneumonia did better if they were kept on their stomachs as much as possible, given steroids immediately after admission, and NOT put on ventilators unless there was absolutely no other choice.

My dad told me that a lot of people had died in the first wave who could have been saved, and he didn't want my grandfather to die like that. Every time I got off the phone with my dad, I found myself choked up. All I could think about was how much love, worry, and concern my father had for my grandfather, even though my grandfather had been so angry at him throughout my parents' breakup.

And I was also angry that my dad didn't have anybody watching over him in that same way.

My dad's fever broke on the fifth day, and my mom started talking about going back to Pennsylvania a couple of days later. I told her I wasn't going anywhere until I had seen my father in person and given him a hug, so we were staying put for another week. I finally got to talk to my grandfather on the seventh day, when a nurse somehow brought a phone charger to his bedside. He was propped up in bed, hooked up to a bunch of IVs and wires, with an oxygen tube under his nose.

"Hi, J," he said, rasping like he had just swallowed a sheet of sandpaper.

"Hi, Gramp," I said. I hadn't called him Gramp since I was five or so, but that's what slipped out. "How are you feeling? Are they treating you okay?" *I'm an idiot*, I thought.

He coughed, then said, "Well, I'm not dead. So, I'm calling today a win. Listen, I can't talk long, so . . . you remember what you promised, right?"

"I'll take care of Grandma. But I won't have to. The doctor told Mom your oxygen has been better and better the past couple of days. You might even get to go home next week!"

I don't know what his response would have been, because it got swallowed up by a coughing fit. When he finally caught his breath, he said, "There's another thing, Jesse. Your father."

The hair on the back of my neck stood up. "What about him?"

"He's been calling here every day, twice a day, to check on me. He . . . I . . . ." My grandfather—my steel-hard grandfather—wiped his eyes on his blanket. When he continued, his voice was even huskier than before. "I was wrong about your father, okay? Please, as soon as you get off the phone with me, call him and tell him that."

"Why don't you tell him yourself, Grandpa? He'd love to hear your voice."

"I, uh, I'm not quite ready to have that conversation, J. But you tell him for me. And don't wait. Your mother told me he's got this damn virus, too, so *don't wait*."

"Got it. I won't wait. I'll take care of everything. You just get better, okay. I love you. We all love you."

"I know," my grandfather said. "I love you, too. Just remember what you promised." He coughed twice and ended the call.

That night, I hung out with Carson in person for the first time since his mom had picked him up from jazz band back in March. It was a warm May evening, which was nice because we were lying on our backs on two picnic tables in the abandoned grounds of the Jewish day camp at the end of his street. I was struck by the length and shagginess of his COVID hair. My mom had made a halfway successful attempt at trimming my hair with the help of an electric clipper and some YouTube videos, but Carson said he wasn't desperate enough yet to let his mother near his head.

"Speaking of your mom," I said, "we got so distracted by the school shutdown that I never even asked you what she said about you playing the vibraphone."

"Ah," he said, "that was interesting. She didn't mention it the whole way home, or, like, all day. She just let me freak out. I felt like I was in a horror movie. You know, when you haven't seen the killer yet, but the camera is following the first victim around the old farmhouse? Or when you're on a roller coaster, and the cart is just . . . slowly . . . inching . . . up . . ."

"*That first hill?* I know exactly what you mean."

"Yeah, so she let me suffer until halfway through dinner. Then she said to my dad, 'Guess what? Carson picked up a new instrument. And he's awesome at it!' So then, my parents asked me all sorts of questions—I mean, my mom didn't even know the difference between a xylophone, a vibraphone, and a marimba. And they were blown away by the fact that I could improvise. My dad, especially, kept coming back to that, because his parents made him take classical piano all through his childhood, and it was *all* reading, right? You wouldn't even think of playing notes that weren't on the page.

"When they finally stopped to take a breath, I asked if they were mad at me, and my mother *laughed.* She asked why in the world they would be mad at me for getting *more* serious about music, and I said, 'Because it's not the piano.'

"She said, 'Oh, Carson, you're so dramatic! You make us sound like the mean Asian stereotype parents in some movie from thirty years ago. You make us sound like *my* parents!' So I said, 'But you make me practice all the time. You make me go to Juilliard every Saturday!' And she said, 'We send you to Juilliard because you like it. Don't you?'"

"So then what happened?" I asked.

"I admitted that I do love Juilliard, and she said, 'Good! I'm glad that's settled.' So I said, 'And it's really okay if I keep playing vibraphone?' And she said, 'Do you really love it?' I said I really do, and she said, 'Oh, Carson, that's all we really want. We just want you to have something you can love and be good at.' So then I said, 'Great! Then can I skip my piano practice tonight?' And she said, 'Progress is slow, my son. Your parents were forced to play instruments they didn't want to play so you could be forced to play the instruments you *do* want to play. Perhaps someday, by the grace of God, your children will be allowed to play whatever instruments they want, as badly as they want.'

"Then my dad said, 'Because *that's* the American Dream,' and dinner was officially over."

"Nice!" I said. "So, all this time, your parents have secretly kind of understood you?"

Carson sighed. "Yeah. Frankly, it's mildly terrifying. Now what am I supposed to rebel against?"

He propped himself up on one elbow and turned to face me. "By the way, you haven't mentioned anything about your little Tall Pines love-triangle situation. What's the latest?"

I sighed. It was exhausting to even contemplate explaining. "It's a whole mess. If not for my grandfather having COVID, Chloe and Ava might have killed me by now. As it is, there's still a chance they will kill each other."

"Don't take this the wrong way, Jesse, but I think you might have to try being honest with both of those girls at once. I know it sounds crazy, but it just . . . might . . . work."

. . . .

Driving back to my mom's through the eerily silent streets, I was struck for the millionth time by how many times everyone around me failed to communicate, even with the people they cared about the most. Maybe *especially* with the people they cared about the most. Maybe Carson was right. Maybe it *was* time to be honest.

As soon as things settle down, I told myself.

I let myself into the apartment, and found my mother sitting at the table, weeping.

31. That Stupid Slogan About the Real World

We should have seen it coming, really. My grandmother had a fever and a cough. Apparently, she had been feeling sick for a couple of days, but "hadn't wanted to worry anybody." My father had called to check in on her and hadn't liked the way she sounded. When he'd asked her about it directly, she had confessed the truth. She hadn't gone out to get tested, but we had to assume she had COVID.

My dad had begged her to tell my grandfather, but she had refused, because she was afraid that worrying about her might make him sicker. According to my mom, the exact quote was, "I'll be fine. I've had colds worse than this, and I'm not going to kill my husband over a cold." She hadn't even wanted to tell my mom, but my dad had said he would do it if my grandmother didn't.

I was lucky enough to walk in just after that first flurry of calls. I rushed around my mother's tiny kitchen, making her a cup of herbal tea, while she sobbed and gasped her way through the recap. As I placed her Sleepytime chamomile with two fake sugars down in front of her, the table vibrated. My dad was calling her again.

She answered on speaker. "Hi, Martin, you're on speaker with Jesse."

"Hello, Jess. I guess you've heard the news. I'm sorry."

"Thanks, Dad," I said.

"Anyway, Stephanie, I've been thinking some more, and I need to know: Have you told your father that your mother is ill?"

"No. I'm still processing this myself. And your son just walked in, so I had to explain everything to him."

"Is your mother intending to call him?"

"She said we should all wait a couple of days and see what happens." My mom winced visibly. She had to know that my father was going to hate that answer.

He released one of his deadliest conversational weapons: the Long Psychiatric Sigh. He followed that up with the Pause for Reflection, then said, "Steph, I really don't mean to alarm you, but we might not have a couple of days. This virus is terribly unpredictable. The odds are, your mother is going to be fine. She doesn't have any of the risk factors that your father does. But she's still a woman in her eighties. In the nursing home, we've had patients with seemingly mild cases crash between breakfast and lunch. Blood clots, cardiac arrest, strokes . . . there's just so much we can't—"

"Marty." My mom said this quietly, but when I heard her tone, I wanted to hide under the table. Maybe that didn't come across on speaker, or maybe my dad was just being as oblivious to my mom's moods as ever, but he steamrolled right along with his point.

"Stephanie, I know this is a hard conversation to have with one's own parent. Do you want *me* to call your father?"

And there it was. My mom switched over from sad to angry. "No, I do *not* want you to call my father. You have given your medical opinion, and I appreciate it, but these aren't your parents."

"Oh, you've made that *quite* clear," my father said. "But no matter what you do, and no matter what they think of me, I still care about them."

I couldn't stand it. "Stop it," I snarled. "This isn't about you—either of you. But I think Dad's right. I know Grandma means well, but Grandpa would want to know what's going on. If you won't call, Mom, and if Grandma won't do it, then *I'll* do it if you'll let me."

That broke up the argument by giving my parents something they could agree on: It wasn't the grandchild's job to break this news. My mom agreed to try reasoning with my grandmother one more time. My father compromised and accepted that this had to be my grandma's call.

I went to my room and listened to Led Zeppelin on shuffle. The first song that came on was "Communication Breakdown." I would have laughed if I hadn't been too busy being overwhelmed with dread.

What happened was that my grandmother had a stroke. She had managed to dial 911 before collapsing, and the ambulance crew had found her sitting up in bed, surrounded by a bunch of photo albums.

My hope was that the pictures had made her feel less alone at the end.

My dad was out of quarantine, so now he was driving me back to Pennsylvania. He had to. He had to get back to work, which meant I couldn't stay with him and risk getting exposed to all the germs he might bring home again. Meanwhile, my mom was on a solo long-distance road trip to Florida, because someone had to be there to get my grandfather home from the hospital. Grandpa was still on oxygen, and we weren't sure whether he could walk on his own or take care of himself yet. Also, I was pretty sure she was afraid he might harm himself if he got home to an empty condo.

It was bad enough Grandpa had lost his wife without being able to see her, without even having any warning that she was sick. It had all happened so fast. And then there was the whole deception factor. My dad was absolutely wrecked about the whole thing. He'd been talking about it for about thirty miles by the time we hit the Delaware River.

"Well, we waited, just like she wanted," he said. "And now we all see what happened."

"You can't blame yourself, Dad," I said. "You tried, right? Plus, you were sick, too."

"I *do* blame myself. I blame all of us except you and Leah."

When we got to the long driveway that led to the gate of our community, my dad glanced up at the big roadside banner proclaiming THE REAL WORLD ISN'T REAL and grimaced. "I've always hated that slogan," he said. "Somebody should tear it down and write WE DON'T FACE FACTS!"

"You know, Dad, I'm beginning to suspect it's a good thing you chose psychiatry over a career in real-estate marketing."

"I'm serious, Jess. Maybe this community just caters to people who already don't face facts, or maybe nobody faces facts and that's why the slogan works. But the denial drives me crazy. When your mom made me buy the house here, she said it would be great because we'd have so much more family time if we had a summer house. But I knew I'd have to pick up a couple of extra shifts at the nursing home so we could afford it, which meant I'd get to spend *less* time with her, and your sister, and you. And that's exactly what happened. Then your mother blamed me for not spending enough time up here, like that was my *choice*. Once, she actually said I was *sulking*! But you know what? The real world is real. The bills are real, and someone has to go out in the real world and earn the money to

290

pay them. If your marriage is falling apart in the real world and you come up here and pretend it isn't, the problem is *still real*. And now, this thing with your grandmother—I can see why your mother went along with it. My God! 'If I don't tell my husband I have a potentially fatal illness, it isn't real!' Maybe somebody should slap *that* up on a billboard."

This scared me. I had never heard my father so bitter. "Dad," I said as we turned onto our little street, "you did what you could."

He hit the brakes in our driveway somewhat harder than was strictly necessary. His voice quivered as he said, "That's just it. I couldn't do anything. I'm a doctor. I'm supposed to try to save people, or at least not harm them. I couldn't save my marriage or keep my family together. I couldn't protect you or your sister from any of this. My patients are dying in waves. And now your grandmother . . . Jesse, your grandparents have been so *angry* with me this year. But I loved them. I love them. I felt like, when your grandfather got sick, I had a chance to be of *use* to them. But now I don't know how I can ever look your grandfather in the eye again."

He leaned his head all the way forward so his forehead was against the steering wheel. "You know, Dad," I said, "when Grandpa talked to me from the hospital, he told me to tell you he had been wrong about you. And he said to *tell* you he was wrong. You know he never says he's wrong about anything, right? So that's a pretty big deal. He can't stay mad at you now."

"Well," he said, sitting upright and opening his door, "we'll see what happens. All I know is, he isn't speaking to me *or* your mother right now."

We grabbed our bags and walked past Leah's car into the house. Leah and Jake had come to be with me for a while until the situation with my mom and grandfather could get sorted out. While my father and Leah shared an unusually long hug, I went back for a second trip to the car. I had brought a cooler filled with ice and some top-secret containers to go in the freezer. Because of COVID health regulations, there hadn't been a funeral for my grandmother, and we hadn't been able to honor her in the Jewish tradition by sitting shiva with the family all together in a house receiving visitors for several days. About the best we would be able to do was the brand-new "tradition" of a Zoom memorial service, and even that would have to wait until my mom got my grandfather home and settled in.

Eventually, though, I had a plan for those containers.

My father tried to jump right back in his car and return to the city, but that was crazy. For one thing, it was pretty clear he was exhausted. For another, he hadn't seen Leah for months. She got him to sit down on the couch while I scrounged up a frozen pizza and some chili my mother had made and frozen before the whole illness crisis.

Jake joined me in the kitchen. "You doing okay?" he asked.

"Not great," I said. "How have you and Leah been? Has it been weird, being up there when the college is all closed up and abandoned?"

He smiled. "Kind of a party scene, actually. All the upperclassmen are still around, and there's no work. So . . ."

I probably should have figured. "So you aren't quarantining?"

"Don't worry, Bird," he said, the smile morphing into a smirk. "We're being careful."

"What do you mean, you're being careful? Are you only seeing a small group of friends?"

"No."

"Are you meeting up outdoors?"

"Well, no."

"Are you using face masks?"

"Not usually," he said. "But, uh, we've got plenty of condoms. And your sister's on the Pill."

"Jake," I said, "can you please warn me before you're going to say something like that about my sister, so I can cut off my ears first?"

"Well, excuse me," he said. "I was just trying to take your mind off all your problems. Speaking of which, I heard you blew it with both of your girls up here at once. Impressive!"

"Oh, shut up," I said. "I'm in mourning."

"Yeah, I would be, too. I mean, they both liked you. And they're both right there, in quarantine, *on your street.* Chance of a lifetime down the drain."

I glared at him. "In mourning *for my grandmother.*"

"I know," he said, hopping up so he was sitting on the kitchen counter. "Your grandma was cool. You know, one time Leah and I were down in Florida visiting your grandparents, and all of a sudden, your grandma was like, 'Ooh, my show is on!' So she rushes over to the TV and it's *Game of Thrones*, right? And immediately, it jumps into, like, a rip-roaring nude love scene between a warrior and a sorceress. They're in a cave, there's steam everywhere, you can hear wolves howling in the distance—crazy stuff. And your sister is like, 'Grandma, cover your eyes! This is rated MATURE!' But your grandmother starts cracking up. She's laughing so hard, she's wheezing. When she finally gets control of herself, she turns to Leah and says, totally straight-faced, 'You know my *life* used to be rated MATURE, right? Because if it hadn't been, you wouldn't be here!' So yeah, I'm sorry about your grandma. She was awesome."

"Yeah, well, maybe you should tell that story at the Zoom memorial."

He ripped open a bag of chips and shoved a handful into his mouth while he thought that over. "I don't think so," he said, spraying crumbs everywhere. "That's only, like, my third-best anecdote about her."

32. Zoom Fight!

I guess you're never too young to start a career as a funeral director, because there I was, at age seventeen, manually letting people in from the virtual waiting room so that my grandmother's memorial service wouldn't be Zoom-bombed by perverts. Or rather, I thought, as I approved the entrance of @JakeFromJerzee, by perverts I didn't know. Jake was actually sitting in the easy chair directly across from me and Leah in our living room in Pennsylvania, but he said Leah and I should share one screen without him so our faces would be bigger for our grandfather.

I thought that was amazingly sweet of him, until he added, "Besides, I should have the whole screen to myself for when I steal the show with my Grandma story. That story *slays!*" For a second, he looked mildly horrified. He added, "I'm sorry, I shouldn't have said *slays*. Bad choice of words. That story *kills*. Oops, my bad. That is just a darn good story. Aww, screw it. Your grandma would agree—it *slays!*"

"Jake," I said as calmly as I could, "you might consider muting yourself. Maybe at least until the rabbi has spoken?"

Luckily, we were the first people on the call, but that

didn't last. Five minutes before the scheduled start time, my mom logged on from her apartment in Staten Island. I was relieved to see that, despite his objections and the miserable look on his face, my grandfather was sitting next to her. Right after that, my dad's name popped up. Then, amid a rush of aunts, uncles, cousins, various old Floridians, and friends of my parents, I saw Carson and Chloe enter the room.

A few minutes later, after the rabbi asked everyone to mute themselves and before he started the opening prayer, Ava and Annie appeared together.

That was the first, but not the last, time I found myself crying.

I have to admit, I spaced out through the praying part of the service, partly because every few minutes, an old person would randomly start talking over the rabbi, and then a whole bunch of other people would unmute themselves so they could stage-whisper helpful things like, "Mute yourself, Harold!" Then the unfortunate Harold would have to say, "What are you talking about, mute myself? What are these people saying?" So all the helpers would be talking over each other, trying to explain the mute function, as the rabbi sadly intoned a blessing nobody could hear.

Meanwhile, my chat sidebar would be exploding with snarky private comments from Carson and Ava about the whole fiasco, while I tried to keep an eye on my mom and grandfather, who were scowling at the screen in a joint father-daughter murderous rage.

Then Carson texted me and pointed out that I, as the host, had the power to mute people. Which would have been an excellent thing to know at the beginning of the festivities.

Eventually, we made it to the memory-sharing portion of the service. I tried to pay attention to the words of the older people who spoke up first, but Leah and Jake had started whispering to ask whether I wanted a snack. I was super offended, because I couldn't believe they were thinking of food at a time like this. Besides, we didn't have any good desserts in the house. Also, I was saving room for what only I knew was coming afterward.

What snapped me back to attention was the trembly voice of my grandmother's Florida best friend, Ruthie. There were so many people in the Zoom that Ruthie's head was tiny, so I switched to speaker view. Her head filled my screen and I choked up. Ruthie's hair was a mess. She was wearing a button-up shirt, but the top buttons appeared to be lined up incorrectly. Her lipstick was smeared on her front teeth. Tears were cutting a channel through her makeup.

I knew I was upset about my grandma, but somehow it hadn't really hit me that her friends would be so shaken up. Of course they would, though. I saw her maybe three times a year. Ruthie had probably seen her twice a day for years and years. They had lunch together three times a week. They had founded a book club together. They were bridge partners.

I knew Ruthie's second husband had died a few years before, so she was living alone. Now, with my grandmother gone, and in the middle of a pandemic, what was her life going to be like? I found myself wiping my eyes again as I tuned out Leah and Jake, and leaned in to listen.

"Jeanie loved her husband, Arthur. She loved her daughter. She loved her son-in-law. She adored her grandchildren. I mean, I'm sure she thought I was all right company for a slow day, but she *really* loved her family. So it didn't surprise me at all when she didn't tell Arthur she had COVID. I told her I thought she should, but she could be stubborn."

Ruthie stared intently into the screen. "Artie, am I right? Wasn't she stubborn?"

My grandfather must have tried to say something, because then there was a whole chorus of people trying to tell him and my mom how to unmute. It probably only took my mom about three seconds to do that, but by then, there were so many people talking at once that I never did get to hear whether my grandfather managed to get out an answer. I literally couldn't mute them all fast enough.

Eventually, Ruthie just said, "But that was Jeanie, and we loved her. She was just that kind of person. If you had a blister on your pinkie, and her entire arm was falling off, she wouldn't say a *word* about her arm until she had gotten you all fixed up with a Band-Aid. Just like

298

three summers ago, when she had her first heart attack. She made Arthur swear up and down that he wouldn't say anything to the children—remember that, Artie?—because they were on their summer vacation, and she didn't want them to worry."

Wait a minute, I thought. *Grandma had a heart attack three years ago? And what did this lady mean that it was her first heart attack? Exactly how many heart attacks did Grandma have?*

I switched out of speaker view and found the scene in my mother's apartment. Big mistake. My mom was visibly interrogating my grandfather, whose head was hanging down. I clicked between screens until I found my dad, who looked totally shocked.

Leah whispered, "Jess, did that lady just say Grandma had a heart attack three years ago?"

I nodded.

"We didn't know that, right?" she asked.

"Nope," I said.

"Wow," Jake said. "Should I see if we have any popcorn?"

After that, the Zoom got pretty awkward, because I think it must have been clear to just about everyone (with the possible exception of Ruthie) that the big heart-attack reveal had not been the world's smoothest funeral social move. My phone was blowing up, presumably with messages from my friends. I mean, I wasn't really talking directly to Chloe or Ava, but they had shown up, so the temporary truce was hopefully still holding. Also, Carson was probably coming up with witty comments faster than his thumbs could type.

I didn't look, though. All I could see was the stunned face of my dad, the heated torrent of words that appeared to be blasting forth from my mom, and my grandfather's look of complete despair.

When the rabbi declared the end of the service, I asked my parents to stay on. As soon as my family's computers were the only ones still connected, my parents both unmuted. "Dad," my father said to my grandfather, "how many heart attacks did she have?" This was painful to hear. First of all, he called my mom's father "Dad." Second of all, he spoke so quietly and gently that it was somehow worse than yelling.

"Two," my grandfather said hoarsely.

Then my mother started shouting at my grandfather and my grandfather began barking back. Leah and my father both tried several times to interrupt, but my mom and grandfather just steamrolled right over them. My grandfather had been enraged since my grandmother's death that my parents hadn't told him about her illness. Now my mom was enraged right back at him for hiding something that seemed even bigger for much longer.

As the funeral director, I couldn't help thinking this wasn't how I'd envisioned the evening. *Screw it*, I decided. *I'm still the host of this thing.*

I muted my mom's microphone. "Mom! Grandpa!" I shouted. "Be quiet! *Please!*" They looked away from each other and stared into the lens. Their lips started moving again, but I said, "Nobody can hear you. I muted you. Now please listen. You can fight later, but this is Grandma's memorial service, and I want to speak about *her.*" They both stopped talking.

"Grandma wasn't good at saying what she wanted for herself. Maybe she didn't even know what she wanted for herself. I'm not sure anybody in this family is good at saying what they want for themselves. But Grandma was very good at saying she loved us, and she was even better at showing it. Mom, when you and Dad were fighting last fall, who came up north and made sure I was going to be okay? Grandma and Grandpa. And Grandma spent hours and hours making the world's biggest batch of matzo ball soup so her grandson wouldn't be hungry when his mother moved out.

"And then, a few months later, when things got really bad up here, and I flew down to see Grandma and Grandpa, she didn't want me to worry about her. What she wanted was to make me promise to take care of Grandpa if she . . ." Here, I had to stop, because I couldn't breathe. I put my head on my knees, and then suddenly, Leah and Jake were kneeling beside me. Leah had her arms wrapped around my neck, and even Jake put a hand on my shoulder. It felt kind of nice.

I sat up again and inhaled deeply. Leah didn't take her arms away, but that was all right. "Grandma made me promise to take care of Grandpa if she died. Okay, so I guess now we all know Grandma wasn't so great at taking care of herself. But that's because what she cared about the most was taking care of *us*. She wanted us to be okay, more than anything else in the world.

"Now, Mom, I'm going to unmute you in a second, but first, I want you and Dad to both go look in your freezers. We're going to do the same thing here. I left each of you some of Grandma's matzo ball soup. Mom, you have two servings: one for you and one for Grandpa. Dad, you have one. We have two here in Pennsylvania, so Jake, Leah, and I will have to split up one of the servings. These are the last servings in the world, but that's okay. I think she would be happy to see the soup bringing us all together.

"So, now I think we should all go find the soup, micro-wave it on high for about three minutes, and then get back on camera to taste it. Okay?"

About three and a half minutes later, we all sat down for our last helping of Grandma's soup. I didn't have to mute anybody, although if I'm being honest, Jake's slurping almost had me reaching for the button once or twice.

I'm not going to say that a Jewish grandmother's chicken soup magically solves everything, but at least it brought a fragile peace down upon my family to end the evening.

33. A New Sport for Me!

I thought my big speech and the matzo ball trick had fixed everything. I mean, I knew we'd all still be in mourning, but I thought the fighting and self-torment would be over. So, imagine my surprise the next day, when my mother told me she couldn't get my grandfather to talk to her. Or brush his teeth. Or wash himself.

I tried calling my dad for advice, but he was at work. I had a few hours to kill before he'd be home, so I did some school reading and fiddled around on my ukulele bass for a while. I was so restless, though, that even music couldn't calm my thoughts down.

When I finally did get through to my father, all he said was, "It sounds like your grandfather is depressed. I don't blame him. Frankly, I'm not feeling so cheerful myself. I know how much you admire your grandpa, Jess, but I have to say, I'm furious at him."

"Because he didn't tell us about Grandma's heart attacks?"

"Not exactly. Because he was hypocritical about it. He was so angry with your mother and me when we didn't tell you and Leah our marriage was in trouble. He said hiding the truth would only hurt everybody. And of course he took the whole thing out on me. Then he called me a coward for not telling him your grandmother was sick. And the whole time, he's been keeping this from all of us! If I had known she had a heart condition, I would have told her she needed medical attention *urgently*. She might still be alive."

"Dad, I'm sorry. I didn't mean to . . . I don't know . . . hurt you with this. I just don't know what to do for Grandpa. I don't know what to do for anybody."

My father was silent long enough to make me uncomfortable. Then he coughed, cleared his throat, and said, "Yeah, well, there's a lot of that going around in this family. I'm sorry I can't help you."

I couldn't deal with my ultra-depressing family any longer, so I texted Chloe and Ava. Individually, because I had the feeling it might be weird to act like we were all still a big, happy trio at the moment. *Hey,* I wrote to each of them, *would you be up for a socially distanced walk? I could use a friend.*

Chloe didn't respond.

Ava did, which was worse. She wrote, *You've been using this friend for a long time. I'm sorry, but I think I need some time away from you and Chloe to think.*

I found out later that Chloe and Ava had gotten into a big argument right after the Zoom the night before, but at the time, all I knew was that my grandmother was dead, my family was in pieces again, and I didn't seem to have any friends within a hundred-mile radius.

That text shattered me. I put on sweatpants and a raggedy old rock concert T-shirt, and fell into my bed without even eating dinner.

Bed is like quicksand. It turns out the more time you spend in bed, the harder it is to get out of bed. And the more you struggle, the worse it sucks you in. After Ava refused to see me, I barely left my room for days. Even staggering to the bathroom was a massive physical and mental effort. Going downstairs for food was nearly out of the question. Leah brought plates up to me a couple of times, but she had just lost her grandmother, plus she and Jake were not the biggest nurturers, so that didn't last long. The kitchen piled up with dirty dishes, the refrigerator got emptier and emptier, and things were just generally starting to get dusty and dingy-looking around the house.

We were sinking into chaos.

Then, way too early one morning, some maniac started banging on the front door. I tried to ignore it. I mean, I put my pillow over my head, figuring that either the person would give up and go away, or Leah would finally answer and chase them away. Imagine my surprise and dismay when I heard my sister saying, in her sweetest voice, "Oh, come right in. Sorry about the mess. He's in his room. I'm sure he'll be *delighted* to see you!"

"Delighted" to see them? Who the heck was this, the Tooth Fairy? Because I couldn't really come up with any actual human beings I'd be delighted to see.

The next thing I knew, somebody very nimble was jogging up the steps. I turned over in bed so my back was to the bedroom door and pulled my blankets up around my head. I heard the person breathing in the doorway. I waited.

"Get up, you big faker," Annie said. Then she yanked the covers off me.

I would have turned dramatically to face her, but I didn't have to because the force of her blanket-yanking had spun me around. "Hey!" I said. "I could have been naked, you know."

She rolled her eyes. "Please," she said. "Like you're cool enough to sleep naked. Now come on, we're going for a run."

I forced myself to sit up, although it made my head spin a bit. Also, I might have let out an involuntary groan. Then I asked, "Why would we do that?"

"I'm in training, and I need a partner. I was thinking, you're the closest thing to an athlete on this cul-de-sac, and you need something to get you out of bed, so this is perfect."

I decided to ignore the *closest thing to an athlete* part. "What are you in training for?"

"I'll tell you on the way. What do you say?"

I didn't say anything. I let my eyelids flutter and close. I was still holding on to a vague hope that this was just a strange dream, and that if I stayed still for another moment, she would fade away and I could rest some more. Possibly until lunch. I was pretty sure I'd spotted three-quarters of a freezer-burned bagel behind the ice tray.

"Come *on*," Annie barked from three inches away. My eyes snapped open. She had knelt down so we were face-to-face. "This is important to me, Jess. It's important to *both* of us."

I sighed. "Okay, gimme five minutes. I just have to brush my teeth and stuff."

She stood up straight, but didn't leave the room.

"Can you give me a minute, please?" I said.

"Get up, and then I'll go out," she said. "Otherwise, you're just gonna roll over and go back to sleep."

"Are you this annoying with Ava?" I asked.

"Oh, no," she said, smiling. "I'm a million times more annoying with Ava!"

. . . .

I hoped that running would invigorate me, but I was weak from days of hibernation. I was gasping like a fish on a dock by the middle of the first hill. Unfortunately, our community has lots and lots of hills. "Why do . . . I . . . need . . . this . . . again?" I asked.

"You have to get in shape for tennis season. Otherwise, you're going to die on the courts this summer." I couldn't help but notice Annie didn't sound winded.

"Who says the courts are even going to be open this summer?" I wheezed.

"Well, they're going to be open someday," she said. "And you're not going to be some pathetic bed lump when the time comes. You're welcome."

We reached the crest of the hill just as a wicked stitch stabbed me in the right side. I stopped running and doubled over. "Give me a sec," I hissed. "Cramp."

"One minute," she said. "Remember, we're in training."

"Yeah," I said, rubbing my ribs. "About that. What are you training *for?*"

"Eighth-grade cross-country. Fall sport. Incredibly demanding."

"Since when are you into cross-country?"

"For your information, Jesse Dienstag, I am a very interesting person, with *many* developing interests."

She looked away quickly, but not before I thought I detected a bit of a blush. Suddenly, I thought I understood. "Is one of those interests, uh, romantic in nature?"

"Maybe," Annie said, brushing at the roadside gravel with the toes of one foot. "There might be a certain *person* on the cross-country team. And I might want to spend more time near that certain person."

"Does this person have a name?"

She looked me in the eye. "I'm not ready to say, because this person doesn't know anything about it yet. But, uh, this person is on the *girls'* cross-country team." She looked away again, and her foot stopped moving. I almost got the feeling she had stopped breathing.

"Okay," I said. My mind was racing. I didn't know what the right thing was to say in a situation like this, but I very much wanted to say it. "That's cool. That's fine. You know, I . . . well, I respect your feelings. I'm so glad you trusted me with this. In fact, I'm honored. Very honored. And touched. I, uh, care about and support you. And I'm here if you want to talk about this. Or if you want help finding, like, support resources."

Suddenly, Annie burst out giggling. "Support resources? Oh my God, please stop talking."

"What?" I said. I was kind of hurt.

"I love you, but you are legitimately terrible at this. Like, *extra* awkward. I knew you were going to support me, so it's fine. I'm just relieved that I got to tell you myself before you heard about it from someone else."

"Why?"

"Because you know I've always looked up to you. Now come on. Nobody ever got in shape by standing around *empathizing*."

When we finally got back to the foot of my driveway— Annie prancing, me staggering—she said, "Same time tomorrow?"

I groaned.

"What?" she said. "You've got someplace else you need to be? 'Cause as far as I can tell, your social calendar is, uh, pretty sparse right now."

I started to snap back, but I couldn't spare enough

oxygen to be witty. Instead, I just asked, "Hey, is your sister okay?"

Annie leaned against a tree trunk and brushed some grass cuttings off her socks. "I don't know. She's spending a lot of time just sitting around. She needs you. She needs Chloe, too. But mostly, she needs you. You're her real best friend."

"Annie, I messed up."

She blew upward to get the hair out of her eyes. "Ya think? I told you not to hurt her. She's sensitive."

"I want to fix it."

"So fix it. I believe in you. I mean, you're a dork. And I don't think you have a future in the cross-country running business. But you're still *you*. You matter to her. See you in the morning!"

"Wait, what am I supposed to do?" I realized it was pathetic, asking a middle schooler for life advice, but I didn't have anybody else, and truthfully, Annie seemed to be wiser than the older people I knew.

"How am I supposed to know?" she said. "Do you want my help finding some support resources?"

"Oh, shut up," I muttered. But for the first time in a while, I found myself nearly smiling. And by the time I had finished eating and showering, I had an idea.

34. All About That Bass

I knocked a second time on the door of the guest bedroom in my mother's apartment. "Go away," my grandfather croaked. "I already told you, Stephanie. I'm not hungry. I just want to sleep!"

"Grandpa, it's me. It's Jesse! I drove here from Pennsylvania to see you."

He didn't respond.

"Grandpa, please?"

I heard rustling sounds, like he was moving around in bed. "Give me a minute, J. You don't want to see me like this."

I looked at my mom, who was standing next to me. She shrugged and said, "Okay, Dad. We'll just be over here at the kitchen table when you're ready."

I sat there awkwardly with my mother. I hadn't told her in advance that I was coming. Obviously, I knew she'd be home. It hadn't occurred to me that she might have wanted to get cleaned up, too. She was wearing gray yoga pants with a large stain on one thigh, a faded shirt from our trip to Disney World when I was eight, and fuzzy bunny slippers. She had hastily pulled her hair up into some kind of scrunchy thing when she'd let me into the house.

There were dark half circles under my mother's eyes. She looked like she needed someone like Annie to yank her out of bed and get her moving, but unfortunately, there was only one Annie.

She looked at the pile of stuff I'd left by the entrance door. There was the backpack I'd carried in, which contained my laptop and portable speakers, as well as my smallest amplifier, plus the gig bag containing my fretless Jazz Bass, plus an overnight bag just in case either she or my father needed me to stay over.

"What is all this, Jess?" she asked. "I'm sure you mean well, but nobody here has the energy for some big—"

"Mom," I said, cutting her off. "I came here because I wanted to give Grandpa a hug, okay? But also, I wanted you both to hear something. Partly, it's because I never really thanked you enough for getting me the Jazz Bass, but partly, it's because . . . well, you'll see."

"O . . . kay," she said, not very convincingly. Then she changed the topic. "Are your sister and Jake getting along okay? I've been reading news stories about how quarantine has been putting strains on relationships."

"Oh, Leah and Jake are getting along great," I said. "The house is getting kinda trashed, and there's an outside chance we're all going to die of scurvy or something from the unsanitary living conditions, but their relationship seems to be thriving."

My mom smiled weakly. "That's nice," she said. Clearly, she really was having a titanically rough day.

My grandfather shuffled out of the bathroom and I tried to suppress a gasp. He looked like a scarecrow. He was wearing one of those ribbed white tank tops that old men wear, and it was absolutely hanging off him. His pajama bottoms looked like they had been bought for a much larger man, which I supposed was basically true. He swallowed, and I could see all the parts of his Adam's apple move.

"Gramp," I mumbled. I stood up and put my arms around him.

"Hi, J," he said. "It's okay. I'm fine. Sit!"

I let go of him without having been hugged back. My eyes stung. Even in her distracted state, my mom noticed, and reached over to squeeze my knee.

"What's on your mind, J?" my grandfather asked, like he was the Pope and I had come to him for a blessing.

"Well, first of all, I just wanted to see you. You know, in person. Grandma said I was supposed to make sure you were okay, remember? Just like you told me to do for her if something happened to you?"

He waved his hand like he was shooing me off. "I told you, I'm fine."

I took a deep breath. "Okay, great. There's another thing, too. Remember how you wanted to take Grandma to the Sarah McLachlan concert, but then COVID happened?"

He looked at me blankly. "You know," I added, "the 'I Will Remember You' lady?"

He nodded. "Oh, right. I like her. I always pretended I didn't, but that was just to tease Jeanie. I mean, your grandmother."

"Well," I said, "I wanted to play the song for you and Mom, since Grandma didn't get to hear it."

I spent the next few minutes getting my laptop connected to my speakers, tuning up my bass, plugging into my amp, and cueing up the backing tracks I had spent hours recording the day before. I had programmed in keyboard chords, drumbeats, and two background bass parts. The melody line—the vocal part—was perfect for playing on my fretless.

The last thing I did before I pressed PLAY was hand my mom and grandfather the lyrics to the song, which I had printed out in advance. You can look them up, but I have to warn you: You're gonna cry.

I tried really hard not to look at my mom or my grandfather while I was playing the song, but my mom's sniffles and sobs were hard to miss, anyway, even over the music. As for my grandpa, he coughed a couple of times, but that was all I noticed. I held the last note as long as I could, and when it finally faded, I turned the volume knob on my bass down all the way before turning everything else off. Then I looked up. My grandfather was staring off into space like I wasn't even there.

I hurried to unstrap my bass and lay it down. Then I stepped over to him. He stood up, threw his arms around me, and made a noise I'd never heard before. It was something like, "Ga-AAAHHHH!" His knees bent, and I found myself supporting most of his diminished weight as he broke into racking, heaving sobs. For what had to have been the next half hour, he alternated between shouting half-understandable, half-nonsense phrases into my shoulder, crying uncontrollably, and gasping for air.

The parts I could make out were mostly "I'm sorry, I'm sorry," and the words "Should have been me," over and over again.

Finally, when my back was starting to spasm and I thought my legs were going to give out, my mother appeared next to me, put her arms around both of us, and said, "Come on, Dad, let's sit for a while."

He allowed her to lead him the few steps to his seat and collapsed meekly into it. She brought him a glass of water and he downed the whole thing, stopping only to breathe. Then he looked at me and said, "Thank you, Jesse. Your grandmother would have loved that."

I was pretty shaken up. I had never seen anybody that distressed before in my life. "Are you okay now, Grandpa?"

"No," he said. "But I think maybe I will be."

35. Sitting in a Tree

I figured the Magic Bass Trick might work one more time, so I wrote what I thought was the best piece of music I'd ever come up with. I knew it was the most heartfelt. The problem was, you can't perform a song for someone if you can't get them to be in the same place as you. I decided Annie was my only hope. A couple of days later, a mile or so into a run, I started begging.

"Let me get this straight," she said. "You want me to convince my sister to meet you in the treehouse."

"Yeah."

"Even though she doesn't want to see you."

"Well, yeah. But you said . . ." I stopped talking to pant a few times. Maybe it was my imagination, but I thought Annie might have picked up the pace. Was she messing with me? She was! A thirteen-year-old was messing with me.

I was not sure what I'd done to deserve that. At least not from her.

I continued. "You said I should . . . direct quote . . . fix it with . . . Ava. So I'm trying to . . . fix it. Which means, be in a room with her."

"Or a tree."

"Or a tree."

"Will Chloe be there?"

"Um . . . how good are your diplomatic skills?"

"No freakin' way, Jesse! You expect me to get them both to come? You know they're not speaking to each other, right?"

I stopped running. "What?"

She stopped, too, and I could tell she was surprised. "Wait," she said. "You honestly didn't know that?"

I wiped the sweat off my forehead. "I honestly did *not* know that. Why aren't they talking to each other?"

She smacked me on one arm. "Are you even *serious* right now? Because of you! You can't just go around kissing everybody in the world and think they won't find out."

"Well, sure," I mumbled. "I know that *now*."

She laughed. "You know what?" she said. "I'm kind of glad I don't like boys. Even the nice ones are kind of unbelievably dumb."

"I resent that," I said.

"But do you *deny* it?"

I didn't say anything.

"No," she said, "I didn't think so."

She started running again. About fifteen yards later, she shouted back over her shoulder, "Seven o'clock tonight, at the treehouse. You better bring your A game!"

After dinner, I sneaked through the woods to the

treehouse like a ninja, if ninjas weighed themselves down with high-tech musical equipment and exuded nervous sweat from every pore because of their complex and uncontrollable love for their two best friends. I was in place and set up by 6:45, and spend the next thirteen minutes freaking out about whether the girls would show. I had no idea what Annie said or did to get Chloe and Ava to come, but at 6:58, I heard twigs crackling and voices murmuring.

Chloe came up the ladder first. She didn't acknowledge me. Ava's head popped up just as Chloe stepped to the side. They were both making a show of being casual, in T-shirts and short shorts. Chloe stretched. Ava yawned.

It was unbearable.

I went for the obvious joke. "You're probably wondering why I asked you all here today," I said.

"Be serious," Chloe said. Ava nodded.

Yay, I thought. *They're agreeing on stuff already. That's progress!*

"Okay," I said. "Thank you both for coming to my grandmother's Zoom. That was huge. I know how mad you both are at me, and Annie told me you were mad at each other, too. That's also on me, and I'm sorry. Please, even if you both hate me . . ." I forced myself to look each of them straight in the eyes. "Please don't give up on each other."

Ava said, "Exactly what are you sorry for, J?"

I forced myself to inhale slowly through my nose. I'd

been thinking about this all day. I imagined that at least one of them was going to drag me through this, and I also figured I deserved it. "I'm sorry that I wasn't brave enough to tell Chloe how in love with her I was all last summer. I'm sorry that, even though I was in love with Chloe, I kept getting distracted by my physical attraction to you, Ava. I kept blurring that line, and it wasn't fair to you. Ava, you are my best friend, and I messed that up. Chloe, I was in love with you—I'm still in love with you—and I messed *that* up. But the worst part is that I messed things up between you."

I looked down at my hands, because I couldn't bear to see their faces if the answer to this next question was no. "Listen, I don't expect you to forgive me today. I just want you to hear a song I wrote for you. Is that okay?"

"Sure," Chloe said.

"Might as well," Ava said, expression unreadable. "We're already up here, anyway."

With that kind of audience enthusiasm, how could I fail? I strapped on my U-Bass, fired up my laptop, and took a deep breath that was only *slightly* shaky.

Then I sang.

> *I wanted your lips,*
> *But I need your words,*
> *I wanted your tongue,*
> *But I need your voice,*

I wanted your taste,
But I need your time,
I wanted your skin,
But I need your soul.

I thought I wanted some big fantasy,
Me and you and me and you and me,
Thought the real world wasn't real,
All I wanted was to feel,
All the love that I could steal,
In a treehouse built for three.

I wanted your kiss,
But I need your smile,
I wanted honey,
But I need a home.

I thought I wanted some big fantasy,
Me and you and me and you and me,
Thought the real world wasn't real,
All I wanted was to feel,
All the love that I could steal,
In a treehouse built for three.

I'm an idiot,
I'm sorry,
I'm an idiot,

I'm sorry,

I'm an idiot,

I'm sorry,

I'm an idiot,

I'm sorry,

I'm an idiot,

I'm sorry.

The backing track ended. I closed my laptop, laid my U-Bass down on its soft case, and looked at Chloe and Ava. For the longest time, neither of them said anything, though they gave each other several significant glances.

Finally, Chloe said, "I don't hate it."

"I really like the last part, actually," Ava said.

"The idiot stuff? I agree. Could use a few more repeats, though," Chloe added.

"And hey, no Taylor Swift influence detected, so that's a plus," Ava said.

"So?" I said, trying not to sound like I was begging.

"So I'd say you're progressing." Chloe smiled at me. It wasn't a big smile, but it wasn't *not* a smile.

"As a songwriter?"

"As a friend."

"So, uh, do you guys think maybe we could all hang out again?" I asked. My palms were sweating. I had to struggle to keep my voice steady. I never worked up the guts to ask Chloe out, but even if I had, I wouldn't have been as nervous for that as I was for this, because now I really understood how much I had to lose. "I mean, socially distanced? No touching? And no flirting? With total, open, honest communication?"

Chloe looked at Ava. Ava looked at Chloe. To my great surprise, they both laughed.

"Oh, I think there's almost no chance we can all pull that off," Chloe said.

"But," Ava added, "it might be fun to *try*."

After: The Real World
Will Be Real

In late May, Annie and I are just getting back from a run. She checks her exercise watch and says, "Not bad, Jess. You just need to shave nineteen more seconds off your 5K time, and you'll totally qualify for eighth-grade girls' cross-country!"

So I figure that's a real feather in my cap.

Ava stomps out of the house and down the driveway. We've been getting along, in a tentative, socially distanced kind of way, so I panic for a moment, thinking I've done something wrong and annoyed her, but this time, I am not at fault. "J," she says, "I've got some bad news. Larry just announced that the rec center's going to be closed for the summer. *Closed!*"

I'm not going to lie: This hurts. It really *hurts*. I want to bury my face in Ava's shoulder and mumble curses into her hair, but I can't do that. First of all, we're not touching because we're not touching. Second of all, we're not touching because, now that people have been making more contact with the outside world, we've gotten strict again about distancing in general. Of course, we want to protect ourselves, and our parents are a bigger concern, but most of all, everybody is very conscious of maintaining a shield around Chloe. She hasn't even been going places with a mask on. Without a spleen, she has to be a lot more careful than anyone else I know.

I hold it together with Ava, say my goodbyes, and set out alone to walk off my run and calm myself down. I think about everything I'm going to miss this summer, everything that could have been, everything that's lost that I won't get back.

But then I start thinking about everything I still have and everything that can be again. I think of my dad, who's been through the worst year of his life, but has never stopped showing up for his patients. I think of my grandfather, who told me I had my own life to live and is now waking up every day and having to walk the long walk through his own advice. I think of Chloe, who's just helped her dad apply for government aid to keep her family's business going and their employees taken care of. I think of Annie, who lost her mom, grew into her own identity in the middle of a worldwide pandemic, and still had the strength to literally drag me out of my bed when somebody had to do it.

I think of Ava, my best friend who needs me to prove I'm her best friend, too.

I reach the top of the highest hill in Tall Pines Landing. The sun is nearly at its peak. I close my eyes and turn my head to bask in it for a moment before I head home.

I concentrate, willing myself to relax and picture a time when this crisis has passed. Every crisis has to pass, right? My dad will move on. My grandfather will smile again without having to force it. There will be new treatments for COVID, maybe even a vaccine by January. People are saying we'll be able to have part of our senior year of high school in person.

Who knows? I might even get to play in another jazz band concert. Live. With an audience and everything!

And then it will be summer again. Maybe Chloe, Ava, and I will all have one last chance to work together at the rec center.

I can see this so clearly that my eyes get kind of misty. It's like a little movie playing behind my eyelids:

Chloe puts in a little visit to Larry's office and convinces him to let her, Ava, and me take the catamaran out for its first sail of the summer. Its first sail in two summers, really. When she tells us about it, I almost laugh. Ava gives her a little raised-eyebrow glance, like *Really, Klo?*

But here we are, stepping out onto the dock side by side. Instinctively, I reach out and brush just the edges of my pinkies against Chloe's and Ava's hands. The sun glints off the water. The breeze picks up. I smell coconut and flowers. It's a beautiful day for a boat ride.

I smile. What can possibly go wrong?

Acknowledgments

I have had incredible luck in stumbling upon amazing, helpful experts when doing book research. For the heat-illness scenes in this novel, I leaned hard on my go-to emergency medical care guru, Bil Rosen, BA, CEMSO, CTO, NJCEM, NRP. Bil is an incredible professional, and if I ever collapse on a very sunny day, I hope it happens while I am standing right next to Bil. (And I very much hope he remembers my kind words.)

Acknowledgment

About the Author

Jordan Sonnenblick is the author of many acclaimed YA novels, including *Drums, Girls & Dangerous Pie, Notes from the Midnight Driver, Zen and the Art of Faking It, Curveball: The Year I Lost My Grip, After Ever After,* and *Falling Over Sideways.* He is also the author of the middle-grade comedies *The Secret Sheriff of Sixth Grade, The Boy Who Failed Show and Tell,* and *The Boy Who Failed Dodgeball.* He lives in Pennsylvania with his family and numerous musical instruments. You can find out a whole lot more about him at jordansonnenblick.com.